HAMMERHEAD

By the same author in PAN Books

LET SLEEPING GIRLS LIE
SHAMELADY

HAMMERHEAD

JAMES MAYO

UNABRIDGED

PAN BOOKS LTD : LONDON

By arrangement with

WILLIAM HEINEMANN LTD

LONDON

First published 1964 by Wm. Heinemann Ltd.
This edition published 1966 by Pan Books Ltd.,
33 Tothill Street, London, S.W.1

330 10461 6

2nd Printing 1966
3rd Printing 1966
4th Printing 1968

Printed in Great Britain by Richard Clay (The Chaucer Press), Ltd.,
Bungay, Suffolk

To

A. D. Forshaw, most generous of friends

1

THE LIGHT IN the entrance of the apartment was subdued. When the servant opened the door to the landing, the dark oblong cut against the bright light beyond.

Charles Hood tied his white silk scarf. To complete the effect, the servant should now say: 'There's a trace of fog, sir.' But the man didn't. He was Haitian and this was Paris, a city of other moods.

The servant stood holding the door open. Hood gave him a smile. 'Goodnight,' he said and went out.

Softly the door of the apartment shut behind him. Hood reflected that Espiritu Lobar, whose flat he had just left, certainly owned some superb things. But then he had the means. Hood had called, knowing Lobar was away, because he had wanted to look at Lobar's pictures, among other things. Rich men were constantly buying the wrong pictures.

His steps were soundless on the white carpet as he crossed to the lift. A glowing ruby showed that it was in use. He waited. The trace of a woman's scent drifted to him. *L'heure bleue,* by Guerlain. Hood hummed a line of 'My Heart Belongs to Daddy' which had been the tune of a lovely Guerlain girl he had loved once.

The lift appeared from below and glided past to a floor above. The place was very quiet. True, this was a millionaire's block. But the roar of the Paris evening traffic outside was efficiently stifled. The Champs-Elysées might be twenty miles off instead of at the door.

The ruby eye flickered. There were sounds of somebody getting in or out of the lift above. Hood pressed the button and when the lift descended, he got in. There was a man inside – small and natty, not one of the resident tycoons. Hood noted the English touches; the cast of features, the greenness of his trilby. He pulled the door to and thumbed the ground floor button.

The lift dropped smoothly. They were enveloped by a faint electric hum. Hood stood just inside the door. His fellow-passenger was in the far corner.

All at once, Hood became aware that there was something wrong. The other passenger was staring at him and trying to control a tremor. It lasted a very short time. The next moment, the man threw himself forward and grabbed Hood's arm.

'C-C-Christ – Oh C-Christ – I —'

His face was grey and sweaty. His false teeth dropped and filled his mouth, shaken up and down by his wobbling chin. He sagged at the knees and Hood thought he was going to fall.

'What's the matter? Are you ill?' Quickly Hood pressed the red button. The lift stopped.

The man's mouth twisted. He raised his hands to his face and dropped to his knees. His hat toppled off.

'Try to lie down,' Hood said, trying to remember what you did for a fit. Loosen his collar, at any rate. The man was making inarticulate noises, staring at him. It was going to be distressing if he started lashing out. Then, as Hood bent over and reached for his neck, the man gave a scream and jerked back.

'No! G-gimme – a chance. . . .'

'What do you say? My poor fellow—'

Abruptly it seemed to Hood best to get them both out of this confined space and he turned and pressed Ground Floor again. The lift slid down and stopped at the bottom. Hood swung the door open. 'Stay here. I'll call the porter. We'll get a doctor.' But before he could step out, the man had sprung to his feet and grasped his wrist. Hood let him hold on.

'Don't call anybody! I'm – I'm all right.'

'You don't look it.'

'Be all right – a minute.' He was breathing heavily.

'Are you sure?' Hood gave him a close look. Then he understood. The man was a very frightened customer.

His hand was still gripping Hood's wrist. 'Stick with me, will you? Chriseake.'

'All right.'

'Sorry. Must've looked – funny.'

'How do you know you can trust me?'

The man's globular eyes were on him. He struggled for breath to reply. 'Somebody who comes down in a lift with you – and don't do anything, he's all right, ain't he?'

'How do you mean, "all right"?'

'I thought you was ... Never mind that. Let's get out of here. Marble, by God.'

They were in the white marble entrance with the statue of a Greek nymph which, Hood knew, Lobar had bought a Roman palace to obtain. He looked at the man. He was short, about fifty, with reddish hair and a horsy or actor touch. His trilby was a size too small. He wore a yellow tie. Retired jockey, Hood guessed.

At the street entrance the man faltered again.

That particular spot at the Rond-Point was not well lighted. The entrance faced the Champs-Elysées gardens. Hood saw the man's protuberant eyes searching the dark shrubbery opposite. Beyond, the thundering surge of traffic up and down the Champs-Elysées, the cars sweeping into the Place de la Concorde below and all the noisy activity of the great city round them seemed to leave the gardens in deeper isolation. Figures passed occasionally under a lamp in the midst of the trees.

The man muttered something inaudible.

'They're just typists, going home,' Hood said.

'Not all typists.'

'What's the trouble?' Hood said. 'Perhaps I can help?'

The man seemed hardly to hear. 'You got a car?' he said.

'Not here.'

'Listen, I hope you never need it like I do, but I'm asking you straight, you're sticking with me, ain't you? I can trust you. Maybe you're the only man in Paris I can trust. You coulda knocked me off in that lift. If you'd been . . .' He did not finish.

'Somebody after you?' Hood said.

The man was peering across at the gardens. 'Isn't there somewhere we can go? Quiet and safe?'

'I dare say there's a bar near by.'

The man passed his tongue over his lips as though a long-lost thought had reached him. 'Yes, a drink. Will you?'

Hood hesitated. He did not go out of his way, as a secret agent, to take chances. He had asked himself already if the frightened man was a plant. He did not remember the man's face from any of the photographs which the Identity Office of Special Intelligence Security had shown him, though that wasn't conclusive. But the most skilful actor could hardly produce that sweat, that greyish tinge of mortal fright on the skin.

'All right,' he said quietly.

They had begun to walk. But the man wouldn't go up the Champs-Elysées and they turned down and into the Avenue Marigny. The man kept close to Hood on the inside. A little way down, on the opposite pavement, a policeman was standing outside a sentry-box in the Elysée wall.

Hood said: 'Want to cross?'

The man shook his head. A moment later he said: 'You English?'

'Yes. My name's Charles Hood. What's yours?'

But the man suddenly gripped his arm and switched round, jerking him to a halt. The street lamp showed his face haggard with fear. His cheeks were working. Steps were approaching from behind. The two were standing in the glare of the lamp which left a pool of darkness beyond on the broad pavement. The man shrank. He began to buckle at the knees. Hood turned. The policeman on the far side wasn't looking. There was a break in the traffic. The steps were coming on quickly. The thought of the perfect targets the two of them were presenting under the light made Hood give the man a shove and step smartly after him. The next minute an army corporal in uniform came into view and hurried past. Hood grinned.

But the other man seemed only half assured. He did not take his eyes off the corporal until he was far ahead. Then shakingly he lit a cigarette. 'Sorry.'

At the beginning of the rue Miromesnil there was a glass-fronted café with a few dining-tables at one side. There were six or eight customers, it was garishly lighted – not the ideal place for a confidential chat. But Hood couldn't see anything cosier at close hand and in fact the place was neutral. They took a corner seat on the red leather banquette opposite the bar.

'Two Scotch, a double and a single,' Hood said to the waiter. Then to the man, 'What's your name?'

'Arthur Tate. Known as Tookey.'

Tookey Tate. It meant nothing to Hood.

The man had his hat on and kept smoothing his hair on one side with the flat of his palm. He was plainly still on edge. He snicked his fingernails against each other. He watched the glass-panelled door. When the drinks came he swallowed most of the double in one. He held the glass with little finger lifted.

'What's the matter with going to the police?' Hood said.

Tate shook his head worriedly. 'We can't sit here. Get me another drink, will you?' He beckoned the waiter. Hood ordered. A couple of youths had moved over to play the pin-table by the door and Tate kept swaying to see past them. Twice he said: 'Listen, I'll tell you —' Then stopped, as if he wanted to say something but couldn't bring himself to launch into it. The new drinks came.

At that moment a time signal pipped out on the radio behind the bar and Hood remembered the message he had to leave. He said: 'I'm sorry, Mr Tate, I have to go. Pity we haven't had a better chance to become acquainted.'

Tate snapped his eyes from the door and looked at Hood with horror. His face twitched. With an immense effort at self-control he said quietly: 'D-do me a f-favour, Mr Hood and stay, will you?'

For a few seconds, Hood considered him. He had to leave the message for Waldock at the Embassy before eight-thirty. It could not be telephoned. He said: 'I have something I must do. It will take me about fifteen minutes. If you like I'll come back.'

Tate didn't say anything; perhaps he couldn't. He fumbled a cigarette out and managed to light it. Shakily he nodded.

'So be it,' Hood said and got up. 'Fifteen minutes.'

It was coolish outside. Hood walked along the Faubourg St Honoré, turned into the British Embassy and entered a part of the building where he would not be disturbed. He wrote his message and left it with a confidential person.

Striding back among the crowds in front of the smart shops, he looked at his watch. It had taken him fifteen minutes; he would be a couple of minutes late.

At the café the two youths were still at the pin-table by the door. Hood turned to Tate with a reassuring smile. But it was another man, a French workman with a pipe and an evening paper. The rest of the banquette was empty.

Hood looked round. Tate wasn't there. He suddenly felt awful. He descended to the lavatory. No Tate.

The waiter shrugged. 'I don't know. Has he gone? I didn't see him.' Hood noticed that it was not the same waiter and appealed to the woman cashier. The waiter called out: 'It was Julot. He's just gone.'

The woman shook her head. 'The waiter who served you has gone. I didn't notice your friend.' She seemed all right. She even gave him a sympathetic smile.

Hood glanced round at the other customers. They were all the most ordinary-looking people. Everything strictly commonplace. He looked back at the table. The workman was puffing away at his pipe. The Martini ashtray was still there and in it an unsmoked cigarette was burning itself into a long ash.

2

THE HEADQUARTERS BUILDING of the North Atlantic Treaty Organization directed itself like a great stone and glass wedge into the trees of the Bois de Boulogne. The most elegant nursemaids in Paris sauntered beneath its walls. Ageing Countesses watched their poodles cock their legs against its railings. From its towering heights, the more persistently vigilant of its staff could sometimes catch glimpses of other things in the dusky thickets. A romantic spot.

On the sixth floor, Sir Richard Calvert, the British Ambassador to the Alliance, stood looking out at nothing more than the tops of the trees. The first green of leaves was beginning to appear. Beyond was the hazy eminence of Mont Valerien. Two short buzzes made him turn and take the red telephone on his desk.

'The Secretary of State, Sir Richard,' the girl announced.

'Oh, Dick,' the familiar voice came over. 'I'm ringing you urgently because I have two appointments waiting . . .'

Richard Calvert spoke at some length with his chief and laughed once or twice before he put the phone down. He was a man with a useful gift of informality; he also lacked a sense of self-importance, a quality of great rarity. As he was making a note on a pad, the internal telephone rang.

'Mr Hood, Sir Richard. Will you speak?'

'Oh yes.' Richard Calvert smiled. 'Charles, my lad. It's been ages. What are you doing here?'

'Just passing through. As a matter of fact, selling a picture or two,' Hood said.

'Selling — ?' Richard Calvert began, then checked himself, knowing better than to inquire closer.

'I have a Chardin that would tempt you. Very indecent.'

'You ought to try tempting some of our splendid business corporations. Think of the money they'd have made buying Van Goghs or Picassos or something thirty years ago.'

'This one features a young woman showing a rosy behind to an admirer. I can just see it in a Lombard Street board room.'

'Well, how are you? Here for long?'

'Off tonight. This is simply to salute you and give you greeting. How's Daisy?'

'Fine. I'd say come to lunch or drinks, my dear Charles, but I shan't have a moment. We have this big thing coming up; a whole series of meetings. Agonizing reappraisal and all that. And I have just been summoned to the presence – London.'

'Of course. We'll do it when I'm through again.'

They chatted for a few minutes, then Hood said: 'Love to Daisy. So long.'

'Goodbye.'

Sir Richard rang off and buzzed for his secretary. 'We have to be home tomorrow morning, Alison. The PM wants the Secretary of State at Chequers at the weekend.'

'You too?'

'No. It seems to be a restricted affair. We shall only be over thirty-six hours. We'll have to take everything, the full accounts of the last meeting, the Military Committee's A2 and A3, the Bases report and – er . . .'

'The Huntzinger file?'

'Yes. How many copies of that are there?'

'We have one. There were only six made. It's graded Cosmic Secret, the latest Cosmic we've had.'

'All right, Alison. Well, there it is. I leave things to you as usual. We ought to go by eight tomorrow morning. By the way, have the Swedes found my overcoat yet?' Sir Richard had lost his coat at a Swedish Embassy reception.

'No. They're very apologetic. They say the same three women were in the cloakroom all the time during the reception. They're all regularly employed at the Embassy. They say some other guest simply took it by mistake and they are going through the list.'

'I dare say it'll turn up. Now go along, Alison, and send Miss Parsons in. I want to dictate.'

3

ON THAT same superb morning, Charles Hood was walking down the rue de la Paix. It is one of the smartest streets in the world. It is not the grandeur of its sweep, nor the magnificence of its buildings. The rue de la Paix is of modest width and the façades are simple. Nor is it the shops, though they offer things of great and rare beauty. There is an inimitable stamp about the rue de la Paix. And then there are the women you see there. They have great chic.

That morning, the first warmth of approaching spring was in the air. Hood was following a girl for the sheer pleasure of seeing her move in front of him – a divinely pretty girl in a braided Chanel suit with a long neck and a lovely sway of the stern.

She paused at Cartier's window. A necklace of diamonds and great square emeralds glistened before them; he recognized it as a piece which had belonged to Eugénie at Louis-Napoleon's court. Their eyes met in an enamelled mirror.

'You are entirely worthy of the Empress Eugénie's necklace,' he said. She gave him a sidelong glance and an amused little smile and continued on her way. He lost her a few yards on when she turned into a dress shop. But her frank smile of pleasure came to him through the glass door. He gave her an admiring salutation and passed on.

The plate-glass window threw back Hood's own reflection – the figure of a tall and powerfully-made man. Hood stood half an inch over six foot and stripped at twelve stone nine, much of it hard muscle. This made him a shade heavy for a natural cruiser-weight, but he had boxed at the twelve stone six cruiser limit and had got a half-blue at Cambridge in both cruiser- and heavyweight classes.

His eyes were dark grey and humorous; when he smiled there were small fanwise creases at the corners. He looked a clean-cut Englishman, experienced in the ways of the world, which was what he was. He had dark brown hair, which was inclined to curl, good teeth and a voice that women seemed to find very attractive.

Women who didn't know him sometimes took him for an idler, a rich seeker after amusement. Yet there was nothing typed in him. He had the touch of the cosmopolitan, the ease – what the French call *aisance* – that comes from living in many countries and knowing many kinds of men and many kinds of women.

He dressed well, with nonchalance, yet not extravagantly. A few shirt-makers in London and New York and Paris and one in Hong Kong had his measurements; so had a boot-maker in St James's, a gunsmith in Berne and a cutter of sports trousers in Rio.

Hood was a cosmopolitan by taste and by profession. He was described in *Who's Who* as a sportsman and art connoisseur. He could still put up a good track performance. One day, for fun, Roger Bannister had given him forty yards in a quarter of a mile and Hood had run like mad but had just not been able to hold Bannister off. He was a good revolver shot and had finished fifth in the Pentathlon at Melbourne in 1956; and with his friend Hans Freuzeck, he could take a two-man sled down the bob run at St Moritz to within point six of a second of the record.

It was also true that he had bought pictures and sold works of art to rich men in the capitals of Europe, America and the East. But this was part of Hood's 'cover'. His old friend Sir George Tread, head of MI5, a member of White's and Boodle's, formerly of Eton and the Horse Guards, had once asked him to undertake a confidential mission and this had led to others. During the war, Hood had been one of Sir William Stephenson's Secret Service men in America and thus Special Intelligence Security and the Foreign Office called on him from time to time now.

Hood was free to say no if he felt unequal to an assignment. On the other hand, if he ran into anything, he was expected to signal it, so that either he or another agent could pursue it. He was provided with a secret agent's amenities when he wanted them; but otherwise left to his own judgement.

But the *Who's Who* description concealed something further.

Charles Hood was undercover man for a consortium of some of England's dominant financial powers. It had happened that influential friends who had known of his work for Tread and the Foreign Office had asked him to disentangle some highly confidential affairs abroad. Hood had agreed, had managed the thing successfully and been called on again. He did not need to do it for reward. His private means were ample; but it entertained him.

The arrangement was known to a small group of men who control great interests in the City. They consulted together. The Circle was rapidly formed and the door locked. It was a very privileged, closed ring. It had only once been opened since, at the government's pressing request, to admit an Arab king as temporary member. But magnates and mighty corporations had been turned away with the answer that 'the Circle' was just a City legend and only existed in the imagination.

In the early days, there had inevitably been difficulties when Hood, on a mission for the Circle, had run into trouble and laid himself open to the law in some foreign country. But it had quickly been recognized in high places in Westminster that the arrangement was not without advantages. As a government Secret Service man, Hood was a tried and trusted agent, known to be discreet, and it was better, as the Foreign Secretary had argued, to have an inside man in this position than someone who might be an embarrassment, if not a danger, abroad.

Furthermore, the Circle's interests were constantly involved in areas in which the Foreign Office was concerned. The two overlapped, coincided. Great things might be at stake. A political coup in a foreign country could be as much the government's affair as the Circle's and vice versa, since the members of the Circle were frequently the means whereby the government exercised influence in these places. Hood could serve both. It was agreed that the Foreign Office and Security would have call on his services when required.

For the Circle, this had the enormous advantage of covering Hood if he had to take extreme measures to defend himself. In a sense, therefore, Hood's small organization was a privately financed Secret Service enjoying the advantages of official immunity and help when necessary.

The diversity of the Circle's membership indicated the extent of its power. There was the ICC, the immense International Chemicals Corporation; Lavery Brothers, the industrial products trust; Rothsteil and Company, the bankers; Kristoby's, the auctioneers and art dealers; Combined Steel; Jordan Mathews and Son, shipping and finance; Lords of London, the great underwriting complex; Royal Banner oil; the Diamond Trust and International Tobacco. Hood could call on the resources of one or all of these as he needed.

But now, on this sunny April morning in Paris, he was not, as it happened, on the Circle's business. He was embarking on another government mission, for Special Intelligence Security.

He strolled into the Place Vendôme. A parked white Rolls with Mexican plates and a girl with red hair in the front seat caught his eye. He had an idea whose car it was and was tempted to have fun, but veered away.

He went into Harvel's gallery and spent an hour looking at Harvel's stock. But Harvel was asking absurd prices.

Outside, he walked down to the rue du Mont Thabor and turned along it. All at once there was a metallic clang behind him, he glanced round and glimpsed a hurtling grey mass at his shoulder. He flung himself to one side, felt his coat tugged by a giant hand, went sprawling and hit a glass door which flew open under his weight. There *seemed* then to be a muffled shot and the glass crashed and showered over him.

Screams from the shop; mingled with shouts from the

street. Slowly Hood picked himself up in a tinkle of glass splinters. He didn't seem to be hurt. As two shop women fluttered up, he stepped into the street. He was just in time to see a grey Citroën van swing round the corner. Chauffeurs and the chasseurs of the Hotel Meurice opposite were exchanging indignant shouts. The women of the shop were exclaiming:

'He must be crazy!'

'Suddenly swerved in like that.'

'The drivers they let out nowadays!'

'He was drunk. Did you see the way he went round that corner?'

The excitement promised to last for some time. Hood took off his coat, examined the tear. The van had violently swerved into the only empty space there was between the cars parked at the kerb. It had mounted the pavement just as Hood reached the spot, swung away again and gone on without stopping. A long limousine had been nosing warily out of a *porte cochère* opposite at the time. The van *might* have swerved to avoid that. Yet Hood had an uncomfortable feeling that it had been an attempt to kill him. The shot had seemed to come from a gun with a silencer.

Having got rid of the glass, Hood cast rapidly round for trace of a bullet. But in the glass debris and the disorder of things cluttering the shop he could see nothing. He looked outside for an ejected cartridge case, but there was none. One of the women handed him his jacket with the tear summarily pinned up. 'I'll get a policeman,' he said, moving briskly out.

'Oh, but Michèle's gone for one.'

Hood pretended not to hear. He was already on the pavement. Out of the corner of his eye he saw the salesgirl approaching with a policeman. He turned the other way. There was an immediate chorus of shouts from the onlookers. He took no notice. The shouts redoubled behind him. 'Here's one, Monsieur. Monsieur!' Any minute somebody would run up and catch his arm.

Hood wanted to keep clear of the French police. There was only one thing for it, the old Hal Roach comedy trick. He lifted an arm, as if he had seen a policeman at the end of the street, yelled '*Monsieur l'agent!*', broke into a run and sprinted to the corner. To the left, a taxi was just ringing its flag up. Hood reached it in a bound. A few minutes later they were out of the district.

Hood paid off the taxi at the Gare du Nord. He bought a ticket for Pierrefitte on the suburban line and then went into the lavatory. From there he went to the buffet, left by the street door and jumped into a taxi moving away from the kerb. He was confident he was not being followed.

When the taxi dropped him at the Porte de la Villette, he was in a relaxed mood. Lunch beckoned. He made his way to a bistro where, besides being reasonably sure he would not meet any acquaintances, he knew he would get a sublime chop. So it turned out. He had a half-bottle of young Beaujolais with it, freshly chilled. Slaughterers from the Villette *abattoirs* with blood-stained aprons came and stood drinking wine at the counter. Regularly and infallibly, to a clientele of connoisseurs, the bistro served finer meat than any of the swagger Paris restaurants. The place was full of life and agreeable, cheerful bustle. The waiters were swift and attentive. There was none of the heavy digestive atmosphere of the Paris restaurants where businessmen concentrated on tripe and pigs' trotters and gigantic steaks and bottles of wine and double brandies afterwards.

But instead of enjoying the place and its fare as he usually did, Hood felt ill at ease. He had dismissed the van incident; nothing could be done about that anyway. But the figure of Tate recurred to him with relentless persistence.

Why had he been so frightened? The peculiar scene in the lift came back. And where had he gone? There had been something typical about the man that he ought to have recognized, he felt. He had probably left to get drunk somewhere else, up in a Pigalle bar with girls or blue pictures. But Hood felt that wasn't true either.

Hood had the afternoon before him. He was getting the night train to Beaulieu and Lobar. The thing was to go to the café and sit there for an hour and see what happened.

He went back to the centre of town and walked up the Boulevard Malesherbes to St Augustin. The great ugly mass of the church rose like a rock among the swirl of cars and the hurrying crowds. For a moment Hood stood watching; then he went along to the rue Miromesnil and turned down towards the café.

He was approaching this time from the opposite direction and it wasn't until he had reached the end of the street that he saw he had missed it. He turned and went back. Slowly he returned to the spot he had started from. There was no café.

Standing there on the corner, Hood felt the faint chill which signalled danger. It had warned him at moments of strangeness like this in the past. His senses became acute.

Hood retraced his steps. He knew he had not made a mistake. The pavement was narrow and there were many passers-by. He recognized the art gallery with the hard-edge abstracts and a picture by Munch. Next was a hat shop, and beyond that an antique shop which he thought he remembered. The Café had been here . . .

Then he saw it. In place of the café was a wooden hoarding. It was the sort of hoarding that went up whenever a shop changed hands and the shop-fitters moved in to refit. There was even a poster of a cabaret girl in a few feathers, promisingly thrusting out her middle.

Hood opened the door in the hoarding and looked in. Three or four workmen were moving about dismantling the place. Most of the interior had already been stripped. The floor was littered, the wall plaster holed where fittings had been torn away. He looked up. The name had gone.

Yet twenty-four hours before, the place had seemed well-established and prosperous enough. The smell of the plastic covering of the banquette came back to him. It had been new. And he remembered the impression of newness there had been in the garish pink neon, the shining coffee machine and the mirrors.

'Monsieur?' One of the workmen had noticed him.

'What's happened to the café?' Hood said.

'Café? How should I know?' He was a big man with a moustache that drooped at the corners.

'Is the owner here? Somebody in charge?'

'I'm in charge. There's nobody else here.'

'There was a woman at the cash-desk last night. She looked like the owner or the manager's wife. You don't know where — ?'

Roughly the man interrupted. 'Don't know. We're just workmen here, Monsieur. Don't know anything.' He turned back to work. The other men, whose faces had all been turned, watching Hood silently, did the same.

Hood looked round the place again. It was full daylight, mid-afternoon in the heart of a great capital city. There were hundreds of people within sight. The policeman on traffic duty was irritably whistling on a slow car. A window-cleaner opposite was chuckling at a private joke. Along the pavement a white-haired man eyed a girl's legs as she got out of a car. The Sûreté and the Ministry of the Interior were just round the corner. Yet the sense of unreality was for a moment overwhelmingly strong. There was a clatter and some plaster fell.

Hood pulled the door shut and walked away.

4

BREAKFASTING NEXT morning as the Paris–Vintimiglia express left the Provençal fields and sped along the Mediterranean coast, Hood went over the situation ahead.

'Espiritu Lobar is a remarkable man,' George Conder of Special Intelligence Security had said. It was Conder who had briefed Hood at SIS after he had seen the Head Man.

'He has some fine pictures, at all events,' Hood said 'What's the matter with him?'

'The pictures, of course, were why we pulled you in. I'm told you've had dealings with him.'

'I put him in touch with Gilderstein for two pictures which were going, a Greco and a David, both for stiff prices. I once corresponded with him about a picture that was up for sale – he asked my opinion – and even talked to him on the phone. But I've never seen him.'

'We'll show you him in a minute. We have him on film. Queer-looking bird. Enormous personality. I suppose you know none of the news agencies of the world has a single photograph of him? Any there were he bought up years ago.'

Conder offered a cigarette. They lit up.

'Lobar was born, so we believe, at Makarov on Sakhalin. His mother or father, we are not sure which, was an Arakanese, originally from Borneo. At all events, the dominant strain in him was not Japanese. As you'll see, his eyes are not the true Oriental's. He spent his boyhood in destitution and got his first break as a pearl diver for the Japs. For some reason he was sent to prison, did a year, then escaped and turned up in Harbin. He became a German citizen. He was still a young man, but quickly flourished. He bought an old steamer, supposed to be derelict, then another, gave them a cursory refit and sailed. He was heavily suspected of piracy.

Nothing could be proved. Then several rich Chinese merchants were kidnapped from coastal steamers and ransomed for fortunes. He was suspected again.

'Next Lobar was a Portuguese, running a fleet of whaling vessels into the Antarctic. There was an international protest about his ships, but he got away with it. He then moved right over to Chile, all set to go big. I won't bore you with his entire career. His real name is probably Urip. He has been known as Hans Hendorf, Ryosuke Takamore, João da Silva, Andros Sakany, Costas Dilos and Henri Duverne. Enemies of his – those who survive – call him Hammerhead. He has been Japanese, German, Portuguese, Chilean, Greek, Haitian, Monegasque and is now a citizen of Liberia. Nationality, country, mean nothing to him. He is certainly a criminal, possibly a great one.'

'I can think of others,' Hood said. 'How does all this hook up with SIS?'

Conder drew on his cigarette. 'Lobar is a destroyer.' It sounded odd, even a little emotional, in that prosaic room. 'He is active evil. I used to believe that evil was simply a negative concept. Now I believe it is an active thing. Lobar seems to be driven by some force which impels him to destroy.'

'He doesn't destroy pictures, at any rate,' Hood said.

'No. Paintings are about the only things he seems to want to preserve. But behind this mask by which he is known to the world – the immensely rich man, the connoisseur, the gourmet, the yachtsman, the strangely famous man without a face, since there is no precise photographic image of him – he is the agent of corruption, breakdown and defeat.

'He has destroyed innumerable women. Loyalty perishes wherever he lays his hand on it. All through his life he has broken men away from their duty. He has wrecked people's courage. At every point in his career you find him corrupting their honour, their honesty, their love. This isn't, I'm sorry to say, just untested assertion. There are specific examples of all these things, which we will give you to read about after this. Lobar would destroy a thing, not for money but just because he is bound to. That is what he is doing now.'

Conder got up and walked to the window and came back again.

'Lobar has a yacht, the *Triton*. It is undoubtedly the finest yacht in the world. It is big, over three thousand tons. That's much bigger than the old tea clippers, you know. She is registered as a four-masted schooner, but she changes her appearance. Lately, the *Triton* has been spending a lot of time in two areas. In the eastern Mediterranean and round Fernando Po, the Spanish island off the west coast of Africa. She has been off the Turkish coast near some of the island zones which are banned, round Cyprus, near the Île de Lerins where the French are doing miniaturization experiments with missiles, and twice clear west to the Malta area.'

'Doing what?'

'That's what we don't know. But Lobar, we do know, has been on board. Why? He is not an idle yachtsman. He is an extremely energetic man.'

'How about a gal?' Hood said.

Conder smiled. 'She'd have to be some gal to hold Lobar that long. For a time he owned the Great World in Saigon – you know, the big gambling brothel – and you can imagine what *that* provided in the way of girls. Anyway, the *Triton*, we have noticed, takes on a lot more fuel than you think she'd need. She is also much faster than she is supposed to be. The second time she was off Malta she was observed by HMS *Holdfast*, one of our subs, which surfaced a few cables away. The *Holdfast* reckoned she was doing over thirty-five knots – which is a hell of a speed.'

Hood nodded.

'Still more interesting is the way she navigates at times. You remember the *Sverdlov*, the Russian cruiser that came to the Naval Review at Portland? Came batting up at a hell of a lick, without a pilot, without a signal, without a chart – the chartroom was locked – slap up to station? Without batting an eyelid?'

'Lionel Crabb?' Hood said. 'We wanted to know how?'

'Right,' Conder said. 'We'd still like to know how. Crabb, of course, was lost examining the *Ordzhonikidze*, but he'd been down to the *Sverdlov* before that. There was some device; it wasn't all just a wonderful feat of memory by the *Sverdlov*'s captain as some of the papers tried to make out. We think there is something like this device on the *Triton*.'

Hood nodded again.

'We're getting Naval Intelligence to go over the technicalities with you. It is possibly a novel version or a development of what the Navy boys call SINS, the Ship Inertial Navigation System which is used in our nuclear submarine. Anyway, the *Triton* has been seen behaving in this curious way once for sure. It was in poor visibility off Aliaga in Turkey. Aliaga can be a difficult entrance; but she came batting in and tied up to a buoy as if nothing had happened and her master didn't seem to be acquainted with the place.'

Hood drew on his cigarette. Incongruously a jazz air came up from somewhere outside.

'But more than any of this is what Crabbie was really after with the Russians. We have certain underwater defences. You may have been told?' Hood nodded. This was highly secret ground. 'The NID people will tell you any more they think you should know. At all events, we don't *think* the Russians have anything to cope with our underwater system. Has the *Triton*? Has she been trying something out?'

'Try any frogmen?' Hood asked.

There was a pause. 'We haven't,' Conder said. 'The Turks did.'

'And he didn't come back?'

'They did not even find the headless body.'

'I understand,' Hood said.

'We are providing you with a Gainsborough, a Romney and three other pictures as bait. Choose whichever you like and take them with you. If Lobar doesn't want any of them, which I suppose is hardly likely, for God's sake don't press them on him. You can imagine the time we've had getting them out of the Treasury. We want everything you can find out about the *Triton*, which we believe is spying, and about Lobar.'

Hood said: 'Who is he working for? The Chinese?'

'Might be anybody. We don't think he has any master. But if you want a name and address, the nearest is Satan, old boy. Lobar is dangerous and he will undoubtedly have you killed if he thinks you are getting too close in to things. Now let's have a look at those film shots we have of him. They're not very good but they'll give you an idea.'

The train passed a cluster of yellow houses. There were olive trees, a beautiful eucalyptus. The folds of the mountains rose behind. A dog trotted alongside a boy on a bicycle going down a dusty red road. The sky was blue. Then they were running into Nice. Boarding-house signs went by: Les Flots Bleus. Pension Beausejour. English Teas.

Conder's recital, the cinema showing, the rooms near St James's Park where the security of the British Isles and many distant parts was cared for, seemed remote.

'Encore du café, Monsieur?' It was the waiter. 'Beaulieu in fifteen minutes.'

'No thanks,' Hood said. He paid and left.

The small open station at Beaulieu was bright with spring flowers. Hood sniffed the familiar mixture of Mediterranean smells with pleasure. The conductor handed down the two carefully packed pictures and the luggage and a porter took charge under Hood's watchful eye. They went through the small booking-hall. At the kerb outside was a long dark green Alfa Romeo convertible with Gianetti coachwork. A liveried chauffeur stepped forward.

'Mr Charles Hood? I've been instructed to meet you, sir. Mr Lobar's compliments; a launch is waiting to take you on board straight away.'

My God, thought Hood, this is fast. He hoped he had controlled his surprise. Lobar had evidently been told of the call Hood had made at his Paris flat. But the rest? Hood thought fast.

'That's very kind of Mr Lobar. But I have a call to make first. Would you go to La Reserve.'

'Certainly, sir.'

They stowed the pictures and luggage and Hood got in. As they drove down to the sea, Hood's mind was mapping out contingencies. This was a brilliant opening move by Lobar; and Hood saw that everything might depend on how he played it. The call they were now making was a subterfuge to give him time.

The car drew into the Reserve drive. Hood told the chauffeur to wait. Inside, the hall porter said: 'Well, good morning Mr Hood. This is a great pleasure.'

'Good morning, Marcel. Tell me, is Dr Arlborg in?'

'Dr Arlborg? Let me see, one or two a's? I don't think he's arrived yet. If you'd like to ask the reception what — '

'No. It's possible he won't be here for a couple of days. I want to leave a note for him.'

'Certainly, Mr Hood.'

Hood went through to the empty writing-room, scribbled a meaningless note to the imaginary Dr Arlborg, and sealed it in an envelope. Then he stood at the window looking out on to the celebrated view of the sea and coast. One question was hammering in his mind. Should he put himself in Lobar's hands in this way? Lobar was obviously trying to take him in charge – with a purpose.

Hood was not a man to colour situations of this sort. Yet, looking out at that dazzling scene – the cold blue water, the rocks, a single sail, he felt something ominous and deadly was very close to him. Like swimming out into that blue water out there, knowing that a hammerhead shark was lying in wait.

He paced restlessly up and down in front of the windows. Yet the opportunity could not be missed. The invitation to go aboard the *Triton* meant that he would be at close quarters at once. He finished the cigarette, stubbed it out, went through and gave the letter to the porter with a tip. He had made up his mind.

'Thank you, Mr Hood.'

Outside, the chauffeur was waiting. He opened the door. 'Very well, now we can go to the boat,' Hood said.

They swung along the sea front, then through the quiet roads behind towards St Jean and Cap Ferrat. On either side were the discreetly screened villas. Lemons and oranges were ripening on trees in the gardens. The palms stirred luxuriantly in the warm breeze. The roads were swept and neat. Through gates he got glimpses of maids and chauffeurs. Men painted bright blue tables. Gardeners with baskets leisurely swept paths. There was still the mark of affluence here all right. It was all good to Hood.

But something nagged at him. He thought it was the chauffeur. It was almost as if he had seen the man before. He kept glancing at the tiny reflection of the man's face in the driving mirror.

Then he got it. It was the army corporal who had hurried past down the street the night he had been with Tate.

5

AT ST JEAN harbour they pulled up. A launch was waiting at the jetty, swaying gently against white corded fenders. The chauffeur and the coxswain transferred the luggage and pictures. Just awash, at the stern of the launch, Hood noticed a long steel tube with twin outlets – a double silencer. That probably meant two V engines; five hundred horse-power or so.

He got in. The chauffeur stood saluting as the launch bubbled off; then, as Hood watched from the stern, he turned and went briskly back to the car and drove away. The launch engines revved and the craft surged forward.

Hood looked about him. The launch was a handsome craft, obviously specially designed. It had a raked two-level cabin, white-covered seats and decks immaculately holy-stoned. The panel of instruments glittered in front of the wheel. The whole thing was obviously a show-piece. Beside the coxswain at the wheel, there were two other hands amidships and a fourth forward. They didn't *need* that many, Hood thought. This launch could be run by two. The men were brown-skinned and hefty, in white drill uniforms and looked more like Malays than anything, though bigger-built. They were all silent and took no notice of Hood.

The *Triton* was lying well out. As they approached, Hood stood on the step and examined her. She was much bigger than he had expected, a beautiful thing. Her four tall masts swayed gently in the swell. She was like a racing clipper of the past, but three times the size. The shimmering dark green of her hull set off the white upperworks. Now and then a brass fitting flashed in the sun.

At the top of the gangway a quartermaster and another hand saluted. A moment later, a steward in a white jacket was leading Hood amidships. He was thin, youngish, going bald, with long pale fingers. 'This way, sir.' Hood could not place his accent. They stepped into a vestibule; the steward opened a door on the far side. 'This is your suite, sir.'

They entered a sitting-room in which the first thing Hood saw was a breath-taking antique fresco. Beyond was a bedroom and a dressing-room with a bathroom adjoining. The whole thing was done with supreme taste and luxury. There wasn't much furniture. Everywhere there were rare pieces. They were disposed not as objects simply to be looked at but to be lived with, used and touched – a Jacob chair, a small Riesener and Oeben desk, a Greek bowl, a jewelled Renaissance enamel cigarette box and a large spray of gold and diamond and rose enamel flowers by Fabergé, one of a pair, the other of which, Hood knew, was at Sandringham. The contrasts were very effective. The little dressing-room, for example, was monastic in its bare simplicity. There was a Cézanne and a Kees van Dongen of a girl, all eyes, in a red hat, in the sitting-room and a gorgeous Courbet nude in the bedroom.

The steward said: 'Mr Lobar is sorry he cannot be here to greet you. He hopes you will be comfortable until he arrives.'

'When will that be?'

The steward shrugged. He looked pretty smooth to Hood. 'If you would care for me to show you our arrangements, sir?' he said. He moved a small panel. 'The buzzers here will call room service, the barber, your valet, a secretary. There are duplicate sets in the other cabins.'

'Fine.'

'Would you prefer a girl masseuse, sir? Or Ching? He is also our acupuncture specialist.'

'I – I'll have to consider that,' Hood said.

The steward touched a switch and another panel slid. 'Here are the radio-telephone, television, dictaphone, stereo, internal telephone, as you see . . .'

Hood was trying to work out where the man came from as they moved round; but he couldn't. 'How many passengers can you accommodate?' he asked.

'It depends, sir.'

'What on?'

'How far we're going and where, sir.'

That was pretty vague, Hood thought. The man wasn't exactly a stool-pigeon.

More demonstrations in the bedroom. 'The bed, sir, if you press this lever, will not roll. It is cradled and will remain independent of the ship's motion.'

Hood glanced at him sharply. Did Lobar intend putting to sea? But the steward was looking upward to the deckhead over the bed. 'You may care for a mirror, sir. This button by the bedside ...' Hood looked up and saw his own reflection. A mirror had moved into place over the double bed.

'It will tilt, sir, at will. Just turn the knob.' The mirror tilted for an angle view.

'Yes, I see.'

'The air conditioning, sir.' They moved on. There were, it appeared, also a Turkish bath on board, a gymnasium, Lobar's picture gallery, and the doctor would naturally prescribe whatever you needed sir – which sounded like an open invitation, if you happened to sniff cocaine or whatever. As a parting shot, the steward said: 'There is this button, sir, which is left blank. It calls a hostess. We have two.'

'Oh yes?'

'They will look after your entertainment in any way you need.'

'Like making a fourth at bridge?'

'Yes, sir.' The man was impassive.

'What are their working hours?' Hood said, as a joke.

'They are at your disposal at all times,' the man said deadpan.

'Do you often have passengers?'

'It depends, sir. Will that be all for the moment, sir?'

'Thank you.'

As soon as the man had gone, Hood exploded with amusement. A girl masseuse, a watch-it-in-the-glass bedroom, a dope-peddling doctor and two hostesses! It was the pure

Oriental touch. Lobar had not run the Great World for nothing! He expected his guests to enjoy themselves without inhibitions.

Hood took a cigarette from a box and lit it. But after the first draw he stubbed the thing out; a reefer. He stood looking at the box for a moment, then put a couple of the reefers in his case. You never knew.

It was still hardly mid-morning. He undressed and took a slow bath. The bath, like most of those in French hotels, was a bit short for him. While he was in it, the valet came into the bedroom and wanted permission to unpack his things. He stood close to the bathroom door and spoke in a loud voice. Hood told him to go ahead, but leave the pictures alone.

The odd reappearance of the corporal as Lobar's chauffeur which had been pushed to the back of his mind by the arrival on board, kept recurring to him. It worried him that he could make no sense of it. It was also curious that Lobar should so obviously expect him and yet be absent.

Wrapped in a bathrobe, he rang room service, ordered a double martini and when it came walked round drinking and examining the suite. There was probably a spy-hole somewhere, but it would be difficult to find. Probably a microphone too. He slid the panel back from the radio-telephone and other instruments. He would have to dislocate them, as a precaution.

He unpacked the two pictures he had brought, a small Gainsborough and a Sickert. The Sickert, an interior, had a lovely dominant green. After a while, he turned from contemplating them. He needed somewhere to hide a gun. He had his Yassida with him, an Israeli pistol that he liked very much, a fourteen-ounce double-action gun with a two-inch barrel and large grip. It fired a ·38 special and fitted easily but not too snugly into the special pocket at his belt. There was a hammerless model like the Smith & Wesson Centennial, but Hood would not have used it for love or money. The art of quick shooting, especially when you were stalking a man or in the dark, depended on double-action – on a gun having a hammer. And anyway, for other occasions, the Yassida, like his favourite Colt, had a hammer hood which clipped over the hammer and stopped it catching in clothing on the draw.

He put the pictures back in the packing and stepped round examining it. It would be possible to hide the pistol inside, but he didn't much like it. He looked round the cabin. The space between the fresco and its mount was too narrow. The cavity in which the port-hole jalousie descended? But there were screws to tackle and the space would be deep.

He went into the bathroom; the removable inspection panel of the enclosed bath looked too obvious. In a corner he saw a small ventilator grille. Lifting the grille off, he felt inside. The outlet narrowed about six inches down. The pistol, he found, would not go beyond this point. He wrapped the gun in a handkerchief, lowered it into the outlet and replaced the grille. That seemed satisfactory.

Then he went back into the cabin and dressed. It seemed like a good opportunity to do a little exploring before Lobar appeared. In the middle of buttoning his shirt he stopped.

He was listening. It struck him that the ship was very quiet. There was the same intense quiet he had noticed at the block of flats in Paris. You couldn't hear anything. There were simply one or two of the creaks a ship makes as she moves at anchor. He was not far below the upper deck, he knew. Yet there were no sounds from it.

He went into the bathroom, yanked the plug clear of the bath and turned both taps full on. Then he shut the door and retreated into the bedroom. He stood still listening. He could only hear the faintest sound of the gushing water.

Soundproofed.

He looked down. Thick carpets everywhere, including the dressing-room. Molto curioso, Hood said to himself. Very curious. He finished dressing and went out. The steward was standing in the vestibule. Just by chance, Hood supposed. With or without Lobar on board, it didn't look as if he was going to get far alone.

'If you'd care for a drink before lunch, sir, the bar is one deck below. The lift is here, sir.'

'Thanks.'

Hood took the narrow lift. He had to duck to get in. It was marked *Deux personnes*. To his mild surprise there was nobody to meet him at the bottom. But as soon as he had shut the door the lift rose again. He stepped forward into a biggish oval bar with white leather walls and leopard-skin banquettes and a few soft armchairs. Soft lights. A little sweet music coming from somewhere. A bar at one end. No barman. The place was empty.

Hood smiled, walked to the bar and mixed himself a martini. He cut a snip of lemon skin, pinched it and dropped it in. He lit a cigarette and wished himself good health.

And then slowly, at the far end of the room, he saw a bare light-brown arm rise above the back of a chair, then another rise and clasp it in a stretch. Slowly they disappeared and the head and shoulders of a girl appeared. She turned and looked at him silently.

6

SHE WAS extremely beautiful.

'Who are you?' she said.

By God, said Hood to himself admiringly.

'Say, who are you? How d'you get here?'

Whew! Hood was thinking, that's the best-looker I ever saw. She rose slowly from the chair with her eyes on him. She was a honey brown with finely defined lips, one of those breathtaking half-breed mixtures which the mingling of Eastern and Western races sometimes produces.

She was tall, a golden dream of a girl. The column of her neck moulded into superb shoulders which were nude except for the slimmest shoulder-straps. She was in a low-cut cream evening dress.

'Are you crazy, you? Hey *you*!' She started forward, suddenly dipped to the floor and Hood dodged as a bottle came sailing at him. It hit the panel behind him with a thud.

'What are you doin' here? Hey – you, who let you in here? Who ask you to come down here in this my-place?' She snatched a glass from a table and threw it ferociously at him.

'Hell to you!' she shouted.

Hood was smiling, bubbling with inner amusement and pleasure at seeing such a lovely girl. Whoosh! Something else came flying through the air and smashed against a bottle-rack behind him. Dodging, he spilt his martini.

'My dear young woman —'

'Get out! Get out! Leave me alone.' She blazed at him, casting furiously round for something more to throw. 'I don't want see you, don't want argue. If Lobar sent you, tell him go to hell.'

'If you'll listen —'

But she suddenly stalked to the glass door at the bottom of the lift-shaft and banged on it so hard Hood thought the glass would break. She shouted a stream of imprecations in some language Hood didn't understand, presumably to the steward above, and rattled the door handle. Then she switched to mixed French and English.

'*Créature que vous êtes!* I told you leave me alone. What the hell you mean, Perrin? Answer me!'

Perrin evidently knew better than to respond.

Just as furiously she flung away, lips parted, her magnificent eyes blazing. She came straight up to Hood and stood before him, a few inches away, her eyes going over his face.

Hood had had experience of many women. But this feeling was new. Her presence was magnetic. She passed her tongue over her lower lip, then took the lip in her teeth.

'I'm sorry,' Hood said. 'I didn't know you were here.'

Her eyes lowered and travelled frankly over him.

'Give me a drink,' she said. She ran a hand through her dark mahogany hair.

Hood gave her a slug of Black Label Scotch and soda. She picked it up and drank it all. He wanted to say: you don't drink whisky like that.

'You still haven't told me who you are,' she said.

'Well, my name is Charles Hood.'

'What you doin' here?'

'I've come to show some pictures to Lobar. If that's all right with you?'

Slowly she smiled – and Hood felt indefinable things. She was compelling and entirely beautiful. If she were one of the 'hostesses' it said even more for Lobar.

'What about you?' Hood said.

'You can call me Ivory. That's my name.' She turned, moved down the bar, turned again and stood looking at him sideways. 'How long are you staying, Mr Hood?'

'I don't know. When is Lobar coming back?'

She didn't respond, but gave a rapid glance away. He saw her mood had abruptly changed again.

'Give me another drink, Mr Hood. And for God's sake

stop that corn. I want some jazz – noise! It's like being buried here – drowned!' She slammed a switch and the sweet music cut. Then she stepped away and did something else – Hood didn't see what – and a panel in the ship's side slid back showing a heavy plate-glass window into the sea. They were just below the water-line. The greenish water was luminous from the sun.

'Didn't you know we're drowned?' She laughed. The next moment the underwater scene was lit up still brighter. Some fish nosed up to the glass and swam on.

'Arcs?' Hood said.

She nodded. 'It is a little game. At night, when we are in the tropics, you see another world through there. All the big things come up, the monsters, squids and giant rays and sharks. It amuses Lobar to have a shark at his elbow, a foot away. He laughs at them.'

'Cosy.'

She drank the whisky, again in one. Suddenly she put her hands under both breasts, voluptuously circled them and slowly lifted her arms above her head in another stretch. She said: 'Turn the stereo on, there. I want to dance.'

Hood turned the dial set into the bar.

Hot black jazz came out of a hidden speaker. Ivory was in the middle of the room. She kicked off her shoes, raised her arms again and began a slave dance. Her haunches moved in a lithe circular movement, slowly at first, with powerful deliberation, then into a little crescendo and down again. Gradually the muscles of her belly kneaded the movement and she began giving small outward thrusts which she accompanied with sharp intakes of breath.

'Louder,' she said, half closing her eyes. Hood turned the volume up. The raucous beat of the jazz filled the room. Every now and then, she lifted her shoulders as her haunches came up and out. She was driving harder and, slightly bending her knees, began pounding with the thrusts, harder, as the whole rhythm of the band seemed to move into one concentrated beat.

'More!'

Hood flicked the dial again. The music was deafening. The beat became faster. Her eyes were shut and her lips half open. There was a tiny film of sweat on her face. One shoulder-strap slipped off and her movements shook the dress down, half showing her breast. Her head was thrown back.

Hood watched fascinated. He was amazed at the completeness with which she had plunged into this erotic mood, without a preliminary.

All at once, his eye was caught by a movement to one side of the room. A door opened, soundlessly in the blazing cover of the jazz, and a man came in. He was in a white steward's coat and black trousers, a small man with rather fluffy untidy hair.

He stood just inside the door looking at Ivory. He did not even glance in Hood's direction. There was something about his expression that was strangely like a peasant's, a simple rough-skinned look. His eyes were alive.

He stood there smiling a little as he watched her. He moistened his lips.

Ivory was driving faster. Now her movement was hard outward and upward and a screw back. She held her arms extended in front of her, as if she were embracing someone. She was breathing hard. Her torso followed the undulations. The rhythmic intakes of her breath were visible in the movements of her bosom and shoulders. She was obviously transported.

To Hood it was obsessive. Her erotic compulsion seemed to communicate itself to him. A still more maniacal beat of the music with drummers and piercing clarinets was working up to a climax.

The shoulder-strap snapped. Then the steward made a movement. For some reason, she noticed it. She turned and saw him; her face changed. She made a trembling effort to get control of herself, then she twisted out of the dance movement and flew at him.

She screamed at him in a fury. The sounds were covered

by the blaze of the jazz. Hood seemed to come out of a blur, turned and twirled the stereo volume down. In the crash of quiet her voice seemed tiny: 'Get out! Get out, you! Filthy spy – you dare come here! I'll kill you, Andreas! I'll —' She was hitting at him. The man had his arms up against her blows and dodged away.

'No, no, Mademoiselle. Be reasonable ... I am good to you. ...' He barked out the words in a half-humorous way, making grimaces.

For a moment it looked as if she were going to catch him. But he ducked away through the door. She rattled and banged on it, calling insults. Then she flung away and flopped in one of the big armchairs, her head on her arm.

Hood leant on the bar gazing at her. If possible, she was more beautiful than before. Her bosom was heaving, her high breasts prominent above the dress. After a moment her eyes opened. She smiled. 'You like Salome's prayer dance?' she said, and laughed.

'What was she praying for?'

'Get me a drink, Mr Hood.' Her voice was like cream on velvet.

He poured her another Scotch and took it over to her.

'Where's yours?' she said.

He mixed a fresh martini and sat on the arm of her chair. Still lying deep in the chair she looked up at him. 'There's a word – wait a minute – for you and me ... affinity.'

'Could be.' In a strange way it was true.

'Not could be, is, Mr Hood.' She turned her head and bit his hand.

'Who was the steward you chased out?'

'Andreas? Oh, he's just Lobar's valet. He's maddening. Always round you.'

There was a faint click behind them. Hood looked round. Perrin, the steward who had shown him his cabin, had stepped out of the lift. He had apparently decided that Ivory's temper was cooler. 'Would you care for lunch to be served here, sir?'

'Why not?'

'For two,' Ivory said. 'And bring a pint of pink champagne. Roederer.'

'Yes, Mademoiselle.'

She bit Hood's hand again.

They had an impeccably served lunch; shrimp cocktail, saddle of lamb with *romarin*, fresh salad, ice-cream. It was prolonged – and Hood found himself not wanting this interlude to end. Ivory drank most of the Roederer and had Perrin bring another pint. She was agreeably and amusingly drunk.

He tried her about the chauffeur, but didn't get anywhere. There were several, she said, they came and went. And what the hell, she said, with her eyes on him over the rim of the glass. He remembered the almost unbelievable seductions that British women agents had brought off during the war and wondered if Ivory had been assigned to take care of him. For some reason, people supposed that technique was old hat nowadays. But Hood knew it wasn't.

Gently he tried to pump her about Lobar. Why, as it had seemed, was she angry with *him*? For an instant she looked as if she were going to flare up. But she threw it off, or forgot it, and the next minute was laughing again.

She was diversely entertaining; and he was constantly held by her beauty. He found he had left his watch in the cabin – it was long after Perrin had cleared away the table and gone – but time seemed of no importance. They sat on the banquette smoking. She had been born at Manado in the Celebes, she said, where her father, 'a blond god from Helsinki', had come trading for a season. He had seduced her mother, aged twelve, the fresh bride of a headman who had killed him and hung him from the top of a cocoa palm. The headman had made her mother sleep below the tree and watch the body till it putrefied and fell. But he had been drowned himself a month later. Ivory had been taken to Canton by a rich Portuguese when she was thirteen. 'He gave my mother fifty escudos for me. That was a lot. He was kind to me – oh, a little perverted. But he knew he couldn't keep me. Men were easy. I ran away. Maybe I'll tell you one day.' She laughed.

'Tell me now.'

She said: 'I feel like getting a little bit tighter, only a little, little bit.'

Her head was close to his shoulder. 'What are you doing here, anyway?'

'I've told you, selling some pictures.'

She put her hand lightly on his arm. 'Have you come to amuse me, Mr Hood?' Her movement broke the shoulder-strap again where she had pinned it. But with another laugh she jumped up, refixed it, while he went to the bar and brought back two whiskies.

Quickly her earlier mood of animation returned. She made him put the stereo jazz on and they danced. Her body was firm against his. But he could feel her wanting to break loose into something wilder and suddenly she twisted away. 'Wait, wait. Make it loud, make it strong.'

Hood turned the volume up again. She was in the middle of the floor, haunching again in the dance; but as he turned round from the stereo, she unzipped her dress, writhed out of it and let it drop.

Hood stood stock still. She was wearing a narrow cup bra, a black suspender girdle and briefs. The drink seemed abruptly to have accumulated its effect on her. There was complete abandon in her movements. She faced him, her arms entwined above her head, then in one rippling move, she stripped off the bra and threw it at him. Her full breasts were firm and magnificent. She held out her arms to him.

'Charles . . .'

She had long beautifully tapering legs. Her mat brown skin would have made any woman. The music was drumming faster. She dropped her hands to her thighs, unfastening her stockings. She rolled one, flipped it off, then the other. Her breasts quivered. Hood saw that she wasn't stripping as a tease, but out of sheer voluptuousness.

She seemed to make bigger lunges with her hips as she slipped down the briefs. She lowered them past her knees, stepped out of one leg, catching the briefs on the other foot and sending them flying. Now she only had on the black girdle with dangling suspenders.

Her head went back. Her extended hands entwined before her, then she brought her hands underneath her breasts, lifting them up, while she ground with her hips. The next moment, as if she was unable to wait any longer, she pulled the girdle down and wriggled naked out of it.

For a fraction longer she kept up the thrusting rhythm. Then she faltered, extended her fingers in a trembling climax, dropped to her knees and tilted gently to the floor.

Hood wasn't sure how he ought to deal with this. He went over and took her arm. She was immobile. 'Come on, Ivory. Maybe you ought to get some rest.' She swayed, and he saw that the alcohol had suddenly overcome her.

He lifted her to her feet. She leant on him, her head on his shoulder. He put his arm round her, took her over to the banquette and laid her down. She looked as if she were out. He covered her up with her dress. But the next minute she threw it off and jumped up.

'Now, Ivory, be a good, nice – sensible — '

'Take me up on deck.' She clung to him, arms round his neck. 'We gon' drown down here.'

Hood had a momentary image of Lobar arriving at this point.

'Much better down here, Ivory. Now you lie there — '

'No, no. You take me on deck. Wan' go on deck, now.'

'All right, but get dressed. You can't go on deck like that.'

'I do what I like here. Who says not? D'you think they don' wan' see Ivory. . . .' She swayed, holding him, persisting. Hood tried to quieten her down. At moments she leant her full weight on him. Her breasts came against his chest. He couldn't avoid holding her.

Then she keeled gently over on to the banquette – out.

Hood contemplated her for a minute and sighed. He

picked up the dress and managed, with a bit of a struggle, to pull it approximately on her. He tucked the girdle under her head, gave her a friendly pat and went to the lift.

He lit a cigarette and exhaled a long jet of smoke as the lift carried him up. 'Some introduction!' he said to himself.

7

IT WAS DARK by the time he had freshened up and gone out on deck. He had not had nearly as much liquor as Ivory had; but he had had enough. The fresh air was good.

The lights on the coast shimmered beyond Cap Ferrat on the left, through Beaulieu to Monaco and Italy on the right. Along the Middle and Upper Corniches they were strung out like garlands across the dark mountains.

The *Triton* lay just in the lee of the Cap Ferrat headland. The dark mass of land was dominated by the light of the semaphore on the highest point. At intervals, the sky was faintly and briefly illuminated as the Cap light, on the far side, flashed round.

Farther down, Hood identified the lights of the Hospice. The little port of St Jean seemed full of animation. Distantly he caught the sound of music from a loudspeaker. Towards Beaulieu, a single light shone in the Villa Leopolda where Leopold II of the Belgians had tickled the fancies of his mistresses and Hood wondered who could be there now among the ancient ghosts? The headlights of cars sped across the road viaduct from Monaco.

Seen from the *Triton*'s deck, it was a glittering and splendid sweep of coast. It would, thought Hood, undoubtedly have pleased Jackie. Jackie Please, his girl secretary, had wanted to come along. But Hood had told her there was nothing doing.

Jackie Please was blonde, American and twenty-one with a resilience and a – he could think of no more exact term for it – a juiciness which Hood at times found sorely provocative. She had lately gone in for a Kim Novak white rinse which suited her. But apart from these attributes, she was good at her job without having the spiky efficiency of the model secretary. To begin with, Hood could not believe she wasn't vain. But when he found she wasn't, it enormously enhanced her value to him and her general attractiveness – a thing that he had found nine women out of ten simply did not understand. She had a sense of humour and, most precious, illusions. Hood could never have stood the hard-bitten secretaries some of the men he knew put up with in the name of 'efficiency'.

Jackie had been produced one day by Robert Whitney, known as Chuck, Hood's assistant. Chuck Whitney had met her in New York where she had been in the cast of a grandiose musical version of *Ivanhoe* which Whitney had lost a small fortune in backing.

Hood and Whitney had known each other for years since a memorable July at Henley when they had twice rowed off a heat in the Diamond Sculls and twice dead-heated, a feat unprecedented in the annals of the event. At the third shot, Whitney, a couple of years younger than Hood, had won by a quarter of a length.

Whitney was Irish, the grandson of a man who had made a fortune at twenty-one by buying up a supposedly derelict gold mine in Australia and striking it rich. Chuck, the only son, had inherited a great deal of money. His father had made him read Law and work in the City and on Wall Street for a time, which had bored him absolutely, since he had his grandfather's taste for risk and the unusual. He had escaped some of the boredom by spending money frivolously on the stage and figuring in several breakneck episodes abroad. When the Circle had made its proposal, Hood had thought of Whitney as a partner. (Besides anything else, Whitney knew a great number of people.) By chance, they had lunched together a couple of days before. Hood proposed they team up and Whitney jumped at the idea.

They had made their headquarters in a quiet house in Curzon Street, at the top of which Hood had a small bachelor flat.

It was cool on deck. The vessel creaked gently as she

moved. The water lapped pleasantly against the side. Hood walked round, crossing from one side to the other. Members of the crew passed now and then, going forward and aft. There was a boom out to port, the landward side, and he saw that the motor-launch was tied up to it. That looked as if Lobar were not coming off tonight.

Hood finished his cigarette and went down to his cabin. He rang room service and ordered *consommé*, toast, cheese and biscuits and a bottle of Vichy-Celestins. When the man brought it, Hood told him he did not want to be disturbed again.

'Very well, sir. What time would you like a call in the morning, sir?'

'Don't trouble, I'll wake.' Hood had the faculty of being able to set his mind like an alarm clock before he went to sleep and waking to within ten minutes of the hour fixed next morning.

As he dined he wondered what Ivory was in the ship's set-up. Not one of the hostesses, at any rate. They were two Danish girls, she had told him, called Karen and Bente. But she hadn't volunteered anything more. She seemed more like Lobar's girl friend. No doubt he would soon find out.

He undressed and got into bed, turned out the main light, leaving the pleasant bedside light on. The bed was supremely comfortable, cool and taut, yet soft – and with space between his feet and the end. Hood cared for good beds. The worthiness of beds was a thing too sketchily dealt with by the philosophers of human happiness. By a miracle, the pillow, too, was not an inconsistent mass which wrapped itself round his ears – Hood would rather have had a Japanese wood block – but softly and supportingly firm.

He yawned and reached for the light-switch, thinking, as he put his head down, seven o'clock. Wake at seven o'clock. Then a thought occurred to him. He looked across the cabin, withdrew his hand from the switch and got out of bed. He crossed to the bathroom, lifted the grille off the ventilator and put his hand into the space.

The gun was gone.

Hood woke next morning at three minutes past seven. Bright sunshine was coming through the curtains over the two port-holes. There was a tap at the door.

'Come in.'

It was Perrin with a tray of silver things and newspapers. 'Good morning, sir. I trust you slept well. May I run your bath?'

'Thank you.' Damn curiously timed, he thought. Hood was beginning to dislike Perrin. Those long pale fingers – they were surely damp too – were like the tendrils of some unhealthy plant.

Perrin put the tray down and crossed to the bathroom. When he came out he said: 'Tea or coffee, sir?'

'Neither at this moment,' Hood said. 'I'll have tea at breakfast, a boiled egg—'

'Mr Lobar would be glad if you would join him at breakfast.'

So he's back, thought Hood. 'Yes, with pleasure,' he said.

'On the small veranda, sir, aft. When you are ready, sir, I'll show you the way.' He took the tray and went out.

Well, thought Hood, shaving, here we go. He wondered when Lobar had come aboard. The launch had been tied up at the boom until after dark, so it had probably been early this morning. Of course he might have been on board all the time.

As he towelled himself with one of the superbly rough hard-dried towels, Hood felt keyed up. He was glad he had had a glimpse of Lobar on the SIS film and was not going to the encounter entirely unprepared. His earlier dealings with Lobar seemed oddly remote.

In the bedroom he found his clothes laid out – evidently the valet had silently come and gone. He dressed. Perrin was waiting in the vestibule. They went on deck, walked aft and up a short companion. There was a semicircular bay with an awning, white-covered chairs and a table. Lobar was at the table eating breakfast.

'Mr Hood. Good morning. I am glad we meet at last.' He rose. 'Please sit down.'

Hood got two shocks in that same moment as he gripped Lobar's extended hand. First, Lobar was overpowering in his physical bulk, much bigger than Conder's film had suggested. He had the massive shoulders, chest and arms of a Japanese Sumo wrestler, but without the belly or, Hood guessed, much fat at all. He had a big bald oval head and three gold teeth at the side of his mouth which was now smiling at Hood. He was wearing a plain flaming scarlet silk Kimono and the impression of power, of personality, was enormous.

But what struck Hood, once he had taken in the bulk, were Lobar's eyes and the red weal running round his neck. The left eye stared. It was lidless.

'I appreciate your coming, Mr Hood. You have brought another Greco perhaps?'

Then Hood saw his Yassida pistol on the table.

'Passion fruit, sir?' Andreas, the valet, who was serving, bent at his elbow. 'Avocado? Papaya? Grapefruit?'

'Avocado,' Hood said, rather mechanically.

'Ah, I see you are wondering what this is,' Lobar said. He held up the pistol. 'Perhaps we are expecting pirates, you say.' Lobar smiled, lifting the side of his mouth and showing his gold teeth again. 'I am told it was found in your cabin. I was a little perplexed. But it is a toy somebody has left behind, don't you think? What else? For one moment I did ask myself – It is not yours, Mr Hood?'

The lidless eye stared at him.

Hood said coolly: 'I had a tip from Scotland Yard. There were some crooks after the pictures I've brought. They told me to take precautions. So I brought that.'

'In that case, of course, allow me to give it back to you,' Lobar said. He waved the gun. 'I tried to make it work. But I do not understand it. You could not hurt your friends much with that, I think, Mr Hood, let alone crooks, eh?' He laughed in his brass voice.

He handed it to Hood. 'Show me how it works. Show me how you would shoot down the villains. It is so entertaining at breakfast.'

Hood glanced at the pennant at the masthead, lifted the pistol. But the trigger fell back loosely under his finger. He broke the gun. The shells were there. He thought he could feel the trouble. The torsion pins on the trigger and the hammer had been broken – an expert little piece of demolition.

'Well,' he gave a laugh. 'It means I shall have to foil them by selling you both pictures.' He laid the Yassida on the deck at his feet.

Lobar was sitting back in his chair, looking at him. 'Tell me, Mr Hood, how have you been keeping? What did you think of my Hals in Paris? I heard you had called.'

Hood poured a tiny pool of vinegar into his avocado and peppered. It was exciting and dangerous, yet, on the surface extremely civilized. There was every attendant luxury. He could look out over the sea sparkling in the sun. The coastline, one of the golden playgrounds of Europe, lay, greenish-grey in the early haze, half a mile distant. The ship where he was so comfortably sitting offered fabulous ease. And Satan himself was seated just across the breakfast-table.

Lobar was eating some sort of specially prepared rice dish. He ate a lot of it and snapped his fingers at Andreas when he wanted more. At one moment, he had to snap them twice and it was the other servant who was also waiting on them who nudged Andreas before he noticed.

Hood found it extraordinarily difficult to avoid the lidless eye. It seemed to be observing him constantly, with its hideous stare.

'I see,' said Lobar, 'that you are interested in' – he ran a finger round the great red weal encircling his neck – 'in this.'

'I was wondering how you got it,' Hood said.

'It was when I was hanged.' Lobar took a mouthful of rice.

'I was young and poor and travelling on a ship in the North China Sea. We were attacked by pirates. They killed the crew and many passengers and took over the ship. They were going to clip off my eyelids. As you see, they began. Then they decided to hang me, with a fishing-line. It was thin but very strong. They have a special method. They lash it round under the skin. They pulled me up. All the same, I was heavy. I managed to break it.' He jerked massively with his neck. Hood winced at the mental picture. 'It left me this souvenir. But it is comforting. They say a man cannot be hanged twice.'

Lobar laughed. 'But now, what have you brought me, Mr Hood?'

'Let's wait until you see them.'

There was a crash behind Lobar and an exclamation. Andreas had dropped a dish. He struck Hood as awkward at his job. Lobar, he noticed, gave Andreas a glare but said nothing.

'What are your plans, Mr Hood? You must stay with us for a few days.'

Hood was helping himself to scrambled eggs and crisp bacon and replying that he would be glad to, when a tall fair girl, in a sailor's blouse and slacks, leapt into view at the top of the companionway. She sang out: 'Hello there!' and bounced up.

Oh dear, thought Hood; English and jolly. He shrank at the complications this promised.

Lobar was on his feet. He kissed the girl on the cheek, took her hand and kept hold of it and had a little low-voiced conversation with her, ignoring Hood, during which he showed his gold teeth and she giggled once or twice. He turned to Hood. 'This is Miss Treadman — '

'Trenton,' she corrected emphatically, blushed, laughed. 'Mr Hood.'

Plainly they were hardly old friends. 'How do you do?' That blonde English freshness, Hood said to himself. She was pretty and appetizing with her pert nose and peaches and cream. A rose that was going to fade at thirty if she wasn't careful. And about the last thing she looked was careful.

They all sat down. Lobar paid the girl a good deal of attention, and had more long low-voiced asides with her as if Hood weren't there at all. Hood supposed Lobar had picked her up somewhere ashore. She was called Sue. She didn't seem very experienced, but she was full of vivacity and laughter and a naturalness which Lobar obviously found charming. Hood did himself.

She obviously thought she had struck life rich. Hood shuddered inwardly at the thought of her fooling with anybody as dangerous as Lobar. But it was not the sort of situation he could do anything about and he tried, rather unsuccessfully, to tell himself that it wasn't his affair.

Then it occurred to him, of course! This was why Ivory was furious with Lobar. She was jealous. He wondered if Ivory were going to show up at the breakfast-table. Somehow he thought not.

In a moment, Lobar said something to the girl and got up.

'Now you will come and see my collection, Mr Hood.' Hood picked up the Yassida at his feet and laid it on the table.

'Do you mind taking this to my cabin?' he said to the steward. He caught the Trenton girl's surprised look as she saw the gun.

It was a brilliant morning. Lobar led the way forward. Working parties of the crew were about. The quarter-master at the gangway touched his cap to Lobar and Hood. Looking up, Hood was struck by the taper of the masts. They seemed to be metal and might, he guessed, be telescopic. Then in a flash he did a double-take.

Lobar had paused, holding his red kimono round him, and was eyeing Hood. In charge of one of the working parties chipping paint was a man who seemed to be wearing heavy insulating gloves. But now, at second glance, Hood saw they were monstrous hands. They hung at the end of the man's bare arms, grotesque in their size. They must be nine inches across the palm, Hood thought, with huge fingers.

'Good God,' he said to himself. 'Elephantiasis.' But surely the disease of elephantiasis was usually in the foot.

'Golos.' Lobar had turned and called to the man. He spoke to him in an Oriental tongue. The man smiled, came over and held up his hands. It was as if he were lifting great weights, the hands of a gigantic statue, but of flesh and blood. And Hood saw that they had not gone the uniform pinky colour of elephantiasis.

Lobar was speaking to him. The man nodded silently and glanced at Hood. He was medium height, with hooded eyes and a skin with a yellow tinge. Hood put his age at thirty-five; he was apparently normal except for his hands.

'Interesting, is it not, Mr Hood?' Lobar said. 'You have never seen such deformity before? Well, it is very rare. It used to be done by the Kirghiz-Ama, a tribe of the Kirghiz which settled in China. But it is forbidden now. A great pity. All the interesting things will soon be forbidden. Then the world will die of goodness and boredom. Don't you think so, Mr Hood?'

'Do you mean they did this on purpose?'

'Of course. Golos, Mr Hood, is a masterpiece. He is rarer than a great work of art – a statue, a picture – for, after all, he is alive. What is more, I am a lucky collector. I have a pair – twins. Golos and his brother. Unfortunately, the brother is not here. But he is even more interesting.' Lobar laughed and said something to Golos and the man turned and went below.

'But how was it done? And why, for God's sake?'

'The Kirghiz-Ama were great showmen, you see. They used to wander through the fairs of China with their jugglers and tumblers and side-shows. They had a secret. It was very difficult to use. The authorities were against it. The deformity can be passed on by heredity.

'The secret was a method of treating the pituitary gland. By constant stimulus, they developed the gland to excess.

Whenever this happens, it produces a disease which is called gigantism. It is known to doctors. The Kirkhiz-Ama found they could produce monsters. Their side-shows were thronged. They perfected the method and created marvellous things, Mr Hood. One of the tricks was to delay the action until the long bones in the body were consolidated. This brought on a state which the doctors call acromegaly. It is what makes enlarged hands and feet – among other things.

'Golos has a power in his hands which no other man alive possesses. At the fair they used to put him in a pit with a wolf. Foolish people screamed, but it was not dangerous at all. The wolf could not open its jaws. Golos could hold them shut with one hand – with thumb and finger. I have seen him tear a pile of eight hides in two, Mr Hood, like a sheet of cardboard. He is very gifted.'

There was a small commotion behind them and laughter. A pig was trotting across the deck with Golos after it. One of the working party caught it and held it for him. Golos lifted it and brought it over. He stood silently with the pig struggling in his arms. Hood suddenly felt something awful was about to happen. Then Lobar nodded.

Golos locked his hands over the pig's head – and squeezed. There was a sickening muffled squelch as the bones were crushed. The pig suddenly stopped struggling and went limp. Drops of blood smacked on the deck at their feet. It was horrible.

Hood took a step back. Lobar was looking at him intently. Then he laughed. 'Come, Mr Hood, we will see the pictures. You will find the nudes are superb.'

8

AT HALF PAST THREE in his cabin, Hood heard the launch swirl away from the side and looked out. It was going shoreward with Lobar gigantically in the stern and Sue Trenton. She was laughing, as if they were on an escapade. They had said nothing about going. Damned little fool, thought Hood. She was engaging, all the same.

Lunch had been a watchful interlude. Ivory had sat there smouldering. Lobar had seemed full of menace, joking with Sue Trenton, making smooth conversational exchanges with Hood. There had been moments when Hood had winced at some bit of hand-patting or by-play between him and the Trenton girl, certain that Ivory was going to erupt. Lobar had provoked her with great skill.

He had been non-committal about the pictures Hood had brought. One unusual episode had occurred in the middle of the meal. Sue Trenton had laughingly asked Andreas, who was one of those serving, to mimic Perrin. Apparently she had seen him do it before and thought it hilarious. Andreas didn't need to be pressed. He put down the big silver dish he was holding. Hood expected a mildly amusing bit of impersonation. But the next moment he was sitting transfixed.

Andreas suddenly *became* Perrin. He did not merely change his voice. He adapted his height, his stance, the very structure of his face. He snatched bits of bread from the side-table, things from his pockets and stuffed them with quick gestures into his cheeks, under his lips. He pulled a pencil from his pockets and marked a deep wrinkle between the eyes and another alongside the nose. His face was transformed. With a flick, he switched his tie. Those pale tendril-like fingers of Perrin's were suddenly mincing about and he was speaking with Perrin's voice. It was brilliant.

Sue Trenton laughed and clapped with delight. Hood

couldn't help joining in. But Andreas only kept it up for a moment before Lobar irritably cut him short and sent him about his business.

The throb of the launch faded. Hood was about to turn away from the port-hole, then caught sight of the grey hull of an American cruiser moving in towards Villefranche harbour. He stood watching her. She was moving slowly. Her forward turrets were chunky-looking blocks, no doubt for missiles; she carried two big covered searchlights, or what looked like searchlights, on her mainmast aft. There was a bright orange-coloured helicopter on the quarterdeck. He could see the crew at stations.

Hood wondered what she was. The single figure 7 was painted in black and white outline on her hull fore and aft. Her arrival, at any rate, would mean an outbreak of American cars, American wives and gob patrols, the whole rather unlikely accompaniment of the American Navy in peacetime. Yet there was something refreshing about seeing her like that. She was counter-Lobar.

Slowly, the grey hull moved out of sight beyond Cap Ferrat. Hood stubbed out his cigarette, crossed to the door and eased it open an inch. The vestibule was empty. He went out and, bending his head, stepped through the draped arch on the far side into an alleyway.

There was no one in sight. He ran down on tiptoe, trying the cabin doors. Some were locked, some empty. In one he found some anonymous clothes in the cupboards and a shelf of books. He scanned the titles: *White Thighs, Rape, My Pretty Typist, The Love Feast.*

Straight ahead led to the gym and the swimming-pool. He took the cross-alley. More cabins. He had his hand on one doorknob when he fancied somebody moved inside. He retreated.

This was still, he believed, the main passenger accommodation. Turning aft, he went down a ladder into a small tween-decks flat. Here the surroundings were different – no carpet, the paintwork less fresh, lights fewer. Probably crew quarters, Hood decided. There were two doors. He tried the first. There was the shuffle of a disturbed sleeper's breathing. Hood glanced in. Andreas was lying on the bunk, shifting in his sleep. Hood pulled the door shut.

Lobar's cabin, he had noted that morning, was above. The companionway from the flat must lead up to it. As he reached the top, one of the deck crew appeared, touched his cap and went down without a word.

The heavy oak door of Lobar's cabin was locked. Hood stepped out on to the open deck. The sea flashed in the sun. There was an awning and a big green sunshade. He could see one or two of the crew forward. He parked the sunshade alongside the port window of the cabin and stood behind it while he squeezed a finger inside the top of the jalousie and flipped the bolt. In two movements he was inside.

The cabin was broad and handsome; white leather chairs, a covered sofa against a decorative drape of curtain, a big desk, a Chinese carpet in a shade of coral that made Hood exclaim, small lamps and various objects. Van Dyck's full-length portrait of Don Ignacio Severa, Duke of Almeria, stood against one wall. Adjoining were a bedroom and a bathroom. Opening a door on the far side of the main cabin, Hood found a butler's pantry. He stood looking round the cabin.

The points of a quick search have to be spotted at once before the first fine edge of observation is blunted. The ash-tray by the sofa was full, the cushions disarranged. Andreas had not yet cleaned up after lunch and would shortly arrive to do so. Hood started with the desk. It yielded nothing. Next he tested sections of the panelling. Apart from concealed control switches for the air conditioning and so forth, there was nothing there either – or behind the drape of curtain.

He pulled out a screwed-up woman's handkerchief stuffed between the cushions of the sofa. It was embroidered with a small S. Hood cursed the foolish child (*was* she such a child?) and stuffed it back.

The bedroom did not provide anything of interest. Thickets of suits were hanging in the big built-in cupboard. Shoving them aside and flashing his pencil light, Hood spotted the unmistakable indentation made by the knob or key of a safe door which has been swung open. He felt round for the control, found it low down inside the door. A panel sprang ajar showing the safe door. The safe didn't look very capacious and Hood decided he had no time to try opening it now. He shut the panel and went back into the main cabin.

Hood knew that Lobar was concealing much more than this jewel safe. But *where*? He stood looking round, now rather tense. Andreas could arrive at any moment. Yet in spite of himself, his eye kept wandering to the Van Dyck portrait. There was something wrong with it. The life-size figure was splendid; but the picture was too tall. It wandered oddly below the feet. It was nothing that would be noticed by anybody but an expert.

Suddenly he stooped. Of course; the canvas had been slightly lengthened. It had been done with great skill. The extension had been fitted to the frame – and Hood saw that the frame was meant as concealment.

He ran his hands round it. After one or two tries, a catch snapped. Hood found he could slide the frame and the portrait to one side. In the space behind was a steel door; locked. All at once, there was a soft buzz behind him. A red eye glowed on the desk telephone. Somebody was ringing Lobar.

Hood went to work on the door. The upper bolt had not been turned. But the lock below checked him. The telephone buzzed again. Hood decided he would have to give up and try to return and tackle the safe and the door later. Then abruptly the door gave. He pushed it wide, flashed his pencil torch inside and stepped through. He slid the frame and portrait back into place.

A metal ladder led down at a steep angle. There was a dim glow of light below. Hood put out his torch and descended quietly. At the bottom was a narrow alleyway running forward. This was where the light came from. Hood turned along it, examining the bulkheads on either side. They were steel. Here and there he sounded with his knuckles and got the impression from the resonance that there were tanks.

All at once, there was a metallic creak and a door opened a few yards ahead. A man came out.

Hood ran back to cover. Four men appeared, all in engineers' overalls. Talking together, they clanged the door behind them, locked it and headed away down the alleyway. Hood watched them turn at the far end. Then he sprinted after them on his toes.

Round the corner of the alleyway, he saw they were standing talking to a young Negro watchman. The Negro laughed and reached out to hang a key on the keyboard, presumably the key the men had just handed him. Hood noted the position of the hook; top right-hand corner. As the engineers drew away towards the ladder leading to the upper deck, the Negro drifted with them. For a moment, Hood hoped he was going to desert the keyboard. But he came back.

Hood turned and raced back down the alleyway. At the top of the ladder he listened. There wasn't a sound from Lobar's cabin. He eased back the frame. Somebody was running water in the bathroom. He stepped into the cabin, softly shut the door behind him, adjusted the frame. In the bathroom, Andreas burst into song.

Back in his cabin, Hood sat down and lit a cigarette. Obviously there was something concealed in the part of the ship where the engineers had come from. You didn't lock an ordinary engine-room. He had to get at that key while he could still locate it.

He drew on the cigarette, thinking of the young Negro. Then he went into the bathroom and took up a glass bottle of shaving lotion which was, in fact, a specially designed container holding certain small essential items of professional equipment – and even some shaving lotion. From this he extracted a small pack; he took out of it a thin sliver of wax and returned the rest of the pack. After kneading the wax soft, he attached it to the palm of his hand, stubbed his cigarette and went on deck.

The companion leading down to the space where the watchman sat was well forward, in the crew area. Hood strolled casually up to it. Then he took one of the two reefers from his cigarette case, lit it and stepped down the companion.

'Hi,' he lifted a friendly hand. 'Looking round. My name's Hood. Pretty nice quarters here, h'm?'

'Uh?' The young Negro was on his feet. Hood repeated it slowly.

'Yussah.'

'You been aboard long?'

'Yussah.'

Hood cupped his hands in reefer-smoker fashion and took a pull. He simulated a deep drag, did not inhale, but let a long jet of smoke escape as if he had. 'Where do you come from?' he said.

There was a momentary blank look on the Negro's face; then he said: 'Oh! oh! Liberia, suh.'

Hood didn't think it was true. (Lobar, he recalled, was now a Liberian citizen.) But what he was much more interested in were the young Negro's longing glances at the reefer.

'Is that so? Whereabouts now? Monrovia?'

Silence. A roll of the eyes.

'I used to know Monrovia.' Hood took another drag, exhaled another cloud. 'I had a house at a place called Congo Crossroads. You know Congo Crossroads?'

'Yussah.'

'And Lumley Beach? Fine place, Lumley Beach, h'm?' These were really references to Freetown in Sierra Leone.

'Yuss.' The big black eyes were staring at the reefer. The Negro was beginning to shake.

'Are there barracuda there, as they say?'

No answer. Hood brought his cupped hands up again. This time he blew the smoke straight into the Negro's face.

The Negro's head darted out as if he was going to snatch the cigarette; but he caught himself.

'What? Oh — ' Hood feigned sudden comprehension. Furtively he passed the reefer to the Negro. The Negro cupped it in his palm, glanced round, then sprang up the companion. He stood three steps from the top, his legs visible. Hood stood absolutely still. Suddenly the Negro ducked his head, threw a glance at him, then, apparently satisfied, straightened up again.

Hood moved fast. He unhooked the key, took a careful impression on the wax and replaced it. The Negro's calves were trembling ecstatically as he dragged on the reefer. His toes curled. The next minute he was down again, hiding the extinguished stub in his hat. He nodded silently, all eye-whites and lips.

'Yussah!' said Hood. 'So long.'

On deck, he almost collided with Andreas half hidden by the pile of linen he was carrying. Hood paused. The opportunity might not come again. He crossed to the side and stood idly looking over at the sea until Andreas reappeared. Andreas was wearing an apron and looked busy. Hood waited until he went along the deck and vanished into Lobar's cabin. Then Hood went below, put the key imprint into a matchbox and tucked it into the toe of his spare pair of shoes. There was nobody in the vestibule. He turned along to Andreas's cabin, ducked his head and slipped inside.

It was in darkness. He switched on the light.

9

THE PIN-UP teasers jumped out at him.

They were the first thing he saw. They were everywhere, in colour, black and white, big and small, with some in frames on the chest of drawers – all of girls in corsets.

Hood looked round for at least one nude, or for just a bosom. There wasn't one. Not a nipple or a *mons veneris* in view. Never a plain buttock or haunch. But pinned to the deckhead over the bunk was a life-size poster of a model called Sizzle with suspender clips in the shape of hands and a cut-away arch in front filled with – well, filled with mysterious shadow.

Well, thought Hood, it's a point of view. Those coyly crossed thighs, those suggestively pushing hips, those careful poses of shame or blushing modesty, were probably sexier than the busts or the curly triangles (the eternal triangle!) of the merely naked. If you thought that way.

Moreover, these luscious corset queens all lived in a half-world where dim lights and shadows were the thing, and the spot was on the goods or comfort-station.

Hood was certainly no connoisseur of these things. Corsets had loomed no larger in his life than in most men's. But standing there he recognized that the girls around him were modelling a variety of form and ingenuity in sexiness that was unlikely to pass his way again. Some were scanties, some like armour, some with zips and some had holes like gruyère cheese. By the spot where Andreas's ear would rest, was a little number called Quickie which could be rolled up to go in the handbag. Alongside, was a creation called Honey-pot with a slogan: 'Your Honey-pot's Your Fortune.'

Yes, thought Hood; wear a Honey-pot and the world will beat a pathway to your drawers.

Apart from this display, the cabin was smallish and

untidy. There were three empty beer bottles on the deck. French newspapers lay crumpled beside them. On top of the cupboard were piled and dusty cartons, boots, a broken vase and other things. Hood looked inside. A few clothes were hanging; there were several pairs of old-fashioned lace-up boots, on the shelves were shirts, underwear, Andreas's ironed white jackets – and then two pairs of women's corsets. One was marked inside Zarubino, in ink. Zarubino? Hood noted it in his mind.

He pulled open a drawer; shirts, socks, a packet of old postcards and more corsets. There was a jumble of more old clothes in the next drawer. The bottom one contained only corsets – black, pink, white, rubber, plastic, zipped and laced. Well, that was quite plain. Andreas was a fetishist. Stuck into the corner of the mirror was an invitation card for a trade show of corset models at the Hotel Albert VI in Paris. The name was left blank. The date was 21 April. Hood wondered if Andreas intended being in Paris then. Apparently he did and that was interesting.

Opening one of the long drawers under the bunk, he stopped, puzzled. There were pressed trousers and laundered shirts, ties, waistcoats, all neatly laid out. Some more below. They were a curious contrast with the untidiness above. He pulled open a small cupboard alongside.

'Well, who would think it?' a voice said behind him.

Hood turned. It was Ivory. She was standing holding the door. She was in a slim white blue-edged dress.

'Hello, Ivory. Come in. I can't find what Perrin has done with my things.' In spite of the invitation, he went to the door. She retreated into the alleyway with her eyes on him.

'What things were they, Mr Hood?' she said sceptically.

'I gave him my gym slacks and a couple of sweat-shirts and so on to get laundered. Anyway, forget it. How are you, Ivory?'

'You know that is not Perrin's cabin.'

'It's not? No wonder I can't find the damned things.' He had to get her moving, in case Andreas came along. 'I was just thinking of a drink. How about you, Ivory? You didn't seem to enjoy lunch much.'

She shot him a blazing look, but moved off down the alleyway. Hood shut the cabin door behind him, then followed her. She went through to the vestibule, where Hood saw his valet was stationed again. Hood told him to bring two double highballs and went after her out on deck.

They sat on the veranda in long wicker chairs. When they had finished the highballs, she rang and ordered two more. It was sunny. Ashore, the white plume of a train moved across the grey and ochre of the rocks. High up on the Corniche the windscreen of a car flashed. Hood was just feeling the effect of the reefer, nothing to worry about. Ivory was in a sultry frame of mind, though he saw she was trying to be agreeable to him in spite of it. She looked exotically beautiful sitting there with the breeze slightly ruffling her hair. A little wisp had strayed down her cheek and heightened the effect.

Hood edged the conversation towards Lobar and Sue Trenton.

'He met her about twelve days ago, picked her up somewhere. Give me a cigarette, please.' She smoked nervously.

'Does she stay on board?' Hood said.

'She comes and goes. She doesn't know Lobar.'

'You mean twelve days is usually enough?' She didn't answer.

Hood said: 'Where do you suppose they've gone now?'

She shrugged. 'How do I know? Maybe the villa. Is she a friend of yours, Mr Hood?'

'No. But she's bright and amusing, don't you think?'

'Oh, bright, pretty, entertaining.' She was holding herself in.

'I didn't know Lobar had a villa.'

She stubbed out the cigarette. 'It's called Les Oliviers. It is quite close, on the little bay behind the Pointe St Hospice.' She turned, pointing. 'You can't see the villa from here; it is hidden by the trees, but it's to the left of that white one, on the road going up.' Hood followed her gesture.

The Pointe St Hospice came out like a rocky finger from the headland of Cap Ferrat, forming a snug little bay with shingle beaches well sheltered from the wind by the reddish-white cliffs and rocks. There were villas overlooking the bay. But many were concealed behind stone terraces and trees or stood back in grounds. On the far side, the cliff fell sheer at one point and below, of all things, was a caravan site, with a couple of caravans on it. A distant window was shining brightly in the sun.

'I suppose there's a beach to it, a private beach?'

But she had risen. 'This wind's getting up. Let's go in.' Hood rose; and all at once, she put her arm in his and pressed close to his side. 'Oh, Charles, be nice.'

'Aren't I being?'

'I mean don't be irritating about that English girl. You know what I mean.'

Hood laughed. The right tactics, no doubt, would have been to go on needling her about Sue Trenton.

Inside, she stepped into the lift and they went down to the bar. But at the bottom she had forgotten something. 'Make mine a Scotch and soda. A lot of soda. I won't be a moment,' she said and left him. He heard her stop the lift above on the cabin floor.

Hood lit a cigarette and went to the bar to mix the drinks. How much, he wondered, did Ivory know? And of whatever she did know about Lobar, how much would her jealousy lead her to betray? *If* she were genuinely jealous. In other words, if she were not taking him for a carefully prepared ride.

The lift came down, she stepped out and did a twirl.

'Now look here, Ivory —'

She laughed, throwing her head back.

'– now look here, this is not going to be another dance session.' He was laughing too. It was an amusing moment. Her mood, he saw, had changed.

'All right,' she said at last. 'But not even a mild cheek to cheek with you?'

'Not even. Drink your Scotch and relax.'

They sat side by side on the banquette. She had on some scent which he found tempting. The dress showed her superb shoulders and neck. She seemed to use hardly any make-up – not that she needed it with that honey colouring.

She said in a slinky voice: 'You have come here to keep me amused, haven't you, Charles?'

'Under special import licence. Why do you keep asking me?' He was thinking: shall I make love to her now or a little later?

'Because I suspect you.' She took his glass and jumped up.

'Wait – Ivory, I haven't finished that drink.'

'You've only ice-water left.'

'*Ice-water?* Anyway, what do you suspect me of?'

At the bar, she laughed. She was mixing the new drinks.

'Well, come on, what of?'

'Two lumps of ice? Water?'

'No! No ice. A little soda.'

'I suspect you of being heartless,' she said.

That was a poor get-out, he thought. She brought the drinks over. 'This is the new Highland Dew we got. What you think of it?'

Hood drank some. 'Great. Were you ever in the highland dews, Ivory?' When she shook her head, he said: 'Where did you join the *Triton*?'

She went into a long and complex explanation, meant to elude an answer. Then she led off into some lighthearted chatter about a Greek millionaire and his party they had had on board not long before. Hood let her talk. She knows plenty, he said to himself. That was clear from her evasiveness. Her joke about suspecting him might be true too.

She touched the tiny creases at the corners of his eyes. 'I like these,' she said.

As she went on and laughed, Hood found her more and more attractive. The idea of making love to her was very agreeable. His looks went from her eyes to her bosom, her middle and her legs and the recollection that he had seen her naked, in an erotic dance, gave him a sudden twinge. If she did that again, he wouldn't be able to resist her.

She crossed her legs. The skirt of her dress drew taut on her thigh. He couldn't help giving it a brief caress. Then he leaned over and kissed her neck.

She said: 'Finish your drink.' He did and she got him another. As she handed it to him, he put his arm round her hips and drew her down beside him, close. He felt tremendously stirred by her. His hand holding her to him felt the full firm contour of her breast.

He drank some whisky, deciding that he was going to make love to her now, without delay. He took another drink, finished it and put the glass down. She turned her head and he kissed her. The coolness of her lips was a shock of excitement. The long kiss made her lean far back When she broke away with a small gasp, he covered her breasts with kisses.

The smoothness of her skin above the stocking top made him ravenous for her. He wanted to tear the dress off. She was gasping with mingled shock and pleasure, resisting to excite him further, her breast heaving in the struggle.

Hood threw off restraint. He was rampant. He saw nothing, thought of nothing but the raging desire in him to have her with force, with infinite urgency, with utmost erotic appetite. Her attitude in the disorder of her semi-nudity drove him to a sort of fury. He pinned her. Her long leg, lying over the edge of the banquette with one heel of her shoe resting on the floor, slowly bent at the knee. The heel left the floor. The fingers of her hand pressed against his back, curled, dug into his shirt. The heel was high.

She gasped. Slowly her fingers scored up his back. There was an instant when they dug into his neck, her knee was tensed and tremblingly hard against him – and then all at once it relaxed, gradually slid down, her hand clasped and was still and then began smoothing his neck.

She reached behind the banquette, fumbled blindly for a

moment, then switched the light off. A small lamp by the bar remained on. It happened again.

Then she said: 'Charles, move, you're too heavy.'

But Hood was holding her hard again. The same wild urgency impelled him. Part of his mind was looking on at himself with dismay. He felt the restraining tugs of reason like something faint and far off. But the desire for her which was filling him obliterated everything. She resisted a little, but this only drove him with more fury.

In a moment her knee was crooked to his side. His reason seemed to make a last effort to send through its message. He felt he had lost control. A wild beast seemed to possess him. Ivory's heel touched his spine. A moment later she was trying to push him away. Hood could not stop. They struggled. She submitted again and at the climax dug her nails into him, bit his shoulder.

She broke away. Hood lay recovering his breath. She shifted and began summarily rearranging herself.

In the dim pinkish light, Hood watched her. When she had got back into the top of the dress, her breasts still showed at the unbuttoned front. She stretched out her leg and pulled the stocking taut and began fastening the suspender. She was a few inches away from him. He grasped her wrist and pulled her towards him.

'Charles – wait. No!' She was half scared, half mocking. She went over under his weight.

And then that mocking inflection, that hint of duplicity carried into his mind through the mad erotic impulse that was surging back and seemed like taking possession of him entirely.

With a great effort he broke away. He got to his feet. He felt drunk. Suddenly he had understood what had happened. She had given him an erotic drug.

'Charles, where you going?'

He reeled. He couldn't walk straight. She was beside him, touching his arm. He pushed her off gently, reached the lift and slammed the door.

Above, there was nobody in the vestibule. He locked the cabin door after him. Images of her filled his mind. He saw her pulling her stockings taut at the thigh. She offered herself to him. The drug was still working on him strongly. Shakily he took a cigarette and lit it, but stubbed it out the next moment.

'Charles,' she whispered at the door.

Hood flung round to let her in; then killed the impulse. She tapped. 'Let me in.' He clenched his fists with the effort not to.

'Charles.'

He went to the door, took the key – turned it.

Her voice was close to him. 'Darling ...' He opened the door a little, caught her scent again. He stood there fighting with himself. Through the crack of the door he could see the swell of her nude honey-coloured breasts at the opening of her dress.

He gritted his teeth and leaned on the door and shut it and locked it again.

'You have to let me in ...' Her voice was pleading on the other side.

He crossed to the far side of the cabin, trying not to listen. He was afraid he wasn't going to keep it up.

Abruptly he turned and went into the bathroom. He took out the concealed pack from the bottle of shaving lotion and extracted a miniaturized hypodermic needle. He gave himself a shot, quickly reassembled the pack and put it back into place.

The effect of one drug combating the other wasn't going to be very pleasant. As he went back into the bedroom, he felt a cold sweat starting.

Ivory was still there. 'Charles, come here, I want to talk to you. Come n over here ...'

Hood flopped on the bed and passed out.

10

THE SUN shone brilliantly in the Place Vendôme. Monsieur Henri Harvel, the owner of the celebrated art gallery, bowed, kissing Lady Calvert's hand. It was a trifle old-fashioned; but women loved it, especially foreign women. Monsieur Harvel liked to believe that a good deal of his success in business could be attributed to kissing hands.

'Thank you, Lady Calvert. Thank you, Sir Richard. Do consider the Delacroix. But at any rate I hope we shall have the pleasure of adding the Loir to your collection. *That* is a delightful picture, *n'est-ce pas*?'

He dropped his voice confidentially. 'Very shrewd choice, Sir Richard,' and nodded sagely.

'Well, we'll think about it. Good day, Harvel.'

'Good day.'

Calvert and his wife crossed to the kerb where their chauffeur was holding open the door of the Rolls. They sat back and the car moved off. Richard Calvert sighed. 'The Delacroix's out of the question. But he's right. That Luigi Loir *is* a good picture. I only wish I were sure he isn't putting it on. Three hundred guineas seems a lot.'

'He did say Loir was in several museums.'

'Yes; provincial museums, where they keep a lot of trash.'

'Oh, but masterpieces too.' Daisy Calvert was thrilled when her hand was kissed.

'True, my dear. Luigi Loir; not a painter I know much about.'

'But you liked it, Dick, didn't you?'

'Yes; but I like three hundred guineas too. I wish we had Charles here to advise us. But we haven't, so there it is.'

The car turned up the rue des Capucines towards the Madeleine. Lady Calvert saw the prospect of having the picture fading. She tried a last shot. 'Where is Charles? Perhaps he is back?'

'Wouldn't think so,' said Calvert absently.

It sounded as if that were that. Lady Calvert sat gazing out of the window. She sometimes tired of the battle with the official world for her husband's attention.

The traffic along the rue des Capucines was slow. 'I didn't know we had an escort,' Daisy Calvert said.

'Escort?' He followed his wife's glance through the windscreen. A crash-helmeted French police outrider was straddling his motor-cycle just ahead, craning to see through the blocked traffic. 'H'm. Probably saw the flag. Is it out?'

'Yes.' The small Union Jack on the wing was unfurled. 'Ought not to be, since we're just shopping.'

'I thought outriders were special duty chaps,' Calvert said. He watched the outrider. He couldn't make it out. There must be some reason. Then he smiled. 'You never know what the French'll do next. Come to think of it, I believe the Americans asked for a motor-cyclist because it's convenient when there are these traffic jams. They said they couldn't have their Ambassador held up, so Sam Hoblen got one. They do get you through. Now I suppose the police have decided we all get one, as and when needed. I must say this fellow doesn't seem to be doing much.' Unlike most of his kind, the outrider wasn't making a lot of grandiloquent gestures and showing his authority. He was sitting with his motor idling. Richard Calvert was all the more puzzled.

At that moment, the traffic ahead began to move. Immediately the outrider edged a van towards the kerb and began blowing the whistle he held between his teeth and beckoning to the Calverts' chauffeur to follow him. A sudden change and rather odd, thought Calvert. However —

The traffic ahead veered away on either side. The black Rolls followed the escort through the lane. They flashed through just as the lights changed and swung across the Boulevard.

'There you are!' Calvert grinned. 'Efficient, these outriders. Wonder why they never thought of it before?'

11

HOOD WOKE UP with a splitting head.

The bedside telephone was buzzing. He reached out and unhooked it. He had to work some saliva into his mouth before he spoke. 'Hello?'

'Good morning, sir. Have you orders for breakfast?' It was Perrin.

Hood was still under the impact of recollecting the events of the afternoon before. He loosened his tie and undid the top button of his shirt.

'Hello, sir?'

'Some fruit juice.' He wet his lips. 'And black coffee.'

'Yes, sir.'

Hood rang off. For a moment he lay there. Then, in spite of his head, he laughed. He wondered what she had given him – Spanish fly? He didn't see what else he could have done, except knock himself out!

His watch had stopped. It must be late. He got up, unlocked the cabin door and then went into the bathroom. He left the door open. He took two Gynergene tablets, a compound of tartrate of ergotamine and caffeine which he found more effective than codeine for severe headaches, kicked his shoes off and undressed and got under the shower. He had to stoop; his head nearly touched the shower nozzle. He turned the water on cold and hard, thinking suddenly of Guy de Maupassant roaming round when he was mad trying to get colder and colder showers – 'the Charcot douche', he called it, 'able to fell a bull'. There was a mad element in this encounter with Lobar, Hood recognized.

Presently somebody brought the fruit juice and coffee in next door. Hood sang out: 'Is Mr Lobar at breakfast?'

'He is not on board, sir.' It was Perrin again.

'Is Miss Trenton?'

'No, sir.'

'Thanks. That's all.' Perrin didn't answer. Hood quickly left the shower, grabbed a towel and stepped out into the cabin. Perrin was just moving to the door holding the pair of brown shoes in which Hood had hidden the imprint of the key.

'You can leave those,' Hood said.

'I'll bring them back at once,' Perrin said. 'Just cleaning them, sir.'

'No matter, leave them.'

'Very well, sir.' Perrin put them back in the cupboard, bowed and went out. Hood bent down; the key imprint was still there. He put it in his pocket. It might have been mere chance. But it might not.

He stood slightly stooped, with the towel round his middle, looking out of the port-hole. The sea flashed and sparkled. One or two pedalos were moving inshore. His eye wandered up the mountainside. On one spur, over a sheer drop, was a big house with columns and a Greek pediment. It was one of the incongruous relics of the Edwardian era when the millionaires and the *demimondaines* of half Europe were building villas like turreted castles and neo-classical temples and Gothic priories all along this coast. Farther to the left, a plane dipped for the approach to Nice airport.

Hood drank the fruit juice and poured a cup of coffee. It was scalding and bitter, very good. He decided to go ashore. He wanted to find out what went on at the Villa Les Oliviers - and more about the chauffeur.

He finished the coffee, had some more and dressed. On deck the usual working parties were about. The man Golos was with one. Hood looked over the side. There were no boats at the boom. The launch had not returned.

He strolled casually aft. At the stern was a small deck-house. The deck on either side was barred by a locked wire grille. Hood glanced back. Golos was watching him. He strolled across the deck to the starboard side, leant over and just caught a glimpse of a boat tied up astern. Golos had crossed over too and moved nearer.

Hood lit a cigarette and leant on the side and relaxed. He hoped Ivory wasn't going to appear! Out of the corner of his eye he could see Golos along the deck. Golos had evidently been told to keep tabs on him. Hood looked at the sea, at the gulls. He scanned the shore. The wire extended towards the stern, enclosing the deck like a cage for about ten feet. 'How about being suddenly overcome by desire for a sea bathe?' he asked himself. He finished the cigarette and tossed it over the side. He could change below into light trousers and polo shirt, take a quick plunge over the side before they could stop him and reach the boat astern. He would have to dry out ashore.

There were shouts from the deck. He looked round – it was some mishap with one of the working parties – and was just in time to see a heavy block and tackle swing towards Golos. Golos saw it inches away and ducked. It smashed against the davit. Golos straightened up; he glared at the men of the working party, who had also overturned an open oil-drum on the deck, and were arguing excitedly. His shoulders hunched threateningly; his face was twitching with rage. He went towards them with his great hands unclasped like grappling hooks.

Hood didn't wait to see what happened. He took one look over the side. About three feet below the deck level, a narrow band of wood ran round the stern to keep rope lines from the hull paint. It would give a bare toe-hold.

He swung himself over, gripped the wire grille and let himself down to the narrow ledge. His fingers through the wire took some of the strain. If he slipped he would break the lot. He was pressed so close to the ship's side that he couldn't look down to see his shoes on the toe-hold. He worked his way along. He knew his feet were soon going to start the tremor which occurs when the weight is carried long on the toes.

A medley of angry voices was still coming from the deck

amidships. Hood's toes felt as if they were going to break. He got to within a foot of where the wire cage ended and reached out. One foot bearing his weight slipped. Hood made a grab. His hand caught the wire brace, just as the other foot went. For a few seconds he hung, scraping the side with his feet, trying to find hold, then got one foot on it, took the weight and hauled himself up.

Hood swung inboard. Ducking into the cover of the deck-house, he went quickly astern. The boat was there all right. It had an outboard motor. A rope ladder dangled to it from where he stood. He straddled the rail to let himself down when somebody grabbed his shoulder from behind.

Hood swivelled. It was one of the coloured seamen, a big fellow with a squashed nose. Hood shoved him off and turned back. But before he let himself over, the man's fore-arm locked under his chin and dragged him back on to the deck. Hood got his balance, broke suddenly at the knee and brought the man face-first against the rail. The man gave a howl and let go.

Hood straightened and stood back. The seaman, one hand to his face, flashed a knife. Hood's eyes went quite cold. He was expressionless. Every muscle of his body seemed to be still, waiting. His mind was sizing up the situation. Impossible to retreat at an angle, the opening for one defence. Then move at the last minute.

Motionless, he let the man come. At the last moment, he turned away half right, presenting less target. The man raised the knife and lunged overhand. As it began to descend, Hood's left shot up, blocked the forearm while it was still high. In the same movement, he ducked in, reached his other, right, arm under the man's shoulder, clasped his own hands and, thus locked, threw his whole weight against the parried knife-arm. The man tipped back, there was a crack as his arm broke. Hood dropped with him, knelt, grabbed both his ears and smashed his head twice against the iron base of the rail stanchion.

The seaman fell back inert. Hood looked round for the

knife, but it must have gone over the side. He climbed over. At the bottom of the ladder he hauled on the line attached to the boat and jumped in.

There was a stern anchor down. Hood hauled this in. He choked the motor, ran forward, cast off the painter, returned and pulled the starter. Sweetly, the eighteen horsepower Johnson started at first go. He slipped the clutch, veered hard over and turned the twist-grip throttle to full.

He steered almost directly astern of the *Triton*, making for Nice. The fuel tank indicator showed half full. Looking back he could see figures on the deck, among them one in a white jacket, presumably Perrin.

Hood lit a cigarette, crossed his legs on the seat and sang to the blue Mediterranean sky.

'Oh, it's only me,
From over the sea,
Cried Bub-bub-Barnacle Bill
The Sailor ...'

They were going to come for him as soon as they could. He stretched. He had enjoyed the exercise.

He ran the boat into Nice, through the commercial port, tied up to another boat at the east quay in the inner basin and climbed ashore.

The little port was charming at this time of the year. The light was clear and the sky was high and blue. The *Napoleon*, the steamer for Corsica, looked a great size at her berth on the far side. The imperial N, wreathed in green laurel, proclaimed itself on her bow. Hood grinned; the French cult of Napoleon, strangler of the Revolution, despot and slaughterer of a generation, tickled him.

Farther along, a group of loafers was watching the big crane lowering a Dragon-class sailing boat into the water. Hood walked round, thinking how pretty the old houses were in their dusty reds and yellows and ochres. They had aged well and looked far more elegant than the modern buildings in stone that bleached and weathered badly. A passing coach full of English faces said Noble Tours. Hopefully an Algerian, loaded with blankets, held up his leather bags and poufs – but the coach swept on.

Hood climbed the steps at the far end of the port and crossed the road. He walked along under the colonnade, turned down the Avenue de la Victoire and thought again how Italian the place looked with its coloured façades. He stopped. There was a plaque on the corner of the rue de l'Hotel des Postes. 'Seraphin Torrin, Franc Tireur, Partisan Francais, FFI, was hanged here, the 7th July 1944 and remained exposed for having resisted the Italian oppressor.' There was already a strange unreality about that.

'*Tirage ce soir?*' A burnt-faced woman thrust a lottery ticket under his nose.

Hood shook his head and went on. There was a hiss and a green-and-white trolley-bus pulled up before him at the kerb. He looked along the long straight Avenue. It was a frontier. The tone of the town had changed. The palms of other parts had gone. Grey plane trees with bare bulbous branches lined the street; the lopped branches looked like fists. It was a real-life district, humdrum and daily and strangely apart from the life of the tourist areas where there was another, subtler, sort of unreality.

He walked on. On the Promenade des Anglais, the flower-sellers were working cafés, chirping '*Fleurissez-ous*' and '*Jolies fleurs*'. They were middle-aged and they wore red-and-white-striped skirts and straw hats like plates. They looked hard on the make. You knew they symbolized the clip-joint approach and were called Madame Hernu or something and led brisk lives with husbands and unsentimental daughters and never gave a sucker a break, even or otherwise. Yet, by some odd convention, by some sucker-agreement, they survived. The French were rarely good at this sort of thing. Almost always their eagerness for money got the better of them and destroyed the appeal. Other people were good at it – the Italians, for instance. Hood grinned to himself.

The gardens as usual were full of the dead and dying.

There were lop-sided men waiting for the next stroke, shaking couples creeping along, aged creatures brought out like mummies to the public benches for a bit of sun. Those actually moving stared as if death were coming along on the next bicycle. A billboard for a block of flats said: 'Spend YOUR retirement, The happy evening of life, in the SUN.'

You bet, thought Hood, I can't wait. An aged creature tottered towards him on two sticks. She wore a black hat, voluminous black veil, black dress, black lace neckpiece, black lace-up boots. Her flaccid jowls looked bloodless. She looked as if she had seen entire generations into the grave. The thought of what her domestic interior must be like gave Hood a jolt. She stopped, peering through her spectacles at something on the ground at her feet. It was an insect. She jabbed at it with one of the sticks, squashed it with immense concentration. Hood shuddered and crossed the road. A lovely brunette was standing under an archway. The sun showed through her skirt. That was better!

At the next rank he climbed into a taxi and told the driver to go to St Jean. They were there by the coast road in twenty minutes. Hood paid the man off on the road behind the port. He walked through the quiet back roads to the small deserted bay and began the climb up to Cap Ferrat.

There was nobody on the road. Most of the villas, standing back in their grounds, were locked and shuttered. A sign on one or two said '*Chien Méchant*'. A rare car passed, an occasional builder's workman on a bicycle.

Les Oliviers. The name was in bronze letters on a door in a high stone wall. Farther on was a narrower door; Service. The top of the wall had spikes and broken glass. Hood walked along to the end. Next door was a garden of another villa with a stack of red tiles left by a workman, and no cover; it did not look promising. He retraced his steps.

On the other side of Les Oliviers was a bushy piece of land enclosed by a broken fence. He could see the half-hidden front of a Victorian villa standing well back. Nailed to a tree was a board '*A Vendre*' and the name of an agency.

Hood let a scooter go by. Then he went through the gate. The villa was like a peeling plaster cake. It had a flat roof with a water-tank on it. The tank had leaked a rusty stain down the front. There was a piano-leg balustrade along the top. A broken Venetian blind hung like a concertina across one window.

Hood went round the side of the villa. The wall of Les Oliviers continued, separating the two properties. Continuing through to the back, he came out on the side of the small bay. Well out, beyond it, he saw the *Triton*. But the overgrown garden only sloped for about twenty yards, then ended in a sheer cliff. Hood looked over the low edging of stones. It was a straight drop to the rocks and the sea below.

To his right, the wall of Les Oliviers ran to the edge of the cliff, ending with a fan of steel spikes. Below, some spiked railings had been fixed in concrete, presumably to block possible climbers. At the water's edge there was another splay of them – the sort of thing used to separate balconies – with more spikes.

Hood thought he might just make it round the spikes on the end of the wall. They looked negotiable and would probably take his weight. Then he remembered the Chien Méchant signs. There had been so many burglaries in these parts that people had taken to letting dangerous dogs free in the grounds of these villas. He would have to take a chance, though a dog in Les Oliviers would probably have been barking already.

He stepped to the edge, wiped his hands and examined the soles of his shoes. He leant out, grasped the spikes firmly, then let himself swing.

His knees banged sharply against the steel but he immediately had feet on two of the spikes, like rungs. The tricky thing was to round the edge. He shifted gradually towards the spiked points. The sea splashed on the rocks beneath. He did not look down. He reached a point at the edge of the fan with only two inches of the spike tip protruding from his grip. He released the outer hand and foot (his left), gripped the spike from the farther side. At the same time he swung his body slowly round, past the points of the spikes, then released right hand and foot. The next moment his other hand had taken hold, he was on the farther side and shifting sideways along the spikes towards the rocks. When he could get no farther, he flexed and sprang, landed on the edge and clambered up into the garden of Les Oliviers.

It was spacious, well kept; lawn, palms, exotic shrubs, a crescent of drive. Quite close to were two garages with living accommodation above, probably for caretakers. Obviously no dog.

The double doors of one of the garages were open. Inside, Hood could see a grey Lincoln Continental with Monaco plates. He stood in the cover of a tree, waiting. Nobody appeared. He walked over to the open garage and felt the car's bonnet. It was warm.

Hood stood looking round. There was a work-bench and tools, spare wheels, tyres, all neat. Everything was quiet. Pairs of overalls were hanging from hooks. He tiptoed to the door and stood listening. There was not a sound. Whoever had left the car had disappeared. The silence was queer. A car passed with a muffled hum on the road beyond; but that was all.

Hood went outside and round to the villa. The place was locked. Hood believed in never neglecting the obvious when he had to get into a house. He bent down and lifted the door-mat – the key was often just there! But not this one. He walked round to the back and found a small window unfastened. He climbed in; as he expected, it was the toilet. Next door was the kitchen, very professional-looking with an open Provençal wood spit, a big range, cleavers, copper pots, and so on.

Hood opened a door and went through into the main part of the house. It was sumptuous. His eye caught a hundred fine things, pictures, furniture, objects. But he disassociated his mind from them; at this moment, they existed in another element.

There was a big comfortable drawing-room, with low chairs and a medieval stone fireplace. Roses in a big crystal vase on the table were not yet faded. Next door were two smaller rooms, a library and a writing-room. Cursorily, Hood flipped through the desk. There were unused postcards of Monaco, a mining company's prospectus, an unused cheque-book, the catalogue of a Paris picture sale, boxes of paper and envelopes headed Les Oliviers; nothing else. On the other side of the entrance was the dining-room and another salon, with a gorgeous blue period Picasso. Hood tiptoed out. The house was utterly still.

He went upstairs. There was a locked room on the first floor; examining the door, he saw it was armoured. He left it and went through the other rooms. There was nothing unusual. He pushed open the door of the last bathroom; a drop of blood on the tiled floor and a smear in the wash-basin.

Hood bent, looking at them. The blood seemed fairly fresh. He pulled open the glass-fronted cupboard. On one shelf was a clean safety-razor. He looked at the towels by the wash-basin; they were all fresh and unused. Curious.

As he reached the landing again, he heard a sound. He stood there trying to judge where it had come from. But it was not repeated. He went up to the next floor; four more empty bedrooms. In one, on the floor, was a bottle of whisky and a glass. He came out and put his foot on the stairs to go up to the top floor. There was a loud thump from above and a sort of gargling sound. Hood stood still. Then he crept up the stairs. He opened the first door; it was an empty bedroom. Cautiously he moved along to the next door and looked in. The room was in semi-darkness.

A figure was slumped on the floor, its back against an overturned chair. It was human. But there was something monstrous about its face. The face was a great splurge of blood. It looked at Hood and emitted a bubbling wail.

'Jesus,' Hood said.

12

IT WAS THE very frightened customer who had vanished in Paris, Tookey Tate.

Hood sprang to the window and opened the shutter. He turned and knelt by Tate. Tate's eyes looked at him in mute horror. Blood was running from his nose. But Hood stared at his mouth. The lips were pouting strangely, covered with blood. Hood said quietly to himself: 'My God.' The lips were sewn together.

He took Tate gently under his arms and lifted him to the bed. Tate's wrists and ankles were bound. Hood went down to the bathroom on the floor below and took the razor-blade. He cut Tate free, then slashed a strip of the sheet. With extreme caution, he wiped some of the blood from Tate's lips and nose. Tate made a feeble gesture of appeal.

'I know, old boy,' Hood said. 'Won't hurt you if I can help.' He cut a fresh strip of sheeting, wet it at the wash-basin and, holding Tate's head in his arms, gently cleaned his face.

Halfway through he laid Tate back and got to his feet. Tate's mouth had seemed to be sewn up with gut. Hood saw it was clipped-up with metal staples. They had used one of those long-handled metal staplers made to clip big packing cartons together.

A froth of blood was bubbling between the mutilated red and blue lips. For a moment, Hood stood looking down at Tate. He saw that Tate wasn't going to last much longer unless something was done fast. He bent down and said quietly at Tate's ear: 'Stay still; don't move. I'll be right back.' Tate didn't give a sign.

Hood went out, shutting the door behind him. The house was still silent. He went quickly downstairs. The key was in the kitchen lock, on the inside; he let himself out and tiptoed round to the garage. Nothing seemed to have been moved. He crossed to the work-bench, found a long-nosed pair of pliers and a wire-cutter and took them back to the house. From one of the bathrooms he collected two towels.

On the top landing he stopped. Had that been a door shutting below? He was tempted to go down. But he heard nothing further and went on into the room. Tate had not stirred.

Hood took off his coat, rolled his sleeves and washed his hands. He cleaned the head of the pliers and the wire-cutters and laid them out on one of the towels. At the bedside, he removed Tate's coat and tie and unbuttoned his shirt. He propped Tate up on the pillow and said to him: 'I'll do my best to get it over quick and not to hurt you.'

Tate's eyes bulged; but he only moved a little.

Hood wiped away the bloody froth on the lips. There were five staples; the ends met inside. The tops were too close to the skin to tackle. It was best to go for the front of each. He approached the first with the lower beak of the wire-cutter. But the flesh had swollen on either side of each staple, leaving it deeply embedded. Hood tried to insert the cutter between the lips. Tate gave a choked scream, sending blood and froth welling out.

'Take it easy, old boy,' Hood said. He wiped away and began again. He managed to touch the first staple with one beak of the cutter. He gave a firm little push. Tate's head jerked back with pain and almost dislodged it. Hood could just see the tip of the cutter under the staple. He closed the cutter, gripped Tate's shoulder – and snipped.

Tate's torso heaved.

Quickly, Hood inserted the cutter again, found the staple inside. He pushed the flesh away, so as not to cut it and snipped once more. Tate moaned.

That was one.

The next staple had been driven in harder; it clamped the fleshy part of the lip tight. The lip round it was blue and a little pus was oozing. Hood wanted a cigarette badly. He ought to carry Tate out and rush him to hospital. This thing needed a surgeon with anaesthetic and proper implements. But the police would come in. It would put an end to any investigation of Lobar. And Tate was a link. He knew something vital, that was obvious.

Hood passed the towel over Tate's forehead and wiped the blood away from his mouth. He took a grip on himself. He leant on Tate's chest to prevent a heave. Then with his fingers he sharply pushed back the lip flesh from the staple and as Tate did heave and clasp his arm, enclosed the staple in the cutters and severed it. The bubbles of blood prevented him from cutting the inside at once. He wetted a clean strip of sheet and held it against Tate's mouth. He felt Tate's pulse; it didn't seem over-strong. Tate lay with his eyes shut.

Hood patted his shoulder. 'You're game, Tookey. If you'll let me finish this, I promise I'll get the bastards for you. I promise.' He severed the inner part of the second staple.

The next one was in the centre of Tate's mouth. But it had been pinched up too hard and had bent. This gave a tiny space to insert the tip of the cutter. Hood did so and snipped hard. But the purchase was too near the tip. The cutter twisted, tearing the staple in the flesh. Tate's scream spattered Hood lightly with blood.

Hood knew that if he stopped now he would not be able to go on. He sopped the blood, pressed the cutter under the staple and cut it. He had to hold Tate down while he opened the lips sufficiently to get at the inside and cut that too.

Somehow he managed to sever the remaining staples. He gave Tate five minutes' rest. At the end of that time he took the pliers and extracted the ends. This was almost worse than the rest. The ends were roughly U-shaped and he had to twist them out. The swollen lip had closed back over three of the ends and Hood had to probe for them and push the tip free before he could deal with them. Tate struggled, but less towards the end.

Hood finished the job sweating. He rearranged Tate's position on the bed and stood for a moment at the window.

Then he crossed to the door, went downstairs and came back with the bottle of whisky. He poured three fingers into a tumbler, added a splash of water and took it over to the bed. He held Tate's head up.

'Try to take this, will you, old boy?' Tate slowly opened his eyes, saw the glass. He opened his mouth. Gently, avoiding the lips, Hood gave him the whisky. Hood got another glass and had a drink himself. He sat on the bed. In a minute, Tate opened his eyes again.

'Another shot?' Hood said.

Tate nodded. Hood poured him a good slug, straight. Tate took it and lay back. 'Thanks,' he said faintly.

Hood got up, opened the window a little and lit a cigarette. He wanted to get everything Tate could tell him, fast. But Tate had had agony. He had to give him time. He finished the cigarette and turned to stub it. Tate was gesturing with his hand. Hood went over. Tate motioned him to sit down.

'Can you tell me about it?' Hood said. Tate nodded.

'Don't try to move your lips. Just whisper. When you want to stop just tap my hand. Want another drink?'

Tate nodded, holding up his fingers to indicate a small one. Hood brought it and gave it to him.

'Did they do that to your mouth here?'

Another nod, and a faint whisper, so faint that Hood couldn't catch it. 'What was that?' He put his ear close to Tate's lips.

'They was goin' to clip me nose up next.'

'Who were they?'

'Dunno. Big fellers. Said they'd stop up all me holes, one by one.'

A pause. Hood raised his head. To his shame and horror, he saw two big tears rolling down Tookey Tate's cheeks. 'It's all right, Tookey. They won't do it to you now. You sure you want to talk?'

'Sure.' He looked a bit better.

'What happened in that café?'

Tate took a moment to start, then he whispered very softly: 'It was like this. It started before I saw you that night. I was doin' a job on me own, in Golders Green. Modern house. They was always away on the Sunday. Looked nice and easy.'

'You mean housebreaking?'

Tate nodded. 'I had all Gawd breakin' in. Mortice locks on the windows; special alarms. I had to cut three different alarms. Took me two hours to get in. I said to meself it means there's lovely grub waiting inside. But there was nothing. I been thirty-two years at the game and I never saw anything so ribby.' He had to stop. Hood waited. When Tate continued, Hood could scarcely hear him.

'There was three pounds ten in cash. But I come across some funny hiding-places – clever. Little camera in one. Then some rolls of film; miniature stuff like.'

'Micro-film?'

Tate made a shrugging motion. 'There was a mini tape-recorder too. Then in the wash-house outside, down by a hole by the sink – it's where the Golders Green class hide the cash and jewels – there was only a bloody wireless set, and ear-phones. I nicked what I could, the camera, set and the other stuff and cleared off.'

He paused again. Hood wiped Tate's face.

'I flogged the set next day. That's how they must have traced me. But Detective-Sergeant Everett at the Yard had been getting some information about another job I done the week previous. I'd already fixed up to have a little holiday on the Continong. So instead of trying to flog the rest of the stuff in London, I sent it by a pal o' mine. He was also coming across. So I asked him to post it to me at Poste Restante, Nice.'

Hood interrupted. 'Tookey, are you sure you can go on? If you can there's a question I want to ask.'

'Yes.'

'You are sure this has something to do with what happened to you?' Tate nodded. 'Go on,' Hood said.

'I didn't want to have the stuff with me if Sergeant Everett picked me up on the cross-Channel. I wish to Gawd he 'ad of done. First time in me life I ever wished I was in the nick. They must have been following me, these people, soon as I got off the boat. Three men come up to me one night in the street. There's a car at the kerb and before I can do anything I'm inside and they got me gagged and tied up.'

In a sharp whisper, Hood said: 'Wait!' There had been a sound from below.

He went to the door and listened. Whoever it was below had stopped too; there was silence. Hood went down to the ground floor. He slipped into the dining-room and looked out of the window. All was as before. In the kitchen the door was still locked from the inside as he had left it. He cursed his imagination and ran upstairs again.

Even though he was prepared for it, Tate's appearance was a shock. The lips were terribly swollen – bloated. Tate looked weaker. Hood sat down and touched his hand. Tate opened his eyes.

'Do you think you can go on?'

Tate nodded weakly. He beckoned with his head for Hood to come closer. Hood bent over him. Tate's whispering was very faint.

'They kept me tied up, kept knockin' me about. They burnt me privates with cigarettes. They had some little Frenchman too, they did horrible things to him. They was going to do me in too. They was after this camera and the wireless and the tape-recorder I'd pinched. I kept telling them, but they said I was telling lies.'

'Where were you?'

'They was always changing addresses, taking me from one place to another, flats they were. Then one night they says they are going to kill me. Wet and sticky like, they says. They takes me up to a room at the top of some — '

'The building where I saw you?'

'Yes. But I managed to give 'em the slip. I was shit-scared. I got the lift. When you stopped it and got in, I thought you was one of 'em and you was going to knife me or something.'

'They came for you afterwards in the café?'

Tate's eyes filled with horror. He nodded. 'They took me away. They tortured me. They hung me up and hung weights on me balls. They got bigger weights every day. They said they was going to — ' He groaned. Hood waited once more while Tate summoned the strength to go on.

'Was there a big man there, man with a staring eye and a red mark round his neck?' Hood asked.

'Once.'

'Whereabouts did they take you after the café?'

'Dunno. Near some place called the Opera. I seen a traffic sign.'

'Near the Opera? Any street or number?'

'All I know it was top floor. There was one of them old-time lifts, on a long steel stalk that comes out of the ground. Then they brought me here.'

Hood poured another drink and gave him a little. Suddenly much was falling into place.

Burgling the Golders Green house, Tate had stumbled across some equipment being used by a spy ring and taken it for want of better pickings. The spies had managed to trace him and tried to recover the material. They had cleared out the café, by money or threats, to eliminate all trace, above all the connection between Tate and Lobar's address. And Lobar, of course, knew that he, Hood, had been the last outsider to talk to Tate. It looked as if Lobar was the ringleader, all right.

'But Tookey, you told them where the stuff was?' Hood said. 'Poste Restante, Nice?'

'I kept tellin' 'em. They said they went there and there was nothing, so I was lyin'. But I was tellin' the truth. Godzonner. Then they says: "You won't talk, eh?" and they puts them staples in me mouth.'

'So your pal double-crossed you and never sent the

things? He must have if the post office people at Nice said they had nothing in the name of Tate.'

'No. Mullins. Name of Mullins. That's me real name. It's on me passport, what they took.'

Tate's whisper faded. His eyes were shut. Hood sponged his face. 'Try to tell me a little more, old boy. I don't follow this about Mullins.'

Tate had to give himself time. 'I never carried letters with Tate on 'em or papers name of Tate on 'em, see, when I went abroad. Precaution. If you do a job and get nicked, you don't tell the police the name you go by at home. Maybe they don't make the connection. Interpol don't know everything.'

'I see,' Hood said. 'But did your pal know you as Mullins?'

Tate stirred a bit. He opened his eyes and slowly raised them to Hood and stared as if something had come to him from a great distance. His head wobbled on the pillow and the bloody froth reappeared between his lips. 'Christ. You mean he sent – he sent – it —'

'He knew you as Tookey Tate, didn't he?'

Tate nodded feebly.

'Then that's how he addressed the parcel. And it's why these people didn't get it when they asked if there was anything for Mullins.'

Tate seemed suddenly much weaker. Hood saw that he was going to die unless he was rapidly given care. He must get him away. The speediest would be to phone for an ambulance. But again that would mean the police, inquiries, the end of his mission.

Looking down at Tookey Tate lying there with his hideously tortured lips, Hood felt fury rising in him against Lobar. He could not let Lobar escape. Somehow, Tookey Tate had made it a matter of personally settling the account.

He put his lips to Tate's ear. 'Don't worry, Tookey. I'll get him for you. You can rely on it.'

Hood stood up. He was going to have to take Tate into Nice in the car below. It would mean risks. He would have to leave Tate at the accident ward and get out fast, without explanation. He would be in Lobar's car, which was probably known locally.

But that was how it had to be. Hood poured himself a shot of Scotch, drank it. He turned and with great care picked Tate up in his arms.

As he turned to the door, there was the sound of a car in the drive below.

13

HOOD RETURNED to the bed and laid Tate down. He stepped to the window but could see nothing. The car had evidently turned by the garage. He went out on to the landing, shut the door softly behind him and waited. In a moment, somebody came into the house.

Whoever it was moved about the ground floor, looking round. The steps crossed the entrance hall and went into the dining-room. Presently they came out. Hood tiptoed to the banisters and looked over. A shadow crossed the patch of sunlight below. The next moment, Hood heard the steps coming softly up the stairs.

He leaned back so as to give himself just the space to see the flight below. The person coming up was moving stealthily. Hood caught a faint tang of tobacco. The steps paused at the first landing, then came on up. At the next landing they turned into one of the bedrooms.

Suddenly a shrill peal came from below. The telephone. It sounded loud in the empty house. Motionless, Hood strained to catch a movement from the person in the bedroom. The shrilling of the telephone was covering other sounds. It went on, with its curious urgency. Why wasn't the newcomer answering? Then he saw a shadow move on the staircase. At the same moment, the ringing stopped and he heard the steps going down again.

Hood waited till there was silence below. Then he crept down. The entrance and the drawing-room were empty. He went silently towards the kitchen, eased open the door and faced the chauffeur.

The chauffeur had a cigarette in his mouth. He did not take it out. He rolled it along his lip with his tongue; rolled it back. He looked at Hood.

‘Good morning,’ Hood said. He pulled the door wide and went in.

The chauffeur was standing in the middle of the kitchen. His brown tunic was unbuttoned at the collar. He was a big man with eyebrows that met over his nose. He was obviously very strong.

‘Is Mr Lobar about?’ Hood said with a smile.

The chauffeur’s eyes travelled slowly down over Hood’s chest down to his trousers and shoes. Hood could see him picking out the bloodstains. The chauffeur put his fingers to the cigarette in his mouth and threw it like a dart in Hood’s face. Then he jumped in and let go a pile-driver right smash.

The lighted cigarette hit Hood painfully in the corner of the eye and momentarily blinded him. In the second before the punch, he managed to pivot right, bringing his left shoulder up and sending the fist high up on the side of his head. He kept his feet. Hardly pausing, the chauffeur threw a vicious low left swing at Hood’s liver. Hood, trying to duck, with one eye watering and the other blinking from the ash, only half countered this. The blow was painful. For a second his head swam. Blindly he butted the man and shoved him off. He was not going in for any bare-knuckle fighting in this sort of contest. Hood knew how hard it is to knock a strong man out even with several blows and how easily the attempt can result in a smashed hand.

Already the chauffeur was swinging for a low blow again. Hood kicked the table over, dodging. He was trying to blink away the ash in the corner of his eye. The chauffeur rushed him. Hood swayed back, grabbed the man’s left arm as it came in, jerked on it violently, pulling the man towards him and, as he did, kneed him in the crutch. He still couldn’t see properly and the knee did not connect as he wanted. But the chauffeur heaved and roared with pain, lifting his chin. Hood upped his bent elbow and gave it to him full force under the chin. The chauffeur’s teeth clicked, he shot backwards, crashed against the sideboard and brought down a shelf of pots.

He scrabbled up, feeling his crutch and gasping obscenities at Hood, and whipped up a meat cleaver. He swung it murderously. Hood thought he was going to strike forward with it and crouched. But the chauffeur threw it, low. Desperately Hood twisted round; the handle of the cleaver scraped his neck. As the chauffeur reached for another, Hood grabbed the nearest thing, a heavy silver tray, and threw it disc-wise. The edge hit the chauffeur between the upper lip and the nose. As it landed, Hood jumped at him feet first. His joined heels rammed the chauffeur's belly. The man's skull hit the stove as he went over.

The overturned table was in the way. Before Hood could get up and go for him, the chauffeur slung a chair in his legs and was limping out of the door. Hood ran after him. The chauffeur surely had a gun in the car. As Hood rounded the corner of the house, he was reaching in the open front door of the car. The car had been moved out on to the drive – that was what Hood had heard.

Hood charged him in the back with all his weight. The chauffeur pitched violently forward, face first. Hood snatched up his ankles, dragged him halfway out and stamped on his spine. He got the man's head in the doorjamb and slammed the door on it full force. The chauffeur bellowed, lashed out with his feet and knocked Hood over. Hood scrambled up and flung himself for the cover of the car. Two shots fired in quick succession, as if involuntarily, kicked up the gravel in front of him. Then there were three or four clicks, the chauffeur swore and flung the empty gun at him. It clanged against the side of the car.

Hood straightened up. The chauffeur was at the garage work-bench. His face was bloody. Hood moved towards him, crouching. The chauffeur grabbed something from the bench and backed away and darted out into the garden. Still half facing Hood, he suddenly increased his pace, putting some distance between them. He was working at some object which he held to his side, out of Hood's sight. Hood advanced. The man backed off.

If it was another gun he was loading, Hood had no cover. He went for the man. The chauffeur backed rapidly, then stopped with one hand extended. It held a bottle.

Something in Hood's mind said: 'Acid.' A thin vapour curled out of the bottle.

It was one or other of them, Hood knew. If he backed off, the chauffeur was going to let him have it. If he went in...

Without shifting his eyes, Hood prospected the space behind the chauffeur. There were two shrubs just behind him and some more to the right. There was a chance that, if by a surprise, he could make the man step back quickly, he would fall or stumble. He scraped the ground with his foot.

Hood made a rapid crouching feint to the right. The man's hand jerked and the acid flew in the air – where Hood had been. Hood ducked to the left, snatched up a handful of dirt, threw it in the chauffeur's face and jumped on him. One hand grasped the chauffeur's hand enclosing the bottle, the other had his neck. The chauffeur staggered back. They fell. In the tension of the moment, Hood noticed that they were both sliding. The ground was sloping. They were near the cliff edge.

The chauffeur's free hand was on his jaw, forcing it back. Both their other hands gripped the bottle. Hood understood that there was still some acid in it.

He put all his strength into the effort to bend the man's arm. Slowly he forced the bottle towards the chauffeur's upturned face. Their mouths stretched wide in the effort. The tendons splayed like a fan in the chauffeur's neck. His eyes were staring. He let out a cry that became louder and louder.

Hood's hand slowly twisted the bottle in his grip. It was level, above the man's eyes. Then the acid poured out. It smoked and made a tiny hissing sound. The chauffeur gave an inhuman cry. His eyes and upper face dissolved under a sort of active foam. The tiny bubbles hissed and multiplied. Hood gritted his teeth. He twisted the bottle upside down until the last drop had fallen from it.

He disengaged himself. The man was quivering on his back. His face under the acid bubbles looked as if it were a mass of tiny crawling insects. He was raising his hands with extended fingers slowly into the air.

As Hood stood up, the man began to slide down the grass slope. He was checked by the low edging. He writhed against it. Hood stood getting his breath back, watching him. The chauffeur twisted against the parapet, half rose – and went over.

Hood went to the wall, knelt on the rocks and looked over. The man had hit one of the spikes, right at the water's edge. He was impaled. An arm moved spasmodically.

Hood turned back to the villa.

14

IT WAS growing dark.

He went up to the room where Tate was lying. He gave himself a shot of Scotch. He was shaky after the fight.

The situation was not good. Somebody was bound to see the chauffeur's body in the morning. That would mean the police, inquiries, Lobar warned. There was an iron stair leading down from the villa grounds to the water's edge. He could go down and get the man, risk being seen. Then he looked at Tate. He would have to take a chance on the chauffeur. He must get Tate to a hospital.

Hood took Tate in his arms and carried him downstairs. He lifted him into the front seat of the Lincoln. He wished there was a smaller car, something more commonplace. He looked into the other garage. It was empty.

Hood lit a cigarette. As soon as Lobar found out what had happened he would send after him. To trace the Lincoln would be child's play. And Hood didn't know how long he might need a car.

He left Tate in the Lincoln and went to the service door. The lock was a Yale, blocked from inside, no doubt by the chauffeur. Hood opened it and looked out. Parked fifty yards down the road was a DS Citroën. Farther off, in the opposite direction, was a grey Fiat 1800.

Hood went back to the garage. In the pocket of the Lincoln he found the chauffeur's gloves and two Yale keys. On the seat was the chauffeur's cap. He pocketed the keys and put the cap on. It was too small. He ripped out the sweatband and tried again. The cap fitted more or less. It was an old trick. By some magic, a cap became an entire uniform with a car. Anybody who happened to see him would swear to him afterwards as 'a chauffeur in uniform'.

Tate was slumped to one side, semi-conscious. Hood lifted

him out and carried him to the service door. There was nobody on the road. With Tate in his arms, he walked down to the Fiat. He could hear a radio playing in the house. He put Tate in the front seat. The Citroën would have been ideal; but you needed a key. With a Fiat 1800 you didn't – and Fiats were common enough in this area.

He drove off without lights. Round the first bend he switched on. At St Jean, he turned left along the sea front towards Beaulieu. Ahead, the lights of Cap Roux and Monte Carlo were blinking in the night. Offshore he could see the *Triton*. The car was fairly new and well tuned. At the Lower Corniche he turned left again along the road to Nice. There was a good deal of traffic and it drove as if it were on a racetrack.

At Villefranche the road was up. They idled in a jam. Hood looked at Tate. He had lurched over against the door. Hood straightened him and wound down the window to give him air.

'How goes it, old boy? Can you hold on a bit longer?'

Tate didn't answer. Hood wiped the blood from his nose. The driver behind flashed his lights impatiently. Hood looked up, hastily threw in the gear and drove on. As the other car blared past, the woman passenger gave them a curious stare. She's seen something, thought Hood. He slackened speed and let the other car draw away.

The suburbs of Nice began. All at once there was a gurgle and Tate pitched over on to him. Hood managed to get him upright, but Tate collapsed the other way. He was making a liquid sound. Haemorrhage, thought Hood; poor devil.

He drew over to the kerb. The sharp blasts of a police whistle cut through the traffic noise. Hood looked quickly out of the window. A traffic cop astride his machine was waving him on. It was a no parking zone. Hood went on. Two hundred yards farther along where the zone ended, he had to search for a place. He passed up two at busy corners. Tate groaned. Hood pulled into a space outside a row of shops. He took Tate's shoulder and gently lifted him up. It had been haemorrhage. There was blood all over his chin and chest.

Hood had a moment of bitter and frustrated rage. He wanted to throw aside everything else in the urgent need there was to get Tate to a doctor. It was a feeling he had had many times before when he had been in some lonely and dangerous action against enemy agents and some ordinary, pitiful, mild human being like Tookey Tate had paid out of all proportion for his transgressions.

But feeling was more than unwise in Hood's world. It was often sheer madness. To yield to it could mean spreading a wide circle of death and ruin and the permanent knowledge of weakness and failure.

Hood felt for Tate's pulse and found that he was dead. 'Poor devil,' he said. 'I hope I killed the one who tortured him.'

'What's the matter with your boss?' A head was in the open window – a jolly-looking woman with a plump red face. Quickly, Hood raised an arm, hiding Tate's face as well as he could. 'Oh, the usual. He loves it but he can't take it.' Hood forced a laugh. 'Anything that comes his way – Bordeaux, Burgundy, red, white, cognac, vodka, pastis —'

'It's good, pastis,' the woman said chummily. Her head was still in the window. The light from the shops shone brightly into the car.

'That's true.' Hood adjusted his chauffeur's cap.

'Still, there's them that can and them that can't. There's no mistake. It's like when I was in hospital. The sister says to me, she says: "This treatment is going to be painful, Madame Crotti." I says to her: "You just go on with it, Sister." It surprised her, it did. And she says to me afterwards, when I was discharged: "Well, Madame Crotti, there's some that can stand it and some that can't." '

'Absolutely.'

She was craning with curiosity to get a better view of Tate. 'Anyway, he don't smell like most of 'em do when they're stewin'. It was one thing my mother couldn't abide, and I must say I took after her there. "You can't get it out of their clothes," she used to say. "I swear your father's boots has the stench of the grape," she said. "The stench o' the grape", she used to call it – that's Victor Hugo, you know, poetry!' She laughed joyfully.

How to escape? He dare not let go of the body. Yet he could hardly twist the car out one-handed, and it would look odd to try.

Hood said: 'Well, Madame Crotti, goodnight.'

But she wasn't having any. 'Reminds me of the old song my grandfather used to sing. "Your feet, your feet, your features are divine."' Another joyful peal.

'We must be going.' He started the car.

'You only just come.' Suddenly her tone changed. She had bobbed down and caught a glimpse of Tate's blood-covered chin and chest. 'Oh. He *is* in a — Whatever's happened to him?'

Any moment now, Hood thought, she is going to scream. We shall then have half Nice here. 'Just drunk, that's all. Madame Crotti, do something for me. The police stopped me just now for my lights. See if my rear light's alight will you?'

'What – what's that all over him, there? Blood – it's bl —'

Hood let out a roar of laughter. 'Oh, that's a beauty! Wait till his wife comes along. You can tell it to her.' He went on laughing.

'What is it then?'

'Tomato juice! If you want it exactly, it's tomato juice and grenadine. He was drunk and he tried to swallow a can of tomato juice topped up with grenadine. Blood! We must tell Madame Valette that one when she comes. She'll be here in a minute.'

She was uncertain, then disconcerted. 'Well,' she withdrew weakly. 'Better to have a laugh out of it than the other way. You're a long time dead.' Suddenly she was gone.

Hood let go the body, wrenched the car out and weaved

into the traffic. He glanced back but couldn't see her. Hadn't she merely pretended to accept what he had said and gone to tell the police? That last joke ... He steered into the thickest of the traffic.

The body was upright against the seat. Tate's head had fallen back and the mutilated, monstrously swollen lips were raised in full view towards the roof.

'Sorry, Tookey,' Hood said and gave him a shove. The body tilted against the door. Hood wound the window up.

He wished the traffic was moving faster. It was scarcely going above walking pace. He was hemmed in. It *was* walking pace. There were people keeping up alongside – ranks of them, marching. Some were carrying lanterns. They were singing.

Hood saw that he was involved in a procession. He flashed his lights, switched over his traffic blinker, eased to one side. The marching ranks alongside simply raised their hands and went on singing. A police motor-cyclist appeared alongside the car. He signalled Hood with a pushing motion of his hand to resume station. Reluctantly, Hood did so. The policeman kept level. He was on the same side as the body. Hood watched him out of the tail of his eye. In a moment, the patrolman pulled forward and, turning in his saddle, jabbed a finger in Tate's direction. He lifted his chin inquiringly. It said plainly: 'What's the matter with him?'

Hood took his hands off the wheel and made mock fisticuffs. Then he curved forefinger to thumb to stand for a glass and tipped it back. The patrolman nodded tentatively as if he had come to that conclusion himself. He dropped back alongside. Hood could see him examining Tate. The body had shifted to an unnatural position. It occurred to Hood that if he were suspicious or even careful, the patrolman would note the number of the car. He hoped word about stolen cars didn't go out *that* fast. He thanked heaven he hadn't taken the Lincoln. Sure enough, the patrolman dropped back. Hood could hear his machine just behind.

The cars and marchers of the procession turned off towards the port. There were plenty ahead of him, Hood saw, and more behind. Many of the cars were strung with fishing nets. It was some sort of fishermen's ceremony, the blessing of the boats or some such.

As they approached the waterfront, a blaze of decorated boats strung with lanterns came into view. The procession was disrupting the ordinary traffic and there were police everywhere, blowing their whistles and doing a lot of waving. They were directing the cars to one side. Hood put his head out of the window. 'Where are we going?'

'Official car park,' the policeman said, jerking his thumb. 'Keep going.' The car park was on the west quay. It was fenced in. There were a dozen or more attendants. One directed Hood to a place. Hood tried to move on. The man began blowing his whistle excitedly. Hood pulled in. The place was under a light. The attendant was stalking round, snarling. Hood sat tight, pretending to be looking for something inside the car. The man cleared off.

Hood took his bearings. There was a gap on the right beween his car and the next one. A quantity of chains was piled up in the gap round a big marker buoy and left no room for another car to be parked. But the light was just overhead.

Cars were still moving into the park and the attendants were all round. The sound of singing was coming from the direction of the boats. As a precaution, Hood searched Tate's pockets but found nothing. He said: 'This is where I have to leave you, Tookey,' and put his hand on the door. At that moment a motor-cyclist chugged up, saw the small gap by the chains and buoy, wheeled in to park and cut his engine.

Hood watched him; a young man, alert-looking, in crash-helmet and zipper blouse. He pulled the machine on to its stand, looked round, looked at the Fiat. Hood got out, shut the door and walked away. He walked briskly towards the entrance, turning between rows of cars in the shadow.

'*Monsieur!*' An attendant in rubber-soled shoes stepped up smartly and touched his arm. Hood flexed for action.

'Well?'

'You left your lights on.'

It would only draw attention to the car if he didn't put them out. 'Much obliged.' He went back. The motor-cyclist was standing by his machine staring at Tate's body. Hood tried to look casual.

'Something wrong with your passenger?' the man said.

'Drunk.' He glanced across. One of Tate's eyes had opened and was staring horribly. Luckily, a strip of shadow fell across the lower part of his face. The motor-cyclist was silent. He did not seem to have accepted the explanation. Hood stepped forward and blocked his view. An icy coldness came into Hood's eyes at these moments. He became indecipherable. His face and body were still. There was not a flicker in him; and the levelness of that look conveyed, for those who could read it, a hard intellectual chill that made Hood extremely menacing. He was the quintessence of a man who is not to be trifled with.

The motor-cyclist fiddled with his saddle-bags.

'Fine night for the service,' Hood said.

'Yes. You from round here?'

'Yes. You?'

The man didn't answer. Hood lit a cigarette. He could see the man noting his clothes, his features. A moment later the man gave him a final up and down glance, turned and walked away.

Hood was quite cool. He moved fast. He circled the car, snapped the lights off, returned and opened the door by the body. Tate pitched slowly out with great dignity. Hood caught him, lifted him free and slammed the door. The overhead light seemed glaring on the mutilated face. There was a dark area on the far side of the park and Hood made for that.

The body was not heavy. Hood took the risk and simply carried it in his arms. Headlights from a car moving in probed towards him. He looked round. The parked cars were close packed. The incoming car was turning to approach.

Hood propped Tate against one of the parked cars and began a silent argument with him, composed of gestures. The headlights swung and came on, full on them. Hood jabbed a finger at Tate's chest, emphasizing a point.

Tate slipped. Hood grabbed his coat lapel as if they were at the height of the discussion, then nodded at something Tate was supposed to be saying. The car passed. Hood gave it time to get farther away. Then he picked Tate up and went on. In the zone of darkness just beyond the range of the lamps he made out some upturned boats and piled gear. Carefully he felt his way among this and lay the body down under cover of a boat.

It's a long way from Golders Green, Tookey, he thought; but I hope they'll give you a decent funeral. Going back between the parked cars, he took the chauffeur's cap off and stuffed it in his pocket. He gave a wide berth to the line where the Fiat was and made for the exit. Then unexpectedly he saw the motor-cyclist ahead. He had left the Fiat and was talking to one of the park attendants and a policeman. They were under a light and the motor-cyclist was holding out a hand, fingers extended, at which they were all looking down.

'If that isn't blood ...' the motor-cyclist was saying.

Hood glanced round. A car was manoeuvring behind him. It was a good way back to the next cross-alley and if they raised the alarm, he might be trapped, whereas ahead, the exit was quite near. On the whole, it was better to continue and walk past them. He walked on. As he came up to them, he lifted one hand to his head and scratched, giving cover to his face.

'... couldn't have been. He was dead, I tell you.'

'Did you see him go out, Georges?' the policeman said.

'Not me,' the attendant said. 'I've been down with Dédé.'

'He's a big type – hefty —' the motor-cyclist was gesturing.

Hood was almost past. He felt the motor-cyclist look across. He quickened his pace.

'Here, wait a minute, isn't that — ? By God, I'd swear — It *is* him. There he is!'

Hood was walking fast. He heard them start after him. He cursed and broke into a sprint. They began shouting. The policeman was going to pull his gun any moment.

Hood barely had a start; the motor-cyclist was fit and a fair runner. Hood was through the gate of the car park when he heard the policeman shout something and they all slacked off. Here it comes, he thought – and dived to one side. There was no cover.

The shot smacked against the stone wall backing the quay, ricocheted and smashed a light. Hood ran on. The mass of lighted boats swayed close together at the quayside and extended out into the port. There was a priest with a crucifix and a statue of the Virgin in front of the crowd at the water's edge. The crowd farther back was shifting about.

Hood sprinted full out. There was another shot and a metallic clang to his left. But now he was too close to the crowd. Unable to fire again, the policeman began blowing his whistle. Hood glanced back. The motor-cyclist and another athletic-looking man were coming hard for him, but he had left them well back.

He ran to the edge of the crowd, stopped and turned round, giving himself a few moments to recover breath. Then whipping out the chauffeur's cap, he scrabbled all the loose change he had from his pocket and threw it into it. With this held out, he eased his way gently among the crowd. 'N'oubliez pas les veuves et les orphelins, s'il vous plait, Messieurs-dames. Widows and orphans, please. Thank you. Widows and orphans. Thank you kindly.' He clinked the coins in the cap, kept his head down. Hands went into pockets. Coins dropped into the cap. He saw the motor-cyclist and the other man run past. Then the policeman with another. He pressed into the crowd.

'*If* you please. Widows and orphans.' Gradually he worked his way back to the far side of the crowd, then to the rear. The pursuers seemed to be active farther along the quay.

Opposite him were steps up to the road above. He strolled casually over to them. As he turned up, a fat policeman dashed down past him. Hood went up.

At the top he crossed the road. He chose side-streets and made his way to the centre of the town. A little shrunken old woman was sitting on a bench by the bus terminal. Hood went up to her and bowed.

'If you will allow me, Madame, I have a gift from the sea.' She gaped with watery eyes. He took her knotty blue old hand and tipped the money into it. She blinked; her hand trembled. Hood said: 'And if you can say a Mass for a fellow called Tate, so much the better.'

A black-and-white police van with siren blaring swung round the corner and sped past. Hood turned and walked away. Now he felt he must take the offensive against Lobar. What had Conder's words been? 'He'll undoubtedly have you killed if he thinks you are getting too close in.'

Hood felt a chill. He was going to get closer. He was going back to the villa.

15

FIRST HE was hungry and wanted a drink. He went past one or two cafés, but decided against them; and he wanted to avoid the immense involvement of a full sit-down meal in one of the restaurants. A sign in a doorway said Le Nichon. That sounded entertaining.

He pushed open the door. Heavy drapes, thick carpet, dim lights. Stale tobacco smoke. A nightclub. He glimpsed the bar and went towards it. A girl appeared, ash-blonde with her hair piled up high, amusing mouth, four-inch heels, lipsticked cigarette.

'We're not open yet. It's too early. Come back at ten o'clock.'

'Can't come back. This is my last night in Europe. Can't I get a drink?'

'There's nobody here. That street door shouldn't have been open.'

'How about having a drink yourself?'

'Where'll you be tomorrow if this is your last night?'

'Ouagadougou.'

'Where's that?'

'Africa. In the Upper Volta.'

'Oh. Black women?'

'They get whiter and whiter. That's what the fellows say at all events, when they've been there a year.' He got up on a bar stool.

'Is it romantic? What are you having?'

'Scotch for me. Thanks. Superbly romantic – palms, mangrove swamps, mosquitoes. Could I get a sandwich too, do you think?'

She poured the drinks. She kept looking at him. She seemed to like him very much. Hood thought she was good-looking. When she had taken a sip of her drink she said: 'I'll bring you a sandwich,' and went out behind.

Hood lit a cigarette and drank his whisky. Through an opening next to the bar he could see the empty dance floor and tables. The décor was good. Everything looked comfortable and well kept. Hood found the place very agreeable. Somebody put a pick-up on. Errol Garner playing 'Love for Sale'; that was all right too.

Abruptly a man in shirt-sleeves came through a service door on to the dance floor, followed by half a dozen girls. The girls were in street clothes and some of them had suitcases. The man was doing a lot of talking and began busily going round switching on lights, moving chairs, ordering the girls to stand over here, stand over there and so on. The girls took their scarves and coats off and, Hood was surprised to see, a couple unbuttoned their blouses and took them off and stood there in bras.

'Oh, they *are* there.'

Hood turned back to the bar. It was the blonde, with his sandwich. She said: 'You're lucky, aren't you? On your last night with the white race too.'

'How come?' He jerked his head. 'Who are these charming friends of yours?'

'Strippers. They're after a job. We're two short for the floor show.'

'Do you mean I get a free bosom with my sandwich?'

'Nipple and all. Unless you want to turn your back and tell me about the economics of Ouagadougou.'

'I think I could stand watching,' Hood said. 'The one on the right doesn't look bad.'

'You'd better get your strength up first with a sandwich,' the girl said.

Hood said: 'Let's have another drink.' He ate. The sandwiches were good, one smoked salmon, one chicken. The shirt-sleeved man, apparently the manager, was still busy. 'This is Black Label Johnny Walker, isn't it?' Hood said.

The girl gave him a smile. 'You should have looked in before your last night, sailor.'

'I'll be back, Madame Butterfly.'

There were loud hand-claps from the dance floor, the manager bawled: 'All right, all right! Now number one. Mademoiselle Arlette. Get out there. Remember I'm paying for this. I'm paying to get an eyeful of my little lady. I don't want any of that snatch it and run. Give the customer what he wants. Go on now.'

Arlette was tall and dark and inexpert. She took off her sweater and skirt and her brassière with scarcely any grace.

'You'd think she was going to bed,' the girl said to Hood. 'Alone.'

'Yes, but she's got something to show.' The girl was lovely. 'All she needs is training.'

'That's all any of us can hope for.'

Arlette crossed her legs and rolled her stockings down. She had on a small pair of panties with little pink bows.

'This is where you have the professional privilege, sailor,' the girl said to Hood.

'What's that?'

'She's got no G-string or anything under that.'

'None of them have?'

'None of them.'

Arlette hesitated just an instant, then with a charmingly saucy smile she took them off. She crooked a knee.

'M'mm,' said Hood. 'She's worth training.'

The manager, who was sitting at one of the tables, made her change her pose once, twice, then again – prolonging it. 'All right. Stand over there.' Then he was calling instructions and clapping his hands for the next girl. 'Rita! Let's have it now. Get out there, girl.'

Rita was smoothly professional and used all the clichés of the game. 'We don't like her much, do we?' the bar girl said to Hood. She was leaning close to him. Their eyes met. Then she lowered hers. Hood thought she was a beauty.

'What do they call you?' he said.

'Kit.'

The next girl was Suzie and she was shy. She was show-girl size and when she started to strip, Hood saw the manager getting excited. She took her skirt off, a chemise, and then very slowly and fetchingly, her bra.

There was a silent gasp. The manager stopped jiggling around in his seat.

'Wha!'

'What did you say?'

'Wow.'

Suzie paused, her face turned to her shoulder. She unhooked her stockings from her suspender belt (back suspenders first) then took a little twist in each stocking-top to keep them up. Hood was still looking at that bosom. With considerable cunning, she was wearing her suspender belt over her pants.

She stepped out of the suspender belt. Her pants were black. She seemed not to know what to do with the suspender belt. The manager was moistening his lips. Finally she just dropped the belt. She blushed, took the top of the pants, rolled them down a couple of inches. Hood gave an amused glance at Kit; she smiled back.

Suzie rolled the pants down another couple of inches – and then peeled them off. She stood there in her black stockings and shoes. A tiny remaining wisp added to the charm. The manager coughed nervously.

'How about that special effect?' Kit said.

'It's a sweet nibbler, you can't deny,' Hood said. She laughed.

But Suzie hadn't done. Pivoting slightly on her high heels, she put her hands on her hips and began to do the splits. Slowly her heel slid across the floor. Her long legs stretched wider. Her knee touched, then her thighs – and with a final movement, she came to rest.

'Now how about that for a special effect?' Hood said. 'I know somebody who's ready to kiss the very ground she splits on!' They laughed together.

Jojo, the manager, had rushed forward and was helping the girl to her feet. He patted her encouragement. He kept patting.

Hood turned to take his drink and saw Andreas in the glass behind the bar. Andreas had his coat collar up as if he had just come in out of the rain. His look was fixed on Suzie. His eyes gleamed; he was smiling to himself.

Hood picked up his whisky and took a drink. His back was turned to the entrance and the valet had apparently not recognized him. Kit was watching the proceedings beyond and had not noticed Andreas come in. For a moment, Hood watched the curiously abstracted immobile tableau in which he found himself; the amusing and lovely girl, the little valet with his fuzzy hair and his indelible look of a peasant. Then Kit moved and saw Andreas. A flicker of doubt and curiosity came into her face.

'Well, well. So we're back. This is unexpected.'

Andreas was totally absorbed in Suzie and the other girls. Jojo was strenuously talking to Suzie and preventing her dressing with some urgent remark whenever she looked like picking up her pants or her bra. Rita was standing by smoking a cigarette, naked.

'And how are you?' Kit said louder.

Andreas came to. 'Ah – er – good evening.' He continued to smile rather mechanically. 'I just – I just – er – called in . . .' Then he saw Hood in the glass. His expression barely changed. The mechanical smile faltered for perhaps two seconds, then was back. 'Good evening, sir,' he said slowly.

'Good evening.'

'Do you want to see Jojo?' Kit said to Andreas.

'Yes . . . I wonder . . . I was going . . . to ask . . . if he had . . . that little . . .'

'Well, there he is,' she said, indicating the other room. 'You'd better wait till he's finished – which won't be too hard, will it?'

'Thank you.' His eyes went from her to Hood; he bobbed, in a sort of bow, still smiling, and went eagerly into the other room. He took a seat on the edge of a chair, feet together, hands in lap, meekly watching the proceedings. Hood finished his drink.

'Who is that little guy?'

'Oh,' she smiled. 'A regular customer, that's all. At least he used to be. The last floor show we had here – it finished ten days ago – he used to come every night. Well, *almost* every night. He used to sit at a table on the edge of the floor and just eat those girls up.'

Hood said: 'They weren't by chance wearing corsets, were they?'

'How did you know? I'd have seen you among the customers, sailor.'

'They wired me in Ouagadougou. There was a big corset act, was there?'

'Three acts. We had a lot of photographs of it somewhere.' She searched perfunctorily for them behind the bar. 'I don't know where they are.'

'What did he mean by Jojo having that little whatever it was? Maybe he's come for a spare corset as a keep-sake?'

She smiled. 'You learn a lot in Ouagadougou, don't you? He tried to buy two from the girls. I suppose what he's come for now is some money. He's an amazing little fellow. He was trying to buy these corsets, so we gave him one in the end. Then he used to come in before the show and say he wanted to do an act and it sounded like one of these – well, queer things, and we said no.'

'Queer things?'

'Twisted. But he said it wasn't. He was a mimic, and all he wanted was to do ten minutes of snap mimicry – mimic anybody in the audience. So we tried him. It was amazing. He used to watch customers. We'd give him a spot – fifteen minutes between the girls – and he'd come out and do some well-known people first, then half a dozen customers, people he'd just looked at like that, or me or Jojo or one of the band and he'd have the place in a rampage. It was – well, unbelievable. They went wild about him. He picks up mannerisms, voice, tricks of personality like lightning. Doesn't matter what language. He just makes noises that turn out like French or whatever. He used to get somebody to come out on the floor and talk to him, send them back – and suddenly turn into them. Magic!'

'Why didn't you keep him on?'

'Well, some of his friends came in one night. Or maybe they weren't his friends. They looked very rough. He told Jojo he wouldn't be coming again. He looked unhappy. Then they took him out.'

'One of them a big man with eyebrows meeting over here?' Hood fingered the bridge of his nose. That was the chauffeur.

She nodded. 'You didn't hear that in Ouagadougou.'

'It's telepathy,' Hood said. 'Just like you were telling yourself we need two more drinks.'

She gave him a look in which there was faintly amused melancholy. 'There are other things I'm telling myself.' She poured two whiskies and passed his over.

'And you paid him for the act, I suppose?'

'Yes. He's a mild little bird in some ways. But he was keen for the cash all right. He said he was doing the act just for fun. But he kept asking for money all the time. We didn't pay him much.'

Hood looked round. 'Hello, where have they gone?' The other room was empty except for Rita, dressed at last, pulling up her stockings.

'The office is back there.'

Hood felt uneasy. There was something unexplained about Andreas. 'Did his friends ever come in again?'

She shook her head. 'Never seen them.'

A couple of waiters were moving round in the other room. Abruptly the music cut off and a moment later Jojo came out of the office. As he crossed the dance floor, he gave Rita a slap on the backside. 'Nice work, Rita. Maybe next time.'

She gave him a sultry look. 'That titsy bitch with her tuft.'

'Let it grow, Rita. Let it grow!' Jojo laughed.

When he reached the bar, Kit said to him: 'What's the miraculous mimic after?'

'Wanted his cash.'

'Do you mean he's gone?' Hood said quickly.

Jojo looked at him in some astonishment. 'Yes. What of it? He was in a hurry. Friend of yours?'

'Friend of a friend.'

Jojo went out through the door behind the bar.

Hood drank his whisky. He wondered where Lobar was at this moment. Probably not on board the *Triton*, if Andreas had come ashore. A redhead of about thirty-five came through the bar door smoking a cigarette. She looked very sure of herself. She barely glanced at Hood, walked to the end of the bar, looked into the cash drawer, poured herself a Remy Martin cognac. She said nothing.

Hood asked who with his eyebrows.

'Jojo's wife,' Kit said in a whisper.

'Well,' Hood said. 'I ought to go.' He pulled out some money and paid. In a soft voice, he said to Kit: 'Those photographs of the last show you mentioned; were there any of the mimic doing his act among them?'

She paused fractionally. 'I think there were.'

The redhead with her back turned and the cigarette in her mouth said: 'All right, Kit; if you want to go.'

'Thanks, Paulette.' She jerked her head for Hood to come with her and went to the bar door. He followed her. As the door shut behind him, he clasped her arm, stopped her. 'Was she saying for you to take me up — ?'

'Idiot!' Kit said in a harsh whisper. 'She takes over the bar until ten. What do you think I am?' Her eyes were blazing.

'Sorry, Kit.'

She leaned up and kissed him. Then she turned and led the way. She had a couple of rooms upstairs in a part of the building adjoining the club. It was snug and smelt faintly of powder and the light was soft. It seemed very attractive to Hood. When they had drinks she said: 'I've been wondering what you did with the body.'

Hood jolted inwardly. Outwardly he grinned. 'I always cut them up and leave them in trunks in railway stations.'

'You must have cut this one up alive.'

'She was struggling a bit.'

She came up to him, pulled the lapel of his coat outward. There were smudges of blood on it. She showed him others. 'And there is a largish one by your knee,' she said.

'As a matter of fact, Kit, I—'

'Don't tell me,' she said in a quiet voice. 'I don't want to know anything. There are things you can only have if you don't know. Why do people want to know so much that they spoil the good moments? You don't get so many.'

'This looks like one to me.' She was standing very near him. She looked up. They kissed. He held her close. She wound her arms round his neck. When it ended, she crushed her face against his chest.

'I like you a lot, sailor.'

'That doesn't spoil anything.'

Hood desired her. He held her and caressed her and she clung to him in a long kiss. She broke away breathless and disengaged herself. She lit a cigarette and turned away across the room as if she were afraid to give way to something she had started.

'You'd better get that blood off. Give me your coat.'

He took his coat off and she came back from the bedroom next door with a bottle of some product and sat rubbing the stains out. Then she removed the one on the knee.

'Could you find those photographs?' Hood asked.

'Oh . . . Yes.' She seemed to come back from a long way off, looking at him. 'All right.' She went to a drawer and brought out a pack; but they all turned out to be shots of the corset girls and a singer. She searched again and at last said: 'Wait, he's on this one. It's the only one.'

It wasn't a photograph of Andreas, but of one of the corset strippers at her most provocative, taken by a floor photographer during the show. She was a pretty girl, wriggling out of the corset with a tilt of bare breasts and a sway of her hips, showing a tiny intimate concealment. Her attitude was incandescent. She seemed to be making a play at somebody in the audience; and just on the edge, just in the penumbra where the spotlights faded, Hood saw that the shot had caught a floor-side table with Andreas sitting there, absorbed. His face was just visible.

'Can I have it?' Hood said.

'If you want it. Any special reason?'

He put it in his pocket. 'It's just for a friend of a friend.'

She leaned over him and undid a button of his shirt and put her hand inside on his chest. She said: 'How about making love, sailor?'

He kissed her.

She said: 'I have a terrible appetite for you. It happened like that, soon as I saw you.'

It had happened to Hood, too, this scene, many times and he had thanked the gods of chance for the tender moments they had given and of which he felt entirely unworthy.

She said: 'I'm a bit scared. I'm not usually like this – in fact never. What have you got, sailor?'

'It must be my staring eyes. Same as Landru.'

'Oh yes – the body, I remember. It seems years ago, that. I've known you for so long. Kiss me.'

Hood kissed her. In a moment he gently disengaged himself. He took her face in his hands. 'Kit, I have to leave you. I hate to, and what you've just said is very precious and means all the good things to me you want to mean. But this isn't something I can help.'

Softly she said: 'You can't light me up like this, sailor, and then just go.'

'It isn't me deciding, Kit.'

She didn't say anything. He released her. 'You have to put it down to chance, Kit. There's nothing else to blame.'

Her eyes were down. 'All right. Thanks, all the same.'

'I'll be back if I can.'

'Sailors don't care.'

'Give you my word,' Hood said. 'Kit, can you show me the way out?'

She got up, smiled, passed her hand down his cheek. 'Sure. Come on.'

16

THE RAIN had stopped. It was a warm night. The black surface of the roads glistened from the shower.

Hood walked along until he saw a taxi rank ahead. Then his steps slowed and stopped. He stood, hands in pockets, looking down at the kerb, aware of the small personal signs of apprehension. He very much did not want to go back to Les Oliviers. The villa was an evil and menacing place. He realized that he had been trying to put off the moment by going into Le Nichon. He cursed. It was a valuable chance to discover more about what Lobar was up to. On the other hand, if Andreas had reported seeing him, they would be waiting for him. What they had done to Tate was probably mere trifling to what they would do to somebody more threatening.

Hood turned decidedly. He went to the first taxi, got in. 'Go to St Jean,' he said to the driver.

He lit a cigarette and sat back. He wished he had Tookey Tate and his thirty-two years' experience of breaking and entering with him to tell him where to search at Les Oliviers. Strange recesses I have known. It sounded like a pornographic title. The Private Life of a Caveman. He realized that these flippant thoughts were simply a counter to his tension.

It was still early and there was plenty of traffic about. They left Nice behind. The lamps over the roadway gave a deathly and sinister light, he couldn't help thinking. Then the road curved, and the American cruiser came into view below in Villefranche harbour. She was dressed over-all in lights. Boats moved to and from her across the water. Hood looked down. Sheer below there were lights and activity in the Darse, the old galley-port of Villefranche, where they had their PX.

The taxi headlights gleamed on a strip of cloth slung

above the road. '*Exposition de Fleurs*.' More reassurance from the commonplace!

Villefranche itself was full of the American Navy. The taxi slowed to a crawl in sudden traffic. To the right, the road leading down to the port was lined with parked cars. A few French tarts were sitting on offer under the coloured lights of a café terrace, all mouth and cleavage. A gob lounged up to an Oldsmobile as wide as a house, spat out his gum and got in. As he pulled away, a petty officer behind eased a Thunderbird into the space. Hood's French taxi-driver was staring, his lips silently muttering.

By the kerb a grey bus said: 'US Navy. Shuttle.' A couple of families sat waiting inside. The fair-haired children in zippered blue rompers were climbing over the seats. The wives smoked. The men had crewcuts and wore civilian suits. A couple of lieutenants in uniform came up the road carrying suits on hangers and got in. The navy had brought an entire American settlement to the area – American flats, American schools and so forth. The wives passed the time boringly together when the men were at sea, irretrievably alien among the French.

One of the bars was full of crewcuts and striped collars. But otherwise the boys' festive joys were discreet tonight.

The taxi eased through the traffic and climbed the rise on the far side. Five hundred yards beyond, on the incline beyond the town, there were blinking red lights in the middle of the road and two black-and-white police vans drawn up at right angles on either side. Here we go, Hood thought.

'Control – police,' the taxi-driver said over his shoulder. He slowed and stopped. Two policemen appeared. One stood a pace back with a tommy-gun. The other said: 'Papers.'

Hood opened the door and got out. It was best to be in the open on these occasions. They were high up over Villefranche bay. The side of the road was edged by a low stone parapet which dropped sheer away to the railway line and the rocks below. The opposite side was a blank stone cliff. They had chosen a good spot.

The French police often made Hood see red. They were an unprincipled lot of thugs. He controlled himself and said: 'Bong swar M'sewer,' in the corniest French he could manage. He reached into his pocket, produced his wallet and took out his Competitions Licence from the *Fédération Internationale de l'Automobile* with the small photograph of the orang-outang's face in the top right-hand corner meant for the portrait of the holder. He had used it on innumerable occasions before. It had never failed, notably with the police. They always looked carefully at the name. They spelled it to themselves with their lips moving, Charles Kildare Hood. They smiled, touched their caps: 'Thank you, sir. Good-night, sir.' Never a glance at the orang-outang.

Hood had his regular licence with identity photograph on him in case of need. But the ape one was a calculated item of his equipment. If it *was* noticed it would give him a chance to build up irrelevancies in the way of jokes and chit-chat about the pass and flattery ('Couldn't get past *you*, officer') and steer away from awkward questions.

He tendered it to the policeman. The man concentrated on it, looked up at Hood, back at the pass.

'Zher — ' said Hood, '—er – zher swee – er – Onglay. Or really Irish by origin, if it interests you.'

The man frowned up disagreeably at the English words. 'Comment?' He had a dark face, lank hair and a military moustache – a notably thick-witted combination.

Hood shrugged. The man was looking doubtful with his deep frown, though he hadn't yet noticed the orang-outang. Yet there was a close affinity between the two, Hood felt. Carefully he dropped the postcard-size photograph Kit had given him, and stooped in a flash to pick it up from the road.

As he had guessed, the policeman wanted it at once. 'Allez. Qu'est-ce que c'est?' He took it from Hood's hand.

'Say – er – ma amie. Or should I say mong amie? You know – girl friend. Tray jollee, eh?'

A glimmer of comprehension appeared on the policeman's

dumb face. His lips formed what purported to be a grin. He held up the photograph to his companion, gave Hood a contemptuous up and down glance and handed back the pass and photograph. 'Allez,' he said and jerked his head for them to go through.

Hood got in, slammed the door and they wound between the obstacle of spikes on the road. Mentally, he could hear the policeman snorting to the other: 'Les anglais, tu parles! Toujours des histoires de cul.' He grinned sardonically. Prejudice and obtuseness, the perfect allies.

On the far side, the driver accelerated and they went on. At St Jean, Hood told him to stop halfway along the sea front and paid him off. The place was quiet. Lights shone from one restaurant. The bar by the port was open. A trumpet solo of 'Them There Eyes' came from a pick-up on one of the boats.

Hood turned up the road towards Cap Ferrat. It took him ten minutes to reach Les Oliviers. He tried the service door first; it was still locked. He took out the Yale keys he had found in the Lincoln and opened the door a foot. The villa seemed to be in darkness. He went in.

The dark mass of the building stood out against the sky. Keeping to the grass, Hood went round to the garage. He stood in a wedge of shadow examining the place and listening. Nothing stirred. The silence was full of unseen threats. Very faintly he could catch the swish of the sea and the rattle of the shingle. There wasn't another sound.

He thought of the chauffeur's body lying below on the spike. He had to recover it. He clenched his teeth at the prospect. But otherwise, it was going to be found and attract all the police in the neighbourhood to the villa in a few hours. Lobar would be questioned – and that would be that. He, Hood, might just as well retire.

He remained standing in the shadow. Everything looked as he had left it. The Lincoln was standing in the drive. The garage was still open. He crossed over and went in and ran his pencil torch round. No change.

Hood snapped off the torch and went outside. He walked down the garden to the shrubs which marked the beginning of the slope towards the edge. Suddenly he froze. He had passed the shrubs in the dark and was on the edge. For a minute he couldn't move. He fancied the wind was fresher on his skin, the sound of the sea and shingle closer. It was a very bad moment. He took a grip on himself. He shone the torch-light and, peering, made out that he was in a gap between the shrubs. He retreated, found the iron stair leading to the water's edge and went down. The sea had fallen a foot or so with the small Mediterranean tide and left a narrow strip of shingle by the nearest rocks. His steps scrunched noisily along it. Farther on he had to climb over rocks.

Ahead the fan of spikes stood out. There was no body. Hood clambered over, searched the water with the torch but could see nothing. He ran his hand over the spikes and his torch showed blood. There were also strands of weed, indicating that the spikes were washed by the sea at some time or other. Had the sea carried the body off?

Hood climbed back to the stair and returned to the top. The kitchen door of the villa was still open. He went inside and stood in the hall listening. Not a sound.

He turned into the drawing-room, switched on a lamp. He found a cupboard full of drinks and mixed himself a stiff highball. He took a drink – and then suddenly hurled the glass across the room. It shattered against the wall. To hell with Lobar and his drinks! The thought of Tate and his agonizing death filled him with cold fury. He was overcome with repulsion. He felt like wrecking the place. All the evil latent in Conder's recital of the facts about Lobar suddenly seemed to surge up into active expression in this house with its lovely things, its pictures and objects. Hood was revolted. Lobar's infamy was all the more loathsome because he surrounded himself with these fine things – which were the expression of love.

The icy look was in Hood's eyes again. He went out to the garage, found a heavy hammer, axe and a cold chisel. Under the work-bench was a short iron bar which would do for a jemmy. He took these back into the house, turned on the lights and went up to the first floor. There was fine wood panelling on the jamb of the armoured door. He attacked it, hacking away the wood with the axe and sending chunks flying. His cold anger possessed him.

Steel showed through. He went to work with the jemmy. He began to sweat, took off his coat. But the door would have tested an expert. After half an hour, Hood saw he was going to get nowhere and threw aside the tools.

He rolled down his sleeves. At that moment he heard somebody arriving outside. The front door opened and slammed and there were voices in the hall. Hood slipped on his coat, lit a cigarette and went to the stairs.

Espiritu Lobar and Sue Trenton looked up at him.

There was a brief pause.

Lobar, in a dark suit and bow tie, different clothes from those he had left the *Triton* in, remained immobile. The girl, who had also changed into a short evening dress, looked oddly puzzled.

Then the tableau, as it were, came to life. The girl dropped her arm from Lobar's shoulder. Lobar smiled and came forward. 'Good evening, Mr Hood.'

'Good evening.' Hood went on down.

'Welcome to Les Oliviers,' Lobar said. 'Glad to see you managed to find the way – and get in. May I ask how?'

'Your chauffeur. I've been waiting some time. I suppose he went to get you?'

Sue Trenton swayed and caught Lobar's arm and giggled. 'Oh no he didn't. *We've* been waiting for him. An' we want him now, don' we, Choo-Choo? He's going to drive us out to the Casino.'

She was tight. They had, it seemed, arrived by taxi. Then something happened which Hood had not seen before. Lobar's massive face became suffused with blood, hideously dark, as if unseen hands were compressing his throat. The red hanging band stood out like whipcord. His body was shaken by tiny vibrations. It only lasted a moment. He didn't make a sound; and abruptly the spasm of fury was gone. Hood had never seen anything like it.

'Come in,' Lobar turned to the main room. 'Let me get you a drink.'

'I wan' drink too,' the girl said.

'I am sorry you find us without servants, Mr Hood. There are usually my caretakers at least. They were in an accident the day before yesterday. People drive so carelessly.' He had a fractional pause, noticing the stain from the smashed glass. 'Whisky, Mr Hood?'

Hood looked at him coolly. 'I was going to have a highball. I'll change my mind and have it.'

'I hope my chauffeur has not had an accident,' Lobar said. 'Would you say he was careless?'

'I am sure you would call him a safe man. Very reliable. Shall I make it a stiff one, Mr Hood?'

'Thanks,' Hood said.

Lobar gave the girl a short one on half a tumbler of ice-cubes and Hood a tall glass full. He poured himself two inches of Scotch. 'To your long life, Mr Hood.'

'To your abounding health, Mr Lobar.' It looked as if Lobar had brought the Trenton girl back to go to bed with. Otherwise, Hood imagined, he would have had a bodyguard. Also it seemed that he did not know about the chauffeur yet.

'I wonder, Mr Hood, did you see the Velasquez? I have a pair. They are in — '

'Oh, pishwish!' Sue Trenton intervened. 'I don't wan' hear about old pictures. I wan' go gambling. I wan' go to the Cas-*ee*-no! I've been telling you all evening – 'n I wan' go *now*!'

Lobar exposed his teeth. It could not, Hood thought, be called a smile. She was at Lobar's side, small beside his mass, pawing his shoulder.

'No. I think not,' Lobar said. 'Not the Casino.'

'What!' She made a pettish, tipsy grimace and pushed herself off from him. She turned to Hood. 'We're going then, aren't we, Mr Hood?'

'Delighted,' Hood said. Lobar, he thought, looked particularly dangerous. The lidless eye was red and staring. Lobar was obviously in a fury at having his evening with the girl spoiled. Hood was anxious to needle him further.

Now Hood wanted to precipitate Lobar into action so as to outplay him and work his destruction. He had a strong conviction that the *Triton* was not all, as Conder had believed. There was something more. The *Triton*, with all its luxury, might even be a blind. He had, if possible, to provoke Lobar into showing his hand.

He finished his drink. 'Let's go, then.'

The girl pealed with laughter. Lobar said: 'One minute. I will see if the chauffeur is here. Help yourself to a drink, Mr Hood.' He went out of the room.

'Give lil' Sue a drink too, uh?' She was holding Hood's arm, swaying at his side. 'You're a good sport, Mr Hood. Mr— What *is* your—? Why do I keep calling you—? Here, why'nt you gimme drink?'

Trying to hear which way Lobar had gone, Hood stepped softly to the door. It was an uncanny instant. The entrance light was out. The house extended above them in darkness. He couldn't hear any sound. Lobar had vanished. He might be hidden somewhere within a few feet. Had he seen the demolition by the armoured door? Then faintly he heard a crackle and a metallic voice. It sounded like a closed-circuit radio. Insecurity was rapidly increasing, Hood felt.

The girl had a cigarette in her mouth and was trying to find matches in her bag. Hood went back, mixed a drink.

'Hey, where's mine?' She came over, puffing out a cloud of smoke.

'Later,' Hood said. 'Where did you go with Lobar, by the way?'

She let out another peal of laughter, with her head back. 'We wen' up to a *won* – derful place way, way, way up in the mountains where they're building a new ski ska – a new *ski* station. Moonli' 'n the mountains. M'mm.'

Out of the corner of his eye, Hood thought he saw a flicker of movement beyond the open door – he was not sure. He wished as never before for his gun.

'Y-know, sometimes you look strange, Mr — What *is* your name?'

'Charles.' Suddenly he had a hunch that Lobar was summoning help and would come back and say something like: 'I'm sorry, my chauffeur is absent. I have called for a car. It will be here in a moment.'

This would be decidedly undesirable. Once in a car with some of his henchmen, Lobar could dispose of them as he wished. Hood wasn't going to let him. He could, of course, say to Lobar: 'The chauffeur was telling me your car was here. We can take that.'

But Lobar would shrug. 'I do not drive. Besides, I have asked for the other one. Some friends of mine are obliging me.'

Hood turned to the girl. 'Come on, Sue. Let's go.'

'Oh – shall we?' She beamed. 'Let's make a grea' big gamble! I'm goin' win *thounds*, you see – thounds.' She crossed the room with tipsy deliberation to where she had dropped her bag on a chair and began poking round in it again. The smoke of her cigarette got in her eyes. She couldn't find what she wanted.

'Charles – gimme a drink.' She turned. 'Why don't you gimme a drink?'

'We'll get one at the table. Come on.' He went to her, took her elbow.

'Now wait a minute.' Perversely she shrugged him off. 'Let me see myself. Got to put some'ing on my face.' She produced a compact and, rubbing powder off the glass, still with the cigarette smoke in her eyes, began applying lipstick.

Hood was tense. Lobar was coming back any minute.

'Sue, let's go.'

'All ri' . . .' She took her time. She finished with her face, dropped the compact back. She lifted her skirt in front and began tightening a stocking on the suspender. Then, looking up, she caught Hood's look, coyly raised a shoulder and turned away, working at the suspender clip.

Hood glanced in great anxiety at the door. There could be hardly an instant to spare. He turned back. She was tightening the stocking at the back.

'My girl, this is no time for fooling.' He stepped over, picked her up and went for the door.

'Hey – wait!' She giggled, protested, kicked her legs.

'But what about Choo-Choo? . . . Wait for Choo-Choo.' They were in the dark entrance.

'Ooh-hoo . . . Choo-Choo, he's taking me —'

'Shut up!' Hood clapped his hand over her mouth. She wriggled. The next moment he had to let go to open the main door. She let out a half-gurgle half-laugh. Heaving her over his shoulder, he ran into the drive.

The Lincoln was still standing there. He pulled the door wide, dumped her into the driving seat, gave her a mighty shove and slid in before the wheel. Suddenly he saw the outer gates of the villa were open. He snapped on the headlights. In the flood of illumination, Lobar stood, obviously waiting, at the gates. He raised a hand, shielding his eyes, stepped back. At that moment, a red Mercedes surged in through the gates and swung into the drive. Hood had time to see four or five heavy-looking men in it. The driver had a broken nose. Unmistakably, Lobar's friends.

He crashed the Lincoln's gears, trod down, and the car leapt forward as the Mercedes slewed with doors opening. Hood took aim. The big Lincoln swooshed past with three inches to spare and the next moment, he was furiously twisting the wheel and they were out on the road, straightening and surging away.

'Whoof! Where's the fire?' the girl said, letting down a window.

Hood didn't answer. His eyes went from the road to the

driving mirror. In a moment the Mercedes was going to appear behind them under the lights of the road.

The road ran straight and downhill. They reached the first bend. Nothing behind yet. Hood kept going smooth and fast. He swung up behind Beaulieu and took the loops to the Chapelle St Michel and the Upper Corniche. At the end of a long clear stretch he looked back. The road was empty. The Mercedes was not following.

He eased down. He lit a cigarette.

Then the trap was the girl – and he was falling into it?

17

IT WAS TWO O'CLOCK. The immense rooms of the Casino with their towering ceilings and their gilt had the overtones of railway waiting-rooms. Was it St Pancras painted on the ceiling or St Lazare?

Sue Trenton had disappeared for some time into the cloakroom. They had played a little roulette. So far nothing else had happened. Hood was quite sure it was going to.

He strolled round. The place had always struck him as slightly inhuman. Yet for generations of Englishmen it had aroused images of fortunes won overnight, intrigue under the palms, buckets of champagne, King Solomon's own mine of high life. In its hey-day, they told you, it had been 'wonderful'. But Hood found it hard to imagine the spectacle there, even at the height of its mode, when the place had been filled with the tarts and the nobility of Europe. Perhaps the cupids had been a bit more furbished then and you could flirt in the poetic flickering of the gas-jets.

But Hood felt it had not been built for human beings but for the desiccated ideas of Money and Favour and Power. He had seen the place at one time or another in all its moods. In the mornings there was a slight snake-pit atmosphere when the system players turned up with their ledgers, notebooks, computation tables and their drugged looks. You were struck by the fascinating possibility that they all believed each other to be quite mad, since clearly there was only *one* rational system.

The afternoons belonged to the trippers, the enlaced couples, the visiting pork butchers and their wives. It was consecrated to the khaki shorts, the open-necked shirt and sandals and the air of enfranchised negligence. But the evenings in the *Salons Privés* were the most absorbing.

Walking round, watching the *habitués*, the shrivelled men,

the sharp emotionless women, Hood felt something joyless and rather terrifying. The ageing, unsuccessful actresses with their dyed hair and their wrists of bangles and their death-mask faces sat beside stiff dames in old-fashioned jewellery, a bit of fur, and lace dresses that had surely been worn decades ago at some long-forgotten foreign General's ball? Some of them seemed to suffer tortures waiting for mysterious 'lucky' portents – the glimpse of a cross-eyed Hindu? A waiter with warts? – before they could bring themselves to play. Others went in for a sort of quick private game of musical chairs, inching towards a coveted place.

The balmy element was there in force. Hood glimpsed the intricate private worlds, the days passed in small back rooms, the bad meals, too many cigarettes, the minds aching for the drug of gambling, the viper knots of superstition. A few ancient figures tottered in from time to time and looked on with watery eyes, never betting, and Hood tried impossibly to guess at their pasts. There were the *vieilles anglaises*, a little pale and pinched but unquenchably perky in a changed world. You could hear stories of how they received their monthly allowance from home, lost most of it in the first days and eked out the rest of the time together in the cosy gentility of disaster.

Hood smiled and lit a cigarette. At that moment, he caught sight of Lobar. Lobar had just entered. He was wearing a white jacket and smoking a cigar. He barely glanced round, walked slowly over to the *tout-va* baccarat table and sat down. The croupier was just dealing. Lobar took cards, glanced at them, lifted his eyes and saw Hood. A trace of sardonic amusement flickered in his face. He made a little bow from the waist, said '*Carte*', and picked up the card dealt him.

Hood glanced round the table. To Lobar's left, two of the men from the Mercedes were watching the baccarat game. The plan was working. Lobar had followed him here and was being drawn into action.

Then Sue Trenton was coming in from the vestibule. The

drive had sobered her up. Hood had decided that she couldn't have been very tipsy. If she's acting, he said to himself, she's doing it beautifully.

'I lost,' she said, coming up.

'What do you mean, lost?' Hood looked puzzled. 'I thought you were — '

'I was. They've put a fruit-machine in there.'

'Good God!'

Her eyes went past him and she saw Lobar. But Hood could read nothing in her look.

'We ought to celebrate our evening out,' he said.

She gave him a faintly guilty smile. 'I'd love an orange juice or something.'

'This is no hour for orange juice, my girl. You'd better have a glass of champagne.' They went to a seat in the far corner of the room and the waiter brought the bottle. The two men looking on at Lobar's table had seen Hood. Between two hands, Lobar whispered something to one of them and the pair moved back again. They were keeping Hood and Trenton in view.

'Have you known Lobar long?' Hood said.

'Are you going to warn me about him?' She smiled. She was certainly pretty.

'You sound as if you expected me to.'

'He's an unusual man, don't you think?'

'Maybe too unusual to be safe.'

'Oh, Mr Hood, you know that girls have built-in self-defensive qualities.' She laughed and drank champagne.

There was something slightly unrealistic about these exchanges with her, he felt. Yet he had no evidence that she was a decoy for him, and his first estimate – that she was simply a foolish child – might be the right one.

She lit a cigarette and as she exhaled the smoke she said: 'Oh, there's that funny little what's-his-name.' He followed her look.

Leaning forward among the roulette players at the nearest table, eagerly placing chips, was Andreas. His fuzzy hair looked slightly comic. His eyes had the same eager gleam with which he had watched the strippers.

'Rien ne va plus,' the croupier sang out and span the ball. Andreas seemed to tingle with anticipation. He could hardly stay still.

'Cinq, rouge, impair et manque,' the croupier sang out. Andreas beamed. He had obviously won. He pushed his way between the players and eagerly took the seat of a woman who had got up.

'Odd, isn't he?' Hood said.

'Have you seen him do his imitations? He's wonderful!'

'Yes.'

'He's got that man on the door so mixed!'

Hood nodded absently. He had just noticed that Lobar's two men had been joined by three others. They were not all together. The new pair, also big men, were watching him from the opposite side of the salon. A third, on his own, was idly cleaning his thumbnail with a match at a nearby table.

Just as Hood spotted this last man, a small commotion broke out at the table where Andreas was playing. The first two of Lobar's men, those who had travelled in the Mercedes, were on either side of Andreas trying to take him away. Andreas was on his feet, resisting. Bystanders at the table began to protest. The men became more insistent. Andreas was trying to collect up his winnings and free himself from their grip.

The *chef de table* supervising the play hurried round and after a low-voiced argument, they all moved away from the table. Hood could see Andreas still arguing protestingly as the two men walked him firmly towards the door. Then, just beyond the baccarat table, Andreas stopped. He wouldn't go on. There were still plenty of people in the salon, playing or watching, moving from one table to another. Hood thought that there was going to be a scene. Andreas looked angry at having his evening's fun interrupted; and it occurred to Hood that this was the reason why he had been so keen to get money from Le Nichon – to gamble.

Hood glanced round at the other three men. They were all slyly watching the scene.

All at once, Lobar's massive figure rose from the baccarat table. Lobar moved casually towards Andreas and the two strong-arm men. He took his time. As he approached, the two men retreated. They drifted back into the crowd as if it were no longer their concern.

Andreas saw Lobar and looked round nervously, but didn't otherwise move. Lobar came up to him. He began speaking to Andreas. Then with extraordinary rapidity, his face became suffused with fury. It was the effect Hood had seen before. The blood darkened his face and neck. The weal stood out. Lobar was shaken by vibrations. Hood had never seen anything so evil. Andreas seemed to shrink. He went deadly pale and hardly dared look at Lobar. The next moment, with the same extraordinary speed, Lobar had recovered.

Andreas slunk out. Lobar looked calmly round. The salon was busy gambling. Nobody seemed to have noticed. Lobar went back to the baccarat table and sat down.

Why was Lobar so furious? Hood racked his brains for an answer. He glanced at Sue Trenton. She picked up her glass and drank. He saw that if he commented on the incident she would pretend she hadn't seen.

'Well,' she said. 'I must try to win something.' She got up. 'Thanks for the drink.'

'I hope you break the bank,' Hood said.

He watched her cross the floor. She sat down next to Lobar at the baccarat table. Hood wanted very much to follow Andreas. He might still be outside. He started towards the door. Out of the corner of his eye he saw the man sitting alone get up and follow. He stopped at a *chemin de fer* table, slowly worked his way round behind the players. The man followed. Hood went back and said to him calmly: 'Why don't you buy yourself some chips and have fun, Mac?' The man looked him up and down, said nothing and looked back at the game.

Hood stepped towards the door. There was a big crowd round the farthest roulette table. As he reached it, the two other men who had been watching him stepped close to him, blocking his path. They were bulky. One had a snick in his upper lip, an inverted V, which showed the tooth behind it. Unpleasant, Hood thought.

They said nothing. Next minute the third man had come up on the other side.

There was a group of players in the way. Hood could not pass. Suddenly a fourth man, whom he had not noticed before, detached himself from those at the table. He was different from the rest; thin, bald, with glasses, a lipless mouth. They were all edging in. As the man with the snicked lip trod on Hood's toes, the thin one made a suspicious movement inside his coat. Hood saw something glint – a hypodermic. He thought fast. He had not credited Lobar with anything of this order. A crowd was excellent cover for quick surreptitious action, especially when it was absorbed in something like roulette. One murder, famous in the Secret Service but passed off to the papers as natural death, had been committed with a hypodermic in a London theatre bar during the interval.

There would be a flurry, which nobody would notice, an exclamation when somebody saw him lying on the floor. Helping hands would lift him up, bring water, a chair and so forth. Not for minutes would they see he was dead. Then somebody would say: 'Heart, poor devil. Wonder if he was winning?' And somebody else: 'Better change seats, Raoul. You know what they say – See a dead man, change your luck.' It would not be for hours, possibly days, that they would see it was not heart – if they ever saw.

'Les jeux sont faits, rien ne va plus.'

Hood shoved with his shoulder. He was listening to the croupier at the table. He felt his arm taken. He could hear the faint hum the ball makes when it is spun by the croupier and whirls round the upper wood of the roulette-wheel. Then the clicks as it rolls down over the numbers. He snatched his arm free, but they had closed up. He saw the hypodermic come out.

'Trente, rouge, pair et passe.'

'My number!' Hood said. 'Must collect' – and with a mighty heave he broke through. He sprang out of range, thrust between the players and, reaching out, snatched up chips and plaques from the table. Before he could straighten up there were loud shouts of protest.

'But Monsieur —'

'That is my *ponte*!'

'How dare you! That's mine.'

'Monsieur le croupier!'

'Was fällt Ihnen denn ein?'

'*Yours*, Madame? I put this plaque on myself!' Hood looked outraged. There was a rampart of players round him.

'Give me that!'

'How dare *you*, Madame?'

'Mais c'est ma femme!'

In a few seconds there was complete confusion. Hood, surrounded, was stoking a blazing dispute with the croupier, the assistant croupier, five of the gamblers and the *inspecteur des jeux*.

'You, Monsieur, are a liar!'

'What! *Mon dieu* . . .'

'It is scandalous.'

'You are a —'

'And you, Monsieur l'inspecteur, you have insulted me. I insist on seeing Monsieur le Directeur. I insist.'

They argued, raged and bulged with fury. Hood laid it on as hard as he could. 'What's more there's an accomplice among these people – two or three accomplices! I've been watching. They are skilled thieves.'

The players were pop-eyed, blue in the face.

The only way to settle the incident, Hood insisted, was to see the director. Messengers were sent. There were comings and goings. The *inspecteur des jeux* returned, pale with rage. 'Follow me!'

'I certainly will!' Hood said.

He fell in immediately behind. The aggrieved players, the croupiers and a dozen onlookers followed in a troop. They crossed the room, stared at by everybody. On the far side was a door marked Privâte. The *inspecteur* turned and raised his hand. 'Please! Not everybody at once. It is impossible!'

A clamour of protest broke out.

'Non, non! I cannot ask Monsieur Casimir, *le grand directeur*, to ... This Monsieur must come with me first.' He was tugging Hood's arm. He opened the door and stopped them, signed to Hood and the chief croupier to go through. As Hood did so, one of Lobar's men pushed through.

'I am Monsieur's partner,' he said. Before the *inspecteur* could stop him he had passed. It was the thin man. The *inspecteur* let the chief croupier by, slammed the door in the face of the rest and locked it.

They were in a corridor. This led into a marble entrance from which stairs wound up. The *inspecteur* went ahead. Lobar's man managed to get immediately behind Hood. The croupier was last. As they reached the stairs, Lobar's man crowded up to Hood from behind. Hood sprang forward. They turned up. Hood kept to the middle of the stairs.

Furious, the *inspecteur* hurried. Hood kept up to him as close as he could. He could have coped with a pistol in his back. But he had a mortal terror of a jab from that hypodermic.

As they neared the top of the flight, he could hear the man behind him increasing his pace. He was almost on Hood. There was only one wild chance – move as for pistol attack and pray he didn't stab himself in the process. Hood jumped forward and spun. His swinging elbow caught the man's hand, knocked it sideways. The man jolted back, gripped the banister with his free hand. The other held the hypodermic.

Hood knew that this was the decisive instant. He had the advantage of being a step above. He stepped right for the swing. His right thumb was out, tensing the bone-hard ridge of muscle along the edge of the hand and he gave the man a crunching chop across the larynx. He did not put his full weight behind it – that was a killer blow. Its deadliness had been demonstrated in a famous murder case.

The man's eyes went up. His head toppled at a queer angle and he crashed down. The syringe flew in the air. He hit the croupier full tilt and they fell together with a great clatter. Hood jumped down after them. The *inspecteur* gave a shout.

At the bottom, Hood cleared the two sprawling bodies and doubled along the hall away from the gambling-rooms. There was a door on an automatic arm. He pulled it open. Another corridor. He raced down it. At the end he got the smell of kitchens. There were swing doors. He went through.

It was obviously the kitchen and service area of the Casino; a dingy vestibule, cement floor, the permanent ineradicable smell of cooking. Just beyond were the stoves, a long serving-counter, now in semi-darkness. He could see a couple of waiters and a chef at a refrigerator.

To the right was a locker-room. Hood crossed it, then saw the time-clock through the farther doorway. He lit a cigarette and went through. A man with glasses on the tip of his nose was sitting reading *L'Equipe*. Hood took his time. He was careful to give no impression of haste. He walked up to the time-clock, took a card, clocked it, looked at it, and then put it back in the rack.

He turned for the exit. 'Bonsoir.'

'Uh?' A rustle of pages. 'Bonsoir, Philippe.'

Shutting the door behind him and looking back through the little oblong of glass, Hood glimpsed the puzzled, faintly speculative look over the lowered paper. Then the man shrugged and returned to the passions of the cycling world.

Hood slipped alongside the building to a patch of shadow. He took a rapid look round. Nobody. He sprinted across the room and continued running hard down the slope towards the sea front. At the Marine Club he slowed down and, making a wide detour, turned up again into the town. It would soon be dawn.

The streets were deserted. Any taxis still working would

be outside the Casino. He paused at the entrance of a hotel. He could see the night porter inside. He went in and got the man to phone for a taxi. An old Renault appeared.

'Where shall I tell him to go, sir?' the porter said, holding the door.

'To Nice. Thanks.' Hood put ten francs in his hand and got in.

'Thank *you*, sir,' the man said.

As they started, Hood recognized the driver who had driven the Mercedes of Lobar's friends.

18

THE CAR picked up speed at once. There were several sharp clicks. Hood leant forward to slide the glass partition separating him from the driver's seat. It was fixed and wouldn't move.

He wrenched the door handles up, then down. No result; the doors were locked. The driver was fiddling with a closed-circuit radio set in the dashboard. Hood saw him speak into a hand mouthpiece but couldn't catch what he said. Then the man evidently switched over. There was a pause, a few crackles, then Lobar's voice was speaking on Hood's side.

'Good evening, Mr Hood. Or ought I to say welcome back? You will forgive the taxi being a little unconventional. You cannot get out of it. Moreover, you will be taken somewhat out of your way. On the other hand, you will not have to tip the driver. Her Majesty's Treasury, I am told, appreciates these small savings. I wish my hospitality could be more generous. But we are pressed for time tonight and are merely improvising. I am sure you will be indulgent.'

There was a click. The voice went off.

The car was travelling at speed. It screamed round the bends. The driver accelerated past a red traffic light.

Hood rolled back on the seat and gave the partition a mighty kick. He braced himself, gripped the metal hand-grip and let fly again with both feet. The partition shook and a fitting fell off. Hood drew himself back, rammed both feet at the panel again.

The driver kept glancing back. Hood kicked with all his strength. The partition splintered. Edged forward, the driver was trying to protect himself; but he was keeping up speed. Hood's right foot went through. Furiously he wrenched it back. He was sweating. He jack-knifed his knees and drove his heels at the panel. There was a shower of fragmented glass and his feet hit the back of the driver's seat. The cab swerved.

Hood sprang up, elbowed out glass and, reaching through, grabbed the wheel. The driver jabbed him with an elbow, wrenched the wheel back. The cab zigzagged madly across the road and back. Hood wrestled with the man, shouldering the upright of the smashed partition to break it down. They screamed round a blind corner on the wrong side, careered the other way. Hood got a blow at the driver's face, gripped the wheel hard. The man violently jerked with both hands, there was a shuddering crunch, a series of jolts and they went full tilt into the ditch.

Hood was flung across the interior. It was a confused moment. He disengaged himself from broken woodwork and glass, sat up, hit his head. He didn't seem to be hurt, but couldn't get his bearings. Then he realized the taxi was on its side. At the same moment, a figure moved across the headlight which was still on. It was the driver. He was making short grunts of pain and had evidently been thrown clear.

Hood pushed at the door over his head. It was still locked. The other door was under his feet. He could see bluish lights outside. The taxi had crashed just off the road. The lights were from a service station on the far side. He was in time to see the driver disappear behind one of the buildings. Almost at once another man came out of the dark and stood in the sinister blue light looking over the road towards the crashed taxi.

Hood realized he had to get out of the cab fast. They were Lobar's men there.

He smashed his way out to the driver's seat, turned to jump down. Something stabbed him painfully in the chest. He winced back. The taxi had overturned among a clump of agaves, the great greenish-grey ornamental plants with their swordlike leaves. Running footsteps came from the road. Quickly Hood looked round. It was one of Lobar's men, with a gun. Hood gritted his teeth and jumped down. Claws like steel on the leaves' edge ripped him. For a moment he stood among them, shuddering with pain and desperation. Then he forced himself to move and wrench free. He could hear the man nearer now.

He crouched. The man appeared at the edge of the road. It was the man with the snick in his lip who had been at the Casino. He was big, powerful and mean. As Hood crept forward, his hand ran into a point on the ground. Wincing, he pulled it out. It was the top of an agave leaf, ripped off by the taxi, about six inches long and rolled like a coil. It ended in a deadly black two-inch spike. Silently, Hood gave thanks to the gods.

Gripping it like a dagger, he moved towards the man. The Lip saw him at an angle. Hood jumped as The Lip's gun came round. His shoulder hit the gun arm. There was a blast in his ear as The Lip fired. Hood went for his eyes. The steel-like point sank in deep. The Lip made an inarticulate sound and heaved. Hood had his fingers over the hammer of the gun preventing another shot. He stabbed again and the spike hit The Lip's cheek-bone. Hood ripped it down. They both fell. As they hit the ground, The Lip gave a violent twist, broke away and tried to roll clear. He had lost the gun and was gasping raucously. With a spring, Hood was on his back, his knee in The Lip's spine. Palms open, his hands went under The Lip's chin, both thumbs locking deep in the man's cheeks. He hauled back. The Lip seemed to realize it was a lethal grip and tried to call out. His head was right back. Hood gritted his teeth and gave it to him – a savage backward jerk. There was a dull crack as The Lip's neck broke. He flopped, twitched once or twice and lay still.

Hood got up. He stood recovering his breath. The stab in the hand was painful. His coat and trouser leg were ripped. He cast round for The Lip's gun, but couldn't see it. Bending down, he went quickly through the man's pockets. There was no other weapon. The man's wallet contained money and a card with something written on it which Hood couldn't read. He put the card in his pocket. No time for more.

The road was empty. He looked across at the service

station. It seemed deserted. Two of the lights over the pumps were out, leaving broad areas of shadow. A single light shone in the empty office.

Hood walked to the darkest point on the road and crossed. He stood in the shadow of one outbuilding, observing. Nothing moved. He slipped along to the angle of the building and looked beyond. It was eerie; the place seemed to be abandoned. What had happened to the driver? He heard a faint sound. It was like a muffled and distorted voice. In front of him was the concrete drive-in. Opposite was the workshop wing of the station. Tiptoeing over, he looked round the corner.

Just beyond, a light was burning in a wooden garage. The taxi-driver, a cut over his eye, and another man were leaning inside a car and working a radio. A voice was coming over against a lot of static. Before Hood could hear what it said, he noticed another man in the shadow outside the garage. He ducked back.

He had a fleeting impression that the man had seen him. He flattened against the wall. A few seconds passed. He caught the click of a gun cocking. Holding his breath, Hood retreated sideways on tiptoe. His extended hand felt the doorway of the workshop behind him. He slipped inside. In a moment there was a tiny scrape of a step outside. The man seemed to be approaching stealthily.

In the dark, Hood felt round for some weapon. His hand encountered a bench and on it a cylinder; a grease-gun. As he raised it, the light came on. Hood had the advantage of surprise and he was at an angle to the door. He smashed the grease-gun down on the man's wrist. The automatic clattered on the floor. Without giving him time, Hood shot a left to the man's solar plexus and, as he doubled forward, brought the grease-gun nozzle up into his descending facc. The man toppled on him, grappling. They fell, slugging each other. Hood could not keep hold of the grease-gun. The man had a big knuckle-duster ring and kept jabbing at his eyes. But above all, he was trying to get enough breath back to shout.

Hood knew he had to stop him shouting. If the others heard it was all up. The man went into a panic struggle to cry out at all costs. Hood was trying to choke him; his hands gripped the thick neck. But with a twist and a blow, the man freed himself. He scrambled away, gasping for enough breath to shout. Hood sprang on him, seeing the grease-gun on the ground. He grabbed it, wrenched himself astride the man and with two hands rammed the nozzle of the gun into the open mouth.

The man gagged. Hood forced it down his throat and pumped hard. The man heaved. He was bolt-eyed. The thick yellow grease came out round the lips. Arching his back, he tried to grasp the grease-gun. Hood held it in, pumped again. The man was choking and coughing and making a sort of creaking sound in his throat. His face became purple. His hand fell. He jerked convulsively, then sagged and was still.

Hood stood up breathing heavily. A pocket of air rose from the man's lungs, bringing a thick gobbet of grease welling out of his mouth. It burst with a splash. Hood turned away. He snapped off the light and stood recovering. Then he went cautiously out of the door. He could hear the radio still crackling. Then from the road came the sound of an approaching car. He walked fast in the shadow to the end of the service station and as he reached it, a black Citroën with three men inside swung into the drive. Hood went hell for leather for the nearest corner, turned it. There was no one in sight. He ran on for fifty yards, then stopped to listen. Nobody behind. He sprinted across the road, took the next turning, tried the cars at the kerb. Two were unlocked, but he couldn't start them. Then he came to an unlocked Simca Mille; no key necessary! He got in, pressed the starter. As he drove off, he looked back. Somebody was standing at the street corner.

It was dawn when he reached Nice. He parked the Simca in the Promenade des Anglais and crossed to the white block of the Hotel Nicolescu. He took a room in the name of Singleton Root.

'Would you mind registering, sir?' Smilingly, the receptionist passed him the usual white card.

'Certainly.'

Name, said the card. Hood wrote Root, Christian name: Singleton Carew. Filling in other details, he made himself a couple of years younger, described himself as Horticulturist, added imaginary passport details, a false address in Torquay and completed the thing with a Steinberg signature. These little white cards amused Hood. They were for the police. Presumably they were put out on the principle that a crook would be so scared when he had to fill one in that he would put down nothing but the truth.

'Thank you, Mr Root. Four-twelve, Mr Root.'

'Oh, one minute!' Hood said, taking the card quickly back. 'Sex. Male – I almost forgot.'

The receptionist smiled. 'Show Mr Root up to four-twelve.'

In the room, Hood ran a bath. He summoned the valet, pointed out the small rips in his suit and gave it to be urgently repaired and pressed. He ordered a double Scotch. He also asked for fruit juice, scrambled eggs on toast, tea, toast and marmalade at eight o'clock.

When the drink came he sat with a towel round him, examining the key imprint. The matchbox had been crushed in his pocket, but had nevertheless preserved the imprint pretty well. Only one corner was a bit flattened; but the outline was there.

He took the towel off and carried the rest of the drink into the bathroom. He stood at the mirror looking over his face. Considering everything it wasn't too badly marked. He had already attended to the cuts from the ring, in the car. One cut on his lip annoyed him. For the rest, there was a biggish mark on the right of his jaw and one just over his left eye that was going to blacken.

He shuddered at the mental image of the man choking on

the grease. 'Oh, the hell,' he said aloud, finished the Scotch, climbed into the bath and lay soaking.

Hood stepped buoyantly out on to the Promenade des Anglais next morning after a superb breakfast and careful attention to his face at the hotel barber's. He had a plaster dressing on his hand and the suit had been repaired reasonably well.

It was a glorious morning. The sun sparkled on the Mediterranean. There was hardly an angina, thrombosis or an arthritis case in sight. The row of blue and yellow sunshades stirred gently in the warm breeze. The grass under the palms was fresh and green. The name-band on an American sailor's arm said *USS Springfield*. So that's what she is, Hood thought. A pretty girl in tight pink trousers cycled by, showing off her bottom. A pavement photographer snapped her glorious globes – one for himself.

Hood turned towards the shopping area, went into a stationer's and bought some ball-point pens, a box of assorted nibs and a holder and a bottle of ink. He sought out another shop, bought two more bottles of ink and headed back. At the kiosk by the Ruhl he bought a paper; but there was nothing in it about discovery of the chauffeur's body. (It was too early for the rest.)

Back in his room, he sat down at the table in front of the sunny window. He took out his passport and his International Competitions Driving Licence. He opened the passport at his name, laid a blank sheet of hotel writing-paper below it, then tried out nibs, inks and ball-points. The idea was to find a reasonable match for the official pen which had written in his name and details – a good passport office pen. When he had one, he practised writing for a few minutes. Then he took the passport and on the line immediately below the name Charles Kildare Hood, he wrote: 'Professionally known as Arthur Tate.' He did the same with the Competitions Licence (the real one, not the ape one).

The passport was slightly chancy, but not very. He had

used the dodge before. Nobody ever thought to look at the back of the passport for the stamp and the inscription with the authenticating frank and official's signature 'Professional Name added . . .' with place and date. There was no risk with the licence.

He put both in his pocket and went down. There were a dozen people in the entrance lobby. Hood gave them a quick scrutiny. A couple of white-robed Saudi Arabians were talking to a young French girl in an extremely tight skirt. They all looked all right. Hood wondered how soon Lobar would be on to him. The taxi-driver had heard him tell the hotel porter he wanted to go to Nice. Presumably Lobar already had scouts out.

He walked to the main post office and went up to the Poste Restante counter. The woman in charge was small and bird-like. She had a bun and glasses. Hood gave her a winning smile.

'Anything for Arthur Tate?'

'Identity card?' she said.

He produced the Competitions Licence. She examined it and looked up at him. 'One moment.' She left the counter and went to a man, presumably the Supervisor, at a table in the rear. He frowned at the licence and they spoke together. The man looked up at Hood. Hood thought; if he picks up the phone I exit fast. The man handed the licence back to the woman and, as she turned back to the counter with it, he picked up his desk phone.

Hood was on the point of swinging round and going for the door. But something about the Supervisor's manner checked him; he couldn't be acting that well. Hood cursed inwardly. It was one of those moments when you had to hang everything on a snap judgement. The woman handed him back the licence. 'That won't do,' she said.

Hood affected to be taken aback. He plunged earnestly into his pocket and brought out the passport. He handed it to her open at the name page. She laid it flat on the counter, holding it open and looking at it. Then she gave him a little birdy V-shaped smile, pushed it back to him and, after searching a moment, produced a smallish brown-paper parcel.

Hood walked out with it as if it held a bomb.

He stood for a moment in the doorway, checking the street. It seemed all clear. On a hunch he decided not to return to the hotel and headed towards the old town. He knew a small café where he could be fairly sure Lobar's men would not find him. At the Boulevard Jean Jaures, he turned right into the complex of narrow alleys. This was a part of Nice where few tourists came. The alleys were deep and chilly; the sun penetrated them only at midday. The houses on either side nearly touched. He passed carved stone portals inscribed with initials of long-gone owners and dates: H.D. 1649, I.S. 1668. Drips from the washing hung out high above smacked on the flags. There were tiny barred windows and fan-shaped grilles over doors and many churches. Some alleys had shops. The bead curtains clicked.

Hood turned through the ruelle de la Halle aux Herbes, crossed the rue Sainte Reparate and made for the ruelle du Maconat. Steps led up, past a public wash-trough. There was a swathe of washing dumped on the side. The water dripped musically. It might be a street in Tunis or Algiers. The café was ahead. He turned in. It was empty. The man nodded. He was small and dark. Hood sat down at the corner table. 'Coffee.' The man nodded again. He said nothing. He made the coffee with care and brought it. When he had it, Hood opened the parcel.

There were two boxes. One held a small camera with no maker's name, probably specially built. There was also a small container of extra lenses and little lense-cleaning tissue pads. Hood was just going to put them back when he saw an edge of film negative. Between the pads were three undeveloped shots which Tate had evidently missed.

Hood held them up. They were small and it was not easy to see the detail. They looked like rather hasty shots of a man taken in the street, two from the side and one from behind.

He was hatless. There seemed something vaguely familiar about him to Hood. He was a smallish man, simply standing there; he might just have got out of a car. Hood put the negatives in his wallet and opened the other box. This contained a miniature tape-recorder complete with spool. But there was no plug or lead.

Hood put the camera in his pocket, wrapped up the lenses with the tape-recorder and went out. Down in the town he found a shop selling records and tape-recorders. The salesman produced a plug and lead to fit.

'Do you mind if I run it a minute?' Hood said. 'Something I want to check on this tape.'

'Certainly.' The salesman took Hood into an audition booth, plugged in the recorder and left. Hood shut the door and switched the machine on. A man was speaking in English.

'I think we all agree that it's essential not to, er, not to hamper the military commanders with over-elaborate political control. In practise, it is possible to give them automatic authority to, er, employ, er, corresponding nuclear weapons immediately in reply to a nuclear attack, a properly verified nuclear attack. Where you need a political decision is when you start to use tactical nuclear weapons to deal with, to repel a conventional attack, that is, an attack which you can't repel with conventional forces. I think we can expect that the circumstances in this case would give enough time for a deliberate decision...'

Hood snapped his fingers. It was Richard Calvert's voice! No mistake about it. There were background noises – an occasional cough, the clatter of a plate or two, a 'hear! hear!', an effect of resonance, as if the recording had been made at some lunch or banquet. The tape was not long. Hood let it run. There was applause, then the sound cut. The tape ran silent. Hood was about to switch off when the voice came again.

'I think we all agree that it's essential not to, er, not to hamper the military commanders with over-elaborate political control. In practise, it is possible to give them ...'

They were the same words. But now there was no background. The words were spoken against silence. Hood's eyes narrowed. There was something queer about the thing. Perhaps Dick Calvert had been rehearsing at home, though why the rehearsal should come second on the tape he didn't see. It certainly *was* Dick – then abruptly the voice was muttering something in a foreign language, it had changed and become ... whose ... *whose*?

Hood groped. It still eluded him. He ran the tape back, played it over and bent forward eagerly listening. Suddenly he got it. Andreas's voice! It was Andreas mimicking Richard Calvert. He whipped out the negatives and held them up. They were of Richard Calvert. There was no question of it. They had obviously also been taken and used for the purpose of perfecting Andreas's imitation. There had probably been a reel or more. Andreas would only need to study a reel or two of Calvert in motion and hear his voice, to become the British Ambassador to NATO. Their physical build was even similar.

Hood gasped. He could hardly take two paces in the small booth and kept turning backwards and forwards in his tense anxiety. Was it possible? *Could* they get away with it? With Lobar's ruthless organization behind them, it looked like it. They must have the occasion planned – and it must be a big one. He remembered Lobar's voice in the taxi, '... I am pressed for time ...' and that earlier voice of Richard Calvert's on the phone from his NATO office. '... This big thing coming up. Whole series of meetings. Agonizing reappraisal and all that. I've just been summoned to London....'

When he was in London, Hood was kept informed of the trend of affairs. He was also allowed to read certain Foreign Office telegrams. Thus he knew that the series of NATO Council meetings now coming up was going to settle an entire new programme for western defence, something it would be impossible to change for years because of the sheer cost and the gigantic industrial involvement, let alone go back on.

His restless turning was shaking the booth. The floor-boards creaked.

Everything seemed to fall into place. They were going to use Andreas to replace Richard Calvert at one or more of the vital meetings where this new programme was decided on. They would choose their moment so as to make the impersonation less technically difficult. They might have some technician inside to prompt Andreas if he failed at some point. Anyway, there were enough enemy technicians *outside* the meetings, in the Paris embassies, to cram him for all they were worth between sessions; and they would have all the secret documents they wanted to work from. If they got nothing else, they would obtain a mass of secret material. It would be a tremendous coup. Hood could imagine the bitter recriminations there would be between the Central Intelligence Agency in Washington, the British Secret Service, the French *Service d'Études, de Documentation et de Contre-Espionage* and the others.

It must mean, of course, that they were going to kill Richard Calvert. Otherwise he would be able to turn up afterwards and expose the imposture. He would have an 'accident', something made to look commonplace which would deflect suspicion. The new programme, elaborated after months, if not years, of work by the military, naval and air experts would then have to be scrapped as insecure.

Yet even so, things would be in a hideous mess. Secret data of the highest importance would have been given away. And the task of mapping out a fresh defence programme would be extremely difficult.

If, on the other hand, they got away with it, they would hold the key to western defence for years to come.

Hood whistled under his breath. Could it be that? He did not know. How could he make sure? The number on the card he had found in The Lip's pocket occurred to him. It was

Opera 4003. Was that the address near the Opera that Tate had been taken to?

He was appalled, shattered. *What* could he do?

'Does it work, Monsieur?' the salesman put his head in.

'What? Oh yes. Much obliged.' Hood took up the things, paid, and left.

A taxi drew up at the kerb alongside. A woman got out, handed the driver the fare and walked away. 'Taxi, M'sieu?'

Hood pretended not to hear. It was absurd, he told himself; Lobar couldn't be running half the taxis in Nice. But he wasn't taking any chances now. He was overcome by anxiety at discovery of the plot.

The taxi ran slowly past him and stopped at the kerb a few yards on. Hood turned in through the door of a department store on his right. He pressed through the crowd of women customers intending to cross straight to a side exit and leave by that. As he passed a hat counter he glanced in the mirror. Craning in the crush behind him was the taximan's face.

Hood turned smartly up the stairs. He was at the first turning when the man started up too. Hood saw a door up the next half-flight. For Queen and Country, he said to himself – and went in. The door swung to behind him with its shining plaque: Ladies.

Two women were admiring themselves in the glass over the wash-basins. Another was adjusting something intimate in the suspender region. Hood hunched a shoulder protectively, dived into one of the cubicles and shot the bolt.

'Agnes, *did* you . . . ?' one of the women said in English. Whispers followed, then: 'No! . . . Do you think . . . You must have made a mistake.'

'I swear it was. And what's more, it *looked* like . . . (whisper) . . .'

'Walter! Walter! You've got Walter on the brain. I know he's jealous, dear, but suspectin' you would slake your passion with You Know Oo in the Ladies Lav – well, reely.'

'It *has* bin done in all sorts of places.'

They went out. But others came in numbers. Lavatorian

waterworks swirled, ball-cocks rose and fell, shooting bolts echoed – and Hood stood poised for the opportunity to dash. At last it came. There was the click of the automatic door-arm as the last lady went forth. Hood shot *his* bolt and darted out. He pulled the outer door – and confronted a hawk-like nose, a dowager of immense dignity. Margot Oxford! he thought for a second, involuntarily piling on the horrors.

Hood swallowed, then peered straight at the icy glare. 'I – uh – seem to have – uh – got lost,' he said with an ecclesiastical gargle. 'Am I – uh – right for socks?'

Before she could recover, he stepped rapidly down the stairs, made his way to a side door. He looked out. The taxi was not visible. He knew he had very little time. He walked quickly down the street.

19

THE TELEPHONE directory listed nine drive-yourself car hire firms. Hood picked one and hired a black DS Citroën, a car both fast and anonymous.

He drove to the British Consulate. It was something he always did his utmost to avoid when he was on a secret mission. For one thing it was risky. For another, it was none of the Consul's business; for a third, a Consul is not to be compromised in any spy business that happens to be going on in his territory. And lastly, he is a busy man. But this was an emergency. There was no choice.

The Consul had glistening black hair, smoothed flat, and a spade chin. After the preliminaries, Hood mentioned the name of the confidential person in the Paris Embassy who would vouch for him.

'I'm sorry to trouble you with this, Mr Purdy. Also I wonder if you wouldn't mind being careful how you communicate?'

Purdy looked all agog. His face lit up with excitement. He managed to beam and look intensely secret at the same time. He was obviously overcome with enthusiasm at the idea of playing cloak and dagger. 'Yes, indeed. What can I do?'

'First of all I'd like you to send two urgent telegrams. I'll write them straight away.' Eagerly, Purdy pushed over a pad. Hood wrote:

RUTHERFORD AD 461B FOREIGN OFFICE FROM HOOD FOR IMPERIAL WATCHCO. URGENT PROVIDE CLOSE PERSONAL PROTECTION SIR RICHARD CALVERT NATO ALL TIMES.

The Imperial Watch Company was the code name for Special Intelligence Security, but Hood did not think it necessary to explain that. The second telegram was also Rutherford from Hood, but it went:

FOR IMPERIAL WATCHCO OVERSEAS SALES DIVISION STOP ANY DOPE ON MAN NAMED ZARUBINO OR ANDREAS WHOSE PHOTOGRAPH FOLLOWS POSSIBLY BALT STOP GIFTED IMPERSONATOR CORSET FETISHIST REPLY MOST URGENT TO PURDY CONSUL NICE PERSONALLY.

The Overseas Sales Division was the Personal Research Department of Conder's office; but there was no point in explaining that either.

'In cypher, please, Mr Purdy.'

Purdy dropped his voice. 'We don't run to cypher. They have cypher in Marseille, but I'm only a sub-office here, sort of thing.'

'Then in code?'

Purdy was reading the telegrams. There was a conspiratorial hunch about him. As he reached the words 'corset fetishist' his eyebrows went up and he gave a low 'Whew!' Hood took the photograph of the stripper and Andreas out of his wallet. 'I'd like this to go to London by the quickest means possible.' He handed it over.

Purdy's jaw dropped. He looked at the photograph close-to, as if he were trying to spot some microdots in the stripper's navel. Then he looked up and shrugged helplessly. 'Can't see how I can get this away. I mean —'

Suddenly, as if it were all too good to be true, he said: 'I say, this isn't a lark, old man, is it? I mean, you and your pal Rutherford, you really are — ?'

'I wish it were, Mr Purdy. I can't offer you any proof it isn't, except that my friend Rutherford doesn't exist and that Rutherford is only the signal name for a communications channel. You can find that out for yourself by checking in Paris, though you won't find the channel. I'm sorry I can't be explicit, but as I said, I don't make the rules.'

'Oh no, no! Of course. I understand that.' Purdy lowered his voice to a whisper. 'I was in G 2 for a bit myself during the war.' He glanced at the photograph again. Hood could see he was bursting to ask questions.

'Can you send it safe hand, messenger?'

Purdy was narrow-eyed. 'I'll see it gets through. Somebody'll be going next week.'

'Next week? It has to be there today, if possible. Tomorrow noon at latest.'

Purdy drew in his breath with a hissing sound. He looked intense, brisk, resourceful. 'Tell you what. We can take it to the airport, give it a BOAC pilot. We'd have to fox 'em about it being secret, of course. Get a plain envelope. Mark it Press Photos.'

'Mr Purdy, this will fully justify your going yourself or sending your assistant as emergency Queen's Messenger – but at once.'

'Yes?' Purdy glowed with secret fire. He glanced at the door out of the corner of his eye as if somebody might be listening. 'My assistant's away. I'll tell the Consul at Marseille I'm on a top secret op. I'll have to go through him. But no need to tell him what it's about. It's a Secret Service matter, he needn't know. I'll tell him I've been seconded. I suppose I'd better take a gun?'

Hood said: 'Will you phone him now? In discreet terms?'

'Yes, yes. You bet discreet, old man. If they're listening in they won't understand a thing. I'll talk like a scrambler. Wait a minute, though. Come to think of it, I can't get him today. They've got trouble with a freighter down at Port Vendres. Sticky business, I don't mind telling *you*. Woman mixed up in it. She says the chief mate — '

Hood said: 'I think you'd better drop the photograph. I'll manage somehow.' He took it back.

'Oh.' Purdy looked very disappointed. 'But Blickersloughh, the Consul, will be back tomorrow, probably.'

'If you'll be good enough to send off those telegrams, I'll come back at six tonight for the answer. Grade them as high as you can for code. What's that, secret?'

Purdy nodded. 'I'll burn these originals as soon as they've gone.'

Hood produced the key imprint. 'Could you get a key made quickly from this?'

Purdy took it. This was another twist! 'I've got a good man. No need to swear him to secrecy; but I'll tell him to keep his mouth shut.'

Hood cursed inwardly. He said: 'As a matter of fact, you needn't. It's only the key to my garage I want copied.'

'Oh.'

'These' – Hood handed over the camera and tape-recorder – 'are more important. I'd be obliged if you would keep them in your safe.'

'Yes, absolutely.' Purdy took them as if they were the Crown Jewels.

'There's one other last thing,' Hood said. He took out the card he had found in The Lip's pocket. 'If you could find out the address of this Paris telephone number, Opera 4003, I'd be obliged.'

Purdy made a note on a pad, suddenly stopped, scratched it out. 'Better write it down backwards. Precaution. Opera 30—'

'I should write it down frontwards, Mr Purdy, and you only have to ask the telephone Inquiries. I've always been amazed that the French should give this information, but they do.'

He got up. Should he or shouldn't he warn Purdy? He said: 'If anybody inquires after me, you don't know anything about me.'

'I never heard of your existence! Not to a living soul.' Purdy was pulsating with secrecy. 'Wish you could slip out of the back entrance, but there isn't one. I always said we ought to have one.'

'Never mind.' They said good-day, Purdy whispering a furtive 'Good luck!' Hood went grinning down to his car.

It was a hot day without a breath of wind. The leaves of the palms hung motionless. Dust swirled in the wake of cars. Hood felt in need of lunch. He drove to Chico's, took a table conveniently masked by a rubber plant and ordered crudités, lobster fine champagne and a '52 Chablis. The waiter brought him the basket of live lobsters to choose from, and Hood picked out a sizeable specimen.

He looked out at the greenish water on the rocks below. Everything would be splendid, he thought, in this little pocket of time, briefly isolated from the violent and evil things he was at grips with – everything would be splendid if he had some pretty and diverting girl as a companion. And then he said to himself: Kit, of course!

He rose and went to the telephone. But Le Nichon was shut. The phone rang and rang. Hood seemed to hear the desolate echo. It depressed him a bit. He wished he hadn't rung. Then the phone was unhooked at the other end.

'Hello,' a sleepy voice said.

'Is Kit there?'

'H'm? ... Who wants her?'

'Is that you, Madame Butterfly? This is Lieutenant Pinkerton. How about coming to lunch?'

'... Who? ... We're shut. Open ten o'clock tonight...' She spoke slowly and sounded as if she had a hangover.

His heart sank. What a fool he was! Imagining she would remember him.

'Wait – who did you say it was?' Her voice was a whisper. 'It isn't ... it isn't you, is it? Sailor, is it you?'

'From over the sea.'

'But I thought you were going— Do you mean you're back?'

'I took a fast boat. Kit, what's the matter? What are you...?'

'Nothing ... Nothing It's all right. What do you know, eh? My God, and I only kissed you a couple of times. How do you do this to a girl, sailor?'

'That's not a subject I can deal with adequately on the telephone.'

'I was asleep. I needn't tell you in whose arms I was locked.'

'Kit, I'm sorry. Of course, I didn't think. What time did you shut? You must be dead.'

'Eight o'clock this morning. And if you think I'm too tired to come out there after you, you're wrong.'

'I have a lobster about to die for you.'

'Where are you?'

'Chico's.'

'I'll be there in half an hour.'

'I'll hold everything. And Kit, do me a favour, will you? Don't tell anybody, even Jojo or Madame Jojo that it's me.'

'No, but they'll see it in my love-lit eyes.'

'Then put your dark glasses on, kid. Come on, get over here.'

'All right . . . Oh, sailor.'

'What?'

'I love you.' She rang off.

Hood told the waiter to reprieve the lobster, chose a bigger one, and said: 'Just hold it for a few minutes. A friend of mine's joining me. Bring me a champagne cocktail now and when the lady comes bring two more.'

'Certainly, sir.'

Hood floated on the sudden up-surge of happiness that she had brought him. She was a woman for a grand passion; and a woman who is made for that usually gets one sooner or later.

She came in looking cool and beautiful. He hadn't noticed till then how blue her eyes were.

'You look as if you'd just had ten hours' beauty sleep,' he said.

'I hope you've got long leave, Lieutenant.'

The occasion came up to all he had hoped. She was amusing and continuously attractive. The food was very good. The background of danger and the dark forces which Lobar stood for receded and Hood felt refreshed and inspirited.

It appeared that she had gone to Le Nichon three years

before after an unlucky marriage had broken up. In spite of all appearances, it had been a haven. She was emotionally immunized, in any event. Paulette and Jojo were wonderfully kind, and she had continued there. Had the immunity lasted ever since? Well, yes, it had. There had been a man or two, she had accepted them; but it had never been the real thing.

When they were having coffee, Hood said: 'Kit, do you know a newspaperman you can trust in these parts? I want to send that photograph you gave me by wire.'

'A newspaperman? ... Yes, there's Bailly or Georges Larue. Georges Larue's the best. He works for *l'Aigle*.' She looked at him. 'Who do you want to send the picture to?'

'Friend of a friend. He collects them.'

She stirred her coffee, looking down at it, silent for a moment. She was intelligent and Hood was sure she understood there was something unusual behind the request. She looked up again. 'You asked me not to tell anybody I was coming to see you—'

'Kit.' He took her hand, trying to head her off. 'I wanted to see you a lot.'

'I just want to know—'

'If I'm a crook or something? Well, they gave me a life sentence last week, but I broke out of jail and you're not going to give me away, are you?'

'All right, I won't ask you.' She gave him a sad smile. 'What difference would it make, anyway?'

'You have adorable eyebrows.'

A little later he returned to Georges Larue. 'Do you know him well?'

'Oh.' She stubbed out her cigarette. 'He's an old boy friend of mine. He wanted to marry me. Still does. He'd do anything I asked him, if that's what you mean.'

'If you'd ring him up, tell him I'm coming round to see him, and ask him to give me a hand, that would be very sweet of you.'

She smiled. 'All right.'

'Don't say anything about the picture; let me deal with

that. And while we're on this, I wouldn't tell anybody else about it or mention that I was in the club.'

'Aren't you coming home to make love to me, sailor?'

'Kit, darling, I can't. You've got the right man, but *I* have to get the occasion, though that will arrive. I think you're lovely and I should have to be insane if I didn't want to. But this is how it has to be for the moment.'

She caressed his hand and nodded. 'I'll hold you to it.'

'Will you ring up Larue now? I'd like to see him straight away.'

'I'll try him.' She took her bag and got up. Hood lit a cigarette. He felt slightly uncomfortable. They had stayed a little too long in the restaurant and were the last customers. He looked round. The restaurant, with its continuous glass windows, extended out over the rocks, exposed on both sides, and if Lobar's men were about they couldn't miss him. Well, it was his own doing. He had chosen the place. But he wanted desperately not to get Kit involved. He thought of getting up and leaving before she came back. But it was too late; she was there.

'He's waiting for you. The office is on the Boulevard Gambetta. Shall we go?'

He made her wait inside the entrance while he got the car. There weren't any noticeable watchers. On the way, he said: 'Kit, could you get out before we reach the club, a couple of streets away? It's a superstition I have.'

'All right. You can drop me at the next corner.'

'And will you just walk away?'

She leaned over and kissed him. At the corner he pulled up. 'Thanks, Kit. I'll be seeing you.'

'So long, sailor,' she said. 'Be careful.' She got out and slammed the door and Hood was already moving as she walked away.

The Boulevard Gambetta was a busy main street. He parked as near as he could to the *Aigle* office and went in. He stood behind a copy of the paper on a stand watching the people who came in after him. He didn't seem to be trailed.

Georges Larue turned out to be rugby full-back size, good-looking and hearty. Hood liked him. Larue roared with laughter at the photograph. 'You mean the English are going to publish this?'

'Well, it's for a private publication. What the English call "curious" literature. Read by connoisseurs, you know.'

Another gale of laughter. 'The nipple fairly hits you in the eye, eh? You want to send it by Belino?'

'Can you do it?'

'Why not?'

'I'd like to see it go over, if that's possible,' Hood said.

'Sure. Wait a minute, though; this magazine of yours must have a Belino tie-up with the Post Office in London. Otherwise it won't go through.'

'It has,' Hood said. 'You ring the Post Office, Headquarters 1234, and say it's for the Imperial Watch Company; they own the magazine.'

They went through the corridors and offices, the worn, cluttered, over-busy, overcrowded and odorous disorder of every newspaper office in the world. The photo transmission-room was as messy as the rest. Larue handed the picture over to two sad-looking men in long grey overall coats, and when they had put through the telephone call to London, they placed the photograph on the drum of the machine and synchronized it, checked the phasing and began the transmission. Hood watched the drum revolving. The operator had switched the modulation to a loudspeaker and the high-pitched whistle went round and round. It took longer than Hood had expected. At last the whistle stopped. The drums had reached the other end of the axle, which meant that the transmission was completed. Larue handed him back the photograph.

When Hood wanted to pay for the cost, Larue waved his hand. 'It comes on a post office account. If you like, I'll tell Kit.'

'Much obliged,' Hood said, as they shook hands.

He reached the car and got in. Where was Andreas now?

he wondered. Out of the blue, he remembered the odd thing Sue Trenton had said the night before at the Casino about Andreas getting the Casino doorman mixed. What had that meant?

That whole incident between Lobar and Andreas at the Casino had been mystifying. Hood felt impelled to go back and find out more.

He drove down the Boulevard Gambetta, turned off at the rue du Maréchal Joffre and bought a paper at the corner kiosk. He sat double-parked while he went through it. There was nothing on the local news pages about anything happening at the Casino. They would naturally hush up any incident at the tables; but the fight on the stairs?

He put the paper down, let in the clutch and turned down towards the sea front. It was four-fifteen. He would have time to get back for the appointment with Purdy. He drove through to the port and turned left to the Moyenne Corniche. It took him half an hour to reach the Casino.

A mixed crowd was drifting in and out. It was the thin end of the afternoon play and too early for the evening session to get going. Hood went up the steps and into the great entrance hall.

He took it cautiously. In the small room off the foyer, the fruit-machines were going. There were grey-haired women pulling the handles and melancholically watching the plums and bars. Hood didn't hear any jackpots. Most of the women yanked the handles as if they knew the machine wasn't going to be good to them.

He couldn't see anybody suspicious. He went out into the foyer again and stood looking at the case of letters on the wall. There were four or five envelopes behind the glass. 'Mrs Verender, The Casino,' said an English one in a schoolgirl hand, and he had the image of a family in some garden city waiting incomprehendingly for the return of Mum. Underneath there was an envelope for Signor Pasquale Pozzi, Industriale del Petrolio Fino, Casino Municipale. The postmark was six months old. What had happened to the

Industriale del Petrolio Fino? They were like the letters you saw pinned up at international airports. Who wrote to people at airports or casinos? It was the edge of a strange and rather desperate world.

He turned and walked slowly across to the door of the *Salons Privés*. The usual idlers were standing about. None of them showed any interest in him.

Hood went up to a Casino employee in a dinner-jacket and asked for the *directeur*.

'Which *directeur,* Monsieur?'

'The *grand directeur*, Monsieur Casimir.'

After a good deal of discussion and infinite name-giving – Hood stuck to Singleton Root – he was taken up the same stairs where he had had the fight. At the top was an elegant office.

Monsieur Casimir rose at his desk, tall and thin and sallow-skinned with heavy-lidded sad eyes. He was dressed with exquisite care and lightly perfumed. His thin silver hair was brushed up from the sides towards his bald crown so that his head looked like an egg wrapped in silver paper.

'Good evening. I don't quite follow what it is you wish to see me about.' From his sad eyes, he might have just lost a million at his own tables. He motioned to a chair.

'I was mixed up in a little trouble on the stairs outside last night. You possibly heard about it.'

'What! You are the man?' Monsieur Casimir looked startled. He reached towards a desk buzzer.

'I wouldn't do that,' Hood cut in. 'There is no need for alarm. I regret I had to cause a disturbance, but it couldn't be helped.'

'But the man is dead! You killed him. You were seen hitting him. You killed him there, outside this very office, broke his neck —' The door behind Hood opened. He spun round in the chair. Two very bulky men came in; Casimir had rung a foot-alarm. Hood was on his feet. He looked the two men up and down. 'I wouldn't try anything if I were you,' he said. One of the men gave an uncertain glance at his companion. Hood turned back to Casimir. He spoke with force. 'What happened to the body, Casimir?'

'The police came for it, of course. Since they are looking for you, I will have you handed over for arrest.' Casimir was trying to keep his nerve. His tired eyes flickered towards the two men; they stepped forward.

'Wait a minute.' Hood held up a hand. He was going to control this situation. 'The police, you say, came and picked the body up. Did they ask you any questions?'

'Questions? What questions should they ask me?'

'When there's been a killing, the police make extensive inquiries, don't they?' Hood snapped. 'They ask how it happened, who was there, a thousand other things. And they take photographs and they take names of those present, and so on and so forth. Did they do any of these things?'

Casimir looked as if he had been worrying about this before. 'They were in a hurry. They had had a lot of calls. They said they would make all their inquiries later.'

'But they haven't?'

'N-no. But that is not my business. I am going to telephone them now.' He reached for the instrument. Hood, who was close to the desk, put out a hand.

'If you do, Monsieur Casimir, you will cause yourself great trouble. I assure you – great trouble. The police, you will find, know nothing about the affair. But they will want to know a lot. Where, for instance, is the body? As a matter of fact, Casimir, you had the body disposed of so as to avoid a scandal and cooked up this story of "police", didn't you?'

'But— How dare you!' Monsieur Casimir's face was grey. He withdrew his hand.

'Very well. Where's the body?' Hood rapped out the words. His voice was harsh and commanding. 'You were the last to see it.'

'The police have the body.'

'Try making them believe they have. Why isn't there any report in the paper? Why hasn't a reporter been round to ask you about the incident?'

Casimir looked profoundly unhappy.

'How many police were there?' Hood asked.

'Two.'

'In ordinary uniform?'

'Yes.'

'No detectives?'

Casimir shook his head.

'Did *your* detectives, the detectives you employ in the *salons*, know the men?'

'No. But they hardly saw them.'

'But your men would have heard from the local people if the police really had the body?'

'That – that is what I cannot understand.'

'Monsieur Casimir, don't you think we had best discuss this alone? There is more in it than meets the eye, don't you think?'

Monsieur Casimir's look of uneasiness intensified. He hesitated, then signed to the two men. They went out. Hood slightly softened his tone – but not much. 'I think you'd find it worth while to forget this business. If ever you are asked about it, you can say that you thought the men who came here were genuinely from the police – as you did. But that won't arise. The body most likely won't ever be found. You will never hear about it again.'

'But – but —'

'Haven't you found moments, Casimir, when it would be so much simpler to explain than not to? It happens that I was acting in self-defence. That must sound highly unlikely to you but it is not something I can change. He had a hypodermic, as your men no doubt saw. As a matter of fact, I did not intend to kill him. He probably broke his neck falling down the stairs anyway. But he would have killed me without scruple. I'm sorry about the croupier. Was he much hurt?'

'Broken leg. He is in hospital.'

'I'll undertake to pay for the treatment and give him an indemnity. Also to the players I disturbed at the table.'

Casimir waved a hand. 'We have already looked after that.'

Hood judged the moment opportune. 'The reason why I came here, Monsieur Casimir, is to ask for your urgent co-operation on one matter.' Without giving him time to consider this, Hood took out the photograph of Andreas and handed it over. 'Do you know this man? Not the girl, the man at the side who is looking on?'

'A face?' Casimir shrugged unhappily. 'How can I tell? I am not the one to say. You must see the physiognomist. There are —'

'Of course! *That's* it!' A great light broke on Hood. 'The physiognomist! The man who reads faces?'

Casimir nodded.

'He won't let people come in if — ?'

'He stands at the door and sees everybody who comes in. If there is anybody undesirable, he gives a sign and we escort them discreetly out. He is Monsieur Ernest. He has been with us for thirty-three years. He knows the faces of every active gambling criminal, card-sharp, forger, con man, dope peddler and sleight-of-hand merchant in Europe.' Monsieur Casimir looked infinitely pained at having to mention these gentry.

Hood said: 'But of course he also knows the faces of celebrities, well-known people from all over the place, isn't that so?'

'Naturally.'

'Is he very good?'

Stiffly, Casimir said: 'He is phenomenal.'

'Will you get him up here? I want to ask him one question.'

Casimir made difficulties, spoke of 'professional secrecy'. He was obviously altogether uncomfortable about the whole interview. But Hood's manner hardened again.

'Do you want trouble, Casimir?'

'Please – Mr Root.' He rang and sent for the man.

Monsieur Ernest came in with a cheerful smile – an alert,

apple-cheeked man with a moustache, wearing a long blue uniform coat. Casimir motioned to Hood. Hood said: 'Monsieur Ernest, when did you last see Sir Richard Calvert?'

'He came in yesterday,' unhesitatingly said Monsieur Ernest with a smile.

'Are you sure?'

'Y-yes . . . I'm pretty sure . . . I think so.'

'What! But Monsieur Ernest!' Casimir looked outraged at this uncertainty.

'Do you mean it wasn't yesterday or it wasn't him?' Hood said.

Monsieur Ernest nursed his cap. 'As a matter of fact, I get a bit confused between Sir Richard and another Monsieur who comes in. They are very similar, same build, same features, same way of walking. Even that little trick Sir Richard has of hunching one shoulder a bit, the other Monsieur does it too. Usually when it's like that, you tell by their clothes, some little feature that's distinguishing – pearl tie-pin or Rotary buttonhole or cutaway collar, those sort of things. But these two wear the same clothes or very nearly. But now you ask me, it was the other Monsieur last night.'

Hood held up the picture with one hand covering the girl. 'Who is that? Sir Richard or the other man?'

Monsieur Ernest peered. 'To tell you the truth . . . No, I *think* that's the other.'

'But that *is* the other man you are talking about?'

'Oh, yes. And I'm sure Sir Richard has been in in the last four or five days. No mistake. I said "Good night, Sir Richard" to him and he smiled back and said "Good night".'

'Do you know Monsieur Lobar?'

'Oh, very well!' Monsieur Ernest smiled. 'No mistaking *him*!'

'Has he been in with Sir Richard? I mean together?'

Monsieur Ernest reflected. 'The first evening Sir Richard was here about a week ago they came in about the same time. Perhaps not together. Wait a minute, now I remember. Sir Richard came in first and I said "Good evening, Sir Richard.

It's some little time since I had the pleasure of seeing you." He said "Yes, Ernest, it is, isn't it? I hope you're keeping fit" and I said Yes I was. He asked after my daughter and stood chatting with me for about five minutes. He always was very sociable. Then he went on in. Then directly afterwards in comes Monsieur Lobar. He never says much. I just said "Good evening, Monsieur", that was all.'

'You're sure it was Sir Richard that evening?'

'Oh, absolutely. No doubt at all.'

'Thank you, Monsieur Ernest.'

Now in its daring ingenuity it was clear. Lobar had put Andreas through the stiffest test he could think of – to pass himself off as Sir Richard Calvert with a professional noter of quirks and mannerisms, a man who had made his living for thirty years as a close observer of personality. And Andreas had triumphed. He hadn't just hurried by. He had stood there talking to Ernest, while Lobar had probably watched from a distance. If Andreas could get by with Ernest, he could get by with Richard Calvert's staff.

It was staggering – brilliant.

And now Hood could see why Lobar had been so furious when Andreas had turned up unexpectedly at the Casino to gamble – as Andreas. It was extremely foolish and might jeopardize the whole enterprise.

Casimir had risen and was accompanying Ernest to the door, speaking to him in a low voice. He turned and said to Hood over his shoulder: 'Excuse me a moment, Monsieur Root. If you would kindly wait one minute.' He went out with Ernest and shut the door behind him.

Hood sprang up. Of course it was a ruse. Casimir didn't trust him; he had been pretending or had only half-swallowed the explanation about the police – Lobar's police. The door was locked! Hood laughed. What a fool to be taken in so easily!

He crossed quickly to the window and opened it. There was a narrow balcony. Below, a long stone terrace, but too far to drop to from above.

Hood stepped back and looked round. There was no way except the window. Well, sorry, Monsieur Casimir, he said. He took the silk curtains in two hands and, swinging to get his full weight behind the movement, he ripped them down with two heaves. They were good and long. He knotted the pair together, tied one end round the balcony support, climbed over and let himself down. It was easy. Reaching the end of the curtains, he dropped three feet on to the terrace below.

There was a row of windows. It was a ballroom. He kicked out a pane by the inside fastening and let himself in. The place had a long empty polished floor with a few potted palms at one end. He crossed to the door. To the left was a cloakroom and a glass-fronted entrance door; to the right a carpeted corridor. The entrance door was locked.

He ran along the corridor hearing running feet above. On the left was a bar – empty. He turned in and sprang to the window. It opened on to a stone balcony with steps down. Outside was a patch of lawn, palm trees, a flagged path. Just as he reached the steps, several figures appeared at the doorway of the bar. Hood sprinted. There were shouts behind him. At the end, the path ran round the building. Beyond, he saw steps and another big door, shut. It did not look promising. He noticed a wheelbarrow. A narrow path branched off into the shrubbery.

He plunged in. Round the curve was a gardener's hut and, beyond, a gate. As he went through, he saw an open padlock hooked over one of the bars. He swung the gate shut and snapped the padlock round the gate and upright.

Confused voices came from the path. Hood moved quickly and watchfully. He seemed to be on a private drive, bordered by flower-beds and palms, probably still the Casino grounds. The drive sloped up. At the top he passed a couple of parked cars. To his surprise, he came out near the Casino entrance.

As he turned away to go down the curving boulevard, a group of men came hurriedly down the Casino steps. They saw him. There was a shout. Then, just ahead, on the boulevard, Hood saw a police patrol car moving up. He hesitated. Between the oncoming group and the patrol car, there was a car at the kerb. He could see two nuns in it. Their car seemed about to move off.

Hood bounded across to them, pulled open a door. 'Mind giving me a lift?'

Their masculine-looking faces were turned to him. They smiled. Their arms reached out to help him in. The door slammed behind him as the car began to move. He received a crashing blow on the head and passed out.

20

THE LIGHT came through a hole in the top of the shutters shaped like the ace of clubs. Hood couldn't see anything else. He was flat on his back, tied down.

It must be about six o'clock in the morning. He had come to some time after they had left him. His head ached and he was very thirsty. He had no idea where he was.

He lay there looking at the ace of clubs. Presently the door opened and three men came in. They had broad un-French faces. They stood looking at him, walked round examining him but they didn't speak. Then two of them untied him and lifted him to his feet.

His hands and legs were tied. They took him by the elbows and hobbled him towards the door. Hood fell. One of the men kicked him heavily in the stomach. Hood thought he was going to faint again; but he managed to cling to consciousness. They hauled him to his feet and dragged him into the next room.

There were four big men lounging in different attitudes. They wore black clothes. Two of them had black top hats on, pushed back from their foreheads. His head thudding, Hood looked round. The place was an undertaker's parlour. There were piled coffins, silver candelabra, a display panel of mourning cards, crape drapery, photographs of hearses, cremation caskets. One coffin stood apart on trestles. It was open. Near it stood wreaths and flowers with inscription labels. The men just looked at Hood. Hood thought he understood. There was a police look-out; so Lobar had devised this safe means of transport. At least, that was putting the best construction on it.

One of the men got off the corner of the desk and came up to Hood. He didn't speak. Very fast, he threw a right smash at Hood's jaw, but Hood had tucked his chin in and dodged, so that the blow missed. As the man's arm came over his shoulder, Hood butted him with full force under the chin. The man's jaw clicked and he dropped. The other two jumped on Hood. A sandbag smashed on Hood's head. He lost consciousness.

He came to his senses with the slight jogging movements. Now there was a small round hole, the size of a pea, just above his face. Otherwise everything was black.

He was on his back. He knew he was in the coffin. He had a moment of panic, thinking they were going to bury him now. Then he heard a car horn, strangely muffled, outside and felt the effect of brakes. He must still be in the hearse. The air-hole might mean they intended him to remain alive as long as possible after being buried. Or it might simply mean they were reserving him for torture.

His hands and knees were tied but not his feet. They seemed to have laid him in the coffin straight after knocking him out. Hood wondered how long he would last if they put him in a tomb. In an ordinary grave, it couldn't be more than a few minutes before he would use up the air in the coffin and then lose his senses. They would be long minutes! Worst of all would be the sound of the earth on the coffin lid. But in a tomb he might last a week or more.

The hearse was periodically checking with its brakes and moving forward again. He heard an occasional lorry engine pass. They were presumably on a fairly busy road. He tried raising his hands. By digging his elbows fiercely into his sides, he could bend them and just squeeze his hands up between the coffin lid and his chest. He ran them round the coffin and suddenly winced at a sharp scratch. The next instant his fingers were feeling for the spot. It was at the side, about an inch below the lid – the point of a nail sticking out. Instead of screwing it down, they had nailed the lid on, presumably for quick action in an emergency. This nail had been driven in off the straight and the point had emerged inside.

Hood began working the cord binding his wrists against the nail point. He rasped his knuckles on the wood, twisting his hands so as to dig the nail point into the cord and shred it. Each time it caught, he tugged, but dared not do it too strongly for fear of bending the nail. But he felt one strand snap, then another.

It was a very slow process. He dug the nail point repeatedly into the ball of his thumb trying to guide it into the cord. After a while the cramp was such that he couldn't go on and had to squeeze his forearms down again.

Presently he went at it again. He got through one cord; there were three. He jagged his wrist and felt blood trickling. The second cord took so long he thought he would never succeed – then suddenly he had snapped it and the remaining one was loose on his wrist. He worked it off.

He lowered his arms and rested. The hearse was still moving. Slowly he brought his knees up against the lid and exerted pressure. The wood gave a loud creak. But he could see a crack of light where the lid had yielded.

There is great power in a man's knees. The confined space of the coffin gave him leverage. Hood added to it by gripping the back of his thighs and pulling. In a few minutes he had forced the lid up two inches and was untying the cord biting into his legs just below the knees. Outside, he could see the wreaths and flowers banked up round the coffin. Beyond that the roadside was going by; it was a glass-sided hearse.

He pushed the lid up farther and craned round. Two big oval wreaths with ribbons across them masked most of the rearward view; but he could see a black DS Citroën following, presumably with the 'mourners'. He wondered how they had inscribed the wreaths. In front were the driver and another man. Hood knew he could get out of the coffin. But the men following would see and wouldn't give him a chance.

Hood peered out, trying to get his bearings. They passed two petrol stations then some houses. It seemed like the approach to Villefranche. In that event, they must have taken him a good way out during the night. They slowed and stopped.

Hood didn't know why – and didn't care. His eyes were fixed on the motor-cyclist who had stopped alongside. It was the motor-cyclist who had seen him with Tate's body in the Nice car park.

Leaning on one elbow, Hood put an arm out of the coffin. It was masked by the wreaths. He was afraid to tap on the glass because of the two men in front. The glass sides of the hearse rested on an openwork silver grille running all the way round.

Hood pulled a berry from the nearest wreath and flicked it through an opening in the grille. It fell on the road near the man. He did not see it. Hood did it again and this time the berry hit the motor-cycle's front wheel. The man was watching a girl on the other side of the road. Immediately afterwards, they moved on. It was a one-way section under road repair controlled by police. The motor-cyclist dropped behind. Hood cursed with dismay.

They continued along the coast road. The hearse was not travelling fast, presumably so as not to attract undue attention. Hood thought that when they came to get him he would be able to shove his way out of the coffin and, with luck, smash through the glass. But he wasn't sure about the last.

Then, as they slowed again, the motor-cyclist sailed by on the wrong side in perfect French form. Three hundred yards on, the hearse dropped to twenty miles an hour and then pulled up just ahead of the motor-cyclist.

A lorry the size of a tank was across the road ahead manoeuvring into a contractor's yard. The motor-cyclist had one foot on the ground and was lighting a cigarette. Hood flicked another berry and another. They failed to attract his attention. The man got the cigarette going, trundled his machine on a couple of feet, watching the gigantic lorry ahead.

The lorry engine hammered like a battery of machine-guns. Useless to tap the window in that din! Hood tried moving his hand behind the wreath. No good.

At last the lorry had manoeuvred round and was backing into the yard. In a moment they would be going on. In desperation, Hood pulled a handful of petals from the wreath and stuffed them through the grille. They fluttered to the ground.

The man saw them out of the corner of his eye. He looked down, slightly puzzled, looked up and saw Hood. He stared. But after the first instant of astonishment, he looked as if he had seen this sort of thing happen with coffins before. His eyes narrowed. Trundling his machine closer, he peered up for a better look.

'Good for you old boy!' Hood said to him silently, beaming.

Lobar's driver in the Citroën behind immediately began tooting his horn, either to draw the man off or to signal the hearse driver on. But the motor-cyclist had recognized Hood and needed no prompting. He turned his machine away, revved up and roared off just as the lorry left a clear passage.

The hearse driver had heard the Citroën's signal and was trying to burst away. But there was traffic ahead, blocking the way and a long line coming from the opposite direction. They proceeded in single file. The hearse driver kept trying to jump forward a place and having to drop back again.

Then, as they came to a built-up area, Hood saw the motor-cyclist at the roadside talking urgently with two policemen in a little black-and-white Renault patrol car. He pointed at the passing hearse. The view was brief and obscured by intervening cars and the wreaths. Hood's impression was that the police were arguing the toss.

The hearse drove on. The traffic was beginning to string out. Hood nursed his rasped knuckles. Well, that was that. Suddenly the Citroën behind began blowing its horn hard. The hearse accelerated. The Citroën surged up alongside. Hood glimpsed one instant of urgent signalling from the occupants before it leapt ahead again. At the same moment, there was a smash of glass as a bullet came through the side of the hearse. One of the mourners having an afterthought.

Hood forced up the coffin lid and squeezed out. He crouched at the back behind the wreaths. He could see the little souped-up Renault astern. Far back came the motorcyclist crouched over his handlebars and undoubtedly having the time of his life.

The Citroën had cleared off. The hearse was travelling fast now. It swerved off on to a secondary road, turning up the steep curving slope between the villas, then branching off on another side road. Hood thought they had lost the police. Then he saw the piebald Renault still coming on.

The hearse put on more speed. All at once it swung aside on to a dirt track between some terracing. The driver must have seen his mistake at once. He was forced to brake, trying vainly to avoid the potholes. They crashed from one to another. Hood clung on. Wreaths and coffin were being tossed about. Then with a crunch, they went over into the ditch.

Hood wrenched open the rear door and leapt into the ditch, flattening out. Over his shoulder he saw the two men breaking for it across an olive orchard. Doubled up, he ran in the ditch back the way they had come until he heard the Renault approaching. He lay flat until it had passed, then resumed his retreat.

At the first bend, he jumped out of the ditch and sprinted across the road and downhill towards the villas and traffic. Presently he reached a shopping area. A garage had a notice: Cars for Hire. He went in. The garage man said he hadn't anything free for an hour. But he undertook to drive Hood to his brother-in-law's in Nice where he could pick up a car at once.

'All right, let's go.'

As they entered Nice, a black DS Citroën came up behind them. Hood said: 'Let this Citroën pass, will you?'

The garage man drew in, slowed and signalled to the car

to pass. For a moment the Citroën stayed where it was on their tail, then slowly it swung out and came alongside.

The driver was a blonde. She gave Hood a beckoning come-on with her head and a smile. Hood sighed and gave her a big smile in return. 'A little later, Josephine.'

'Yes sir,' the garage man said. 'We have 'em motorized down here now.'

21

PURDY, all eager beaver, said: 'Take a seat. Hello, hurt your hand?'

'It's superficial.'

'The answer to your telegram has come. I decoded it myself. I thought you were coming last night, waited till ten.'

Hood lit a cigarette. 'I nearly got buried.'

'What! Really?'

'Oh, under a pile of work.'

Purdy quarried into this for a moment, his eyes glinting; then he unlocked his safe, took the message out and gave it to Hood. Hood read:

HOOD CONSULATE NICE FROM IMPERIAL WATCHCO STOP CONFIRM PICTURE IS OF IGOR ZARUBINO AGED 49 BORN CHITA MARRIED ANNA HU'ONG WHO BELIEVED DIED 1938 STOP ZARUBINO FORMER MUSICIAN AND CIRCUS PLAYER ONCE STAR KIEV CIRCUS KNOWN AS THE GREAT ZARUBINO STOP MIMIC OF GENIUS STOP LAST HEARD OF VLADIVOSTOK SEPTEMBER 1939 POSSIBLY NOW LOCATED SHANGHAI STOP ENJOIN STRICTEST SECRECY ON CONSUL PURDY.

That settled it. A mimic of genius. Andreas was certainly that. Hood remembered how awkward Andreas had seemed as a valet on board the *Triton* and how untidy; it was easy to see now that it had been merely his cover.

Purdy opened his desk drawer. 'Your key has been done. Don't worry about that last sentence, you know. My lips are sealed.' He passed the key over.

'Good.' Hood put it in his pocket. He thought of the Gainsborough and the Sickert which the Treasury had supplied so grudgingly, sitting out there on the *Triton*. And all Lobar's pictures. It was a strange combination, evil and beauty in that intensity. Yet, as Hood knew by experience of life, it was not unique.

It was nearly eleven o'clock. Hood felt he must find out where Andreas was. Lobar might already have started up the mechanism of his fantastic plot. He realized that he had been sitting in silence for several minutes.

'Thinking of other things,' he grinned. 'Do you know when the NATO Council meeting starts in Paris?'

'NATO? That's right out of my line,' Purdy said. 'But I can find out.' He picked up a telephone and asked somebody in the outer office. They waited while it was looked up. 'Tomorrow? Oh, that's the Military Committee. The Council begins the day after? Thank you.'

The day after tomorrow! Hood said to himself. My God. He felt the shock of urgency.

Purdy was reaching into his desk drawer again. 'I was forgetting. That Opera phone number, I found it out. The address is Fourteen rue Dubosc.'

Hood made a mental note. He got up. 'Thank you, Purdy. One last thing. Do you have a gun to lend me?'

Purdy went pinkish with pleasure, bounded up. 'Got the one we've always kept here. Never used it. Hope you're not going to?'

'I'll give you a signature for it, if you like, in case I have to?'

Purdy went to the safe and brought out a Webley ·45 and a carton of cartridges. 'Here we are.'

'Good God!' It was too heavy and bulky but to Hood it was better than his present state of nudity.

Purdy wouldn't hear of him signing for it, 'not a Service man'. As Hood made to leave, he gripped his shoulder. 'Sure you don't need any help, old man?'

'I think I can manage. Thanks all the same.'

Purdy opened the door for him to slip through and, still pink, nodded a conspiratorial farewell.

The Peugeot 404 Hood had hired was outside. He got in, loaded the Webley and tucked it into his belt. Somehow he must get out to the *Triton* again, find his way to Andreas's cabin and – what then was in the lap of the gods. But the time had come to attack. Attack!

He drove back, by side roads when he could, to Beaulieu, parked the car in the forecourt of a hotel and took the footpath winding along the sea front above the rocks towards St Jean.

He reached the end and walked towards the square by the port. There were plenty of fishermen about, some early tourists. Then, at a table outside the Mascotte café, he saw Sue Trenton. She was alone, drinking a Coca-Cola. He hesitated; but she saw him and he went over.

'Well, well,' she said. 'The man I last saw in trouble. That was a confused exit the other night.'

'It got much more confused.'

She invited him to sit down. Hood did and ordered a Campari-soda. 'What did Lobar say when his friend was hurt?'

She gave him a level look, then shrugged. 'I don't know anything about it. I was playing baccarat.'

'How did you come out?' Hood was watching her. *Was* she just foolish? He couldn't believe she was so skilled in duplicity.

'Oh, I won. It was very amusing.'

'And Lobar lost?'

'How did you know?'

Hood grinned. They both drank their drinks.

'Oh, what's happened to your hand?' She had noticed his raw knuckles. She looked and sounded genuinely pained. 'Both of them!'

'That was a party I had with Lobar's friends early this morning.'

'You ought to get something put on them. Come with me, there's a chemist's right here. Leave the drinks.' She said to the waiter: 'We're coming straight back.'

Hood let himself be led across to the chemist's next door where the assistant applied an antiseptic. They returned to the table outside. The incident seemed to have put them on a closer footing. All at once, Sue Trenton said: 'Are you all right? I mean, I know something is happening but I've been trying to shut my eyes to it. Now I have a feeling it's something awful and —' she gave an uncertain laugh, as if she were embarrassed.

Hood lit a cigarette. Could he or could he not trust her? 'Where is Lobar now, do you know?' he said.

'He's at the villa. A dead man's been found and he has had to see the police about it. It was his chauffeur.'

'You're not waiting for him?'

'No.'

'Sue – can I call you Sue? I don't think it's good for us to be seen sitting here together. Let's go to my car, will you?'

She nodded and got up. They walked along the footpath to the car and sat in it. 'Do you know Lobar well?' Hood said.

'Not that well.' Their eyes met; she shook her head at his unasked question. No bed.

'He's a pretty dangerous man to fool with.'

'Oh!' She laughed self-protectively. Nevertheless her tone was more subdued when she said: 'All the same, I think I'll go on board and collect my things this afternoon and say I'm leaving. I have to go home anyway. Oh dear, oh dear, back to the salt-mines.' He thought she was trying to make light of her sense of uneasiness.

Hood decided to take the chance. He was going to trust her. 'Do you know whether Andreas – you know, the little valet – is on board now or not?'

'He was yesterday afternoon. I haven't been there since.'

'Then he probably still is if Lobar's busy. Sue, listen to me. It's important that Andreas comes ashore tonight and I want to ask you to help get him ashore before Lobar returns. Will you?'

'Why?'

'It's a long and complex story. I wish I could tell you but I can't. You'll just have to take me on trust. I give you my word that I'm not asking you to be a party to anything crooked, quite the reverse. I'll be frank – there's risk attached to it. Perhaps not more risk than you've been running already. I can't even offer you any spectacular rewards if you bring it off. But I promise if you do to give you the most glamorous evening that's attainable in London or Paris when it's all over.'

She gave him a long look. Then she said: 'I'm not afraid of risk.'

Hood took her hand. 'Good girl. How were you reckoning to get on board?'

'They always send the motor-launch in at one o'clock.'

'You don't know if Lobar is going off with you?'

She shrugged. 'I suppose it depends on the police, but I shouldn't think so. They were talking about having to go into Nice later.'

'All right. Now look, Sue. When you get on board, make some excuse for sending for Andreas. Get talking to him and then mention that you're going to see a new cabaret show tonight in Nice or Antibes or somewhere. Say it's a small, intimate show, in a new *boîte* that's just opened, and very, very exciting. If you can laugh and manage a blush it would be perfect! Tell him that as a matter of fact it's daring, and that corsets come into it a lot.'

'*What* come into it?'

'Corsets, you know – girdles, stays, suspender belts, foundation garments and what-all. No, no I'm serious. Andreas is a keen collector of these things, a connoisseur, I may say. If he thinks there's a chance of acquiring more expertise on them he'll be very interested and fall in with whatever you say. He will certainly want to know all about this new *boîte,* where it is and what time the show begins and so forth. You'll have to have those details ready, at your fingertips. Don't hesitate, don't give him a chance to smell a rat. He'll want to go to the show and what you have to do is to offer to take him with you. That is the whole point of the thing – you have to get him ashore. Say he won't be able to get in alone, that the show is private, friends of yours –

anything you like, provided you get him to come with you. I suppose you can ask for the launch to bring you ashore when you want it?'

She nodded.

'*If* Lobar's back on board – which looks improbable – you'll have to smuggle Andreas ashore. That won't be difficult since he'll be eager to come. Tell him to hide in the launch before you get in. But with any luck you should manage it before Lobar appears. You can say you have a car waiting to pick you up and take you to the *boîte* straight away, the car will bring him back and so on. It's important to make him feel he won't be missed on board, that he won't be back late. But the corsets will outweigh all that if you make them sound enticing enough. Can you do it, Sue?'

'Easily,' she said. 'He likes me.'

'All right then. When you get ashore with him, I shall be waiting for you in this car. You can drive, can't you? Good. It may be necessary for you to, if Andreas is reluctant to come along. But once he's with us, I don't anticipate much trouble. We shall have to separate soon afterwards. Is it all clear?'

'Yes. Where do we meet?'

'At St Jean. When you land you turn left away from the Mascotte café and along the port as if you were going to the other side of the St Hospice peninsular. You'll find a narrow cutting, a sort of alley which starts in the wall across the port. There's an oval Citroën sign, blue and yellow, above it which says "Chemin des Fosses" on one side and "Pointe St Hospice" on the other. It's a short cut with steps leading up. It leads you to a road running along the back. I'll be waiting just at the top of the alley.'

'Leave it to me.'

Hood said: 'Good. Shall we make a rendezvous there for five o'clock?'

'All right. And you may as well think out something impressive for our night out in Paris.'

'Sue, I'd like to begin with an instalment now and take

you for a superb and exotic lunch. But we ought not to be seen together, as the divorcees say. Do you mind?'

She was smiling. Hood thought again how pretty she was.

'I'll walk back. Till tonight, then. Goodbye.'

She got out and he watched her walk away. Hood lit a fresh cigarette. If she were playing him along he had well and truly set the trap for himself. And if one thing was more certain than another, it was that Lobar wouldn't let him get away this time.

22

THE ROLLS-ROYCE headed through the Paris traffic. It was moving with comparative speed, its path cleared at intervals by the two motor-cycle outriders blaring their police horns and blowing their whistles. It was raining and although it was still only mid-afternoon, entire streets were wedged with vehicles. There were spots where no amount of blaring or blowing made any impression. The Rolls had to nose through foot by foot.

Sir Richard Calvert sat in the back with the detective they had insisted on assigning to him. His briefcase was beside him. He had not seen the outriders for some days. Now they had suddenly turned up again. They seemed to be pretty erratic in their appearances.

His mind began running on the big Foreign Office change-over that was in the wind. They had tentatively offered him Delhi. But he wanted to remain closer to home, say Cairo at the farthest, until his chance for Washington matured. Besides, Daisy had never been well in India. He sighed. He was too tired to face the wire-pulling campaign necessary to get what he was after. With one thing and another, he had had no leave for twelve months, and now this series of Council meetings they were working up to was proving intensely exhausting. Daisy, too, was feeling the strain.

The outriders, trying to avoid the blocked traffic in the narrower streets, turned up the rue de Courcelles into the Boulevard Haussmann. But that was choked too. They crawled to the crossing, then swung towards the rue Washington which was one-way. Before they had got into it, however, the leading outrider was waving them back; there was apparently a jam farther down. The driver of the Rolls pulled up and the outriders headed off to the left down the rue d'Artois, which was almost doubling back the way they had come.

'Something terrible, ain't it, sir?' the detective muttered.

'What? The traffic, you mean? Oh, yes.'

By chance, the rue d'Artois was reasonably clear. Halfway down it, the first outrider swerved right into the rue Bastiat, then sharp right again. The second outrider had dropped back level. Fleetingly, Sir Richard Calvert noticed a street plaque; Impasse something. It was a narrow dead end with a garage in the far corner. They seemed to be losing themselves in their endeavours to make headway. He looked at his watch.

A yellow van moved across the road behind them, blocking their way. 'Now that's a damn silly thing to do,' the detective said. 'Can't back out now.'

They had stopped. At that moment the doors were opened on each side and two men pointing sub-machine-guns climbed in. Another man was beside the driver. The outriders were revving their engines to cover any noise, any shots that might be fired. The Rolls moved slowly into the garage. A steel blind rolled down behind it.

Hood looked at his watch. It said quarter past six. Sue Trenton had not appeared.

As a precaution, he had parked the car along the road from the short cut alley and was standing behind it. He could see her and Andreas the moment they emerged. He had been on the watch since four-thirty. But there had been no sign of them.

He cursed himself for choosing a spot which gave him no view of the sea front. He couldn't tell whether she had come ashore in the launch or not. Half a dozen times he had run down to the end of the alley to see if he could spot her or the launch, but they hadn't been there. He could see the *Triton* well out. He was afraid of staying away from the car too long in case she appeared there from some other direction and didn't find him.

Hood felt tense and extremely uneasy. The girl couldn't have double-crossed him or Lobar would have sent men after him already. She was in trouble on board. If Lobar suspected that she knew something even superficial about Andreas, he would have no mercy.

They would be poised and taking no chances now. They must have Andreas all ready to leave for Paris, if he had not already left. Lobar undoubtedly had everything timed to the minute. Andreas would lay up in Paris until, some time during the next twenty-four hours or so, the moment came for him to move out into the world in the personage of Sir Richard Calvert – for just so long as to collect all the secret data they could want.

He wondered what Conder had done about protecting Dick.

A woman came down the road exercising her dog. Then two young men with fishing rods emerged from the alley. Hood waited. When he looked at his watch again it was ten past seven. She was obviously not coming.

All of a sudden, Hood was coldly furious. He felt guiltily that he had led the girl into a risk which she could perhaps have avoided. He felt an intense loathing for Lobar. Now he understood Conder's emotion that day in speaking of that evil man. Hood hated Lobar with all his strength.

The icy look came into his eyes. He was going on board and he was going to get the girl and get Andreas – and the hell with Lobar.

He left the car and went down to the port. There were the usual fishermen dilatorily painting boats, tinkering with motors or talking. After being passed on from one to another, Hood found a young man who was willing to take him out for a stiff price. But when Hood said start at ten that night, the man wasn't interested.

All right, Hood said, make it five o'clock in the morning. Where was the boat? The man agreed and pulled in the boat to show Hood. It was one of the locally-built jobs, a solid boat with a high stem-post. A good motor? Hood asked. The man jumped down into the boat and started it. Fine, nodded Hood. She would be at the same mooring tomorrow morning? Excellent. He gave the man half the price in advance.

He went back to the car and was just about to get in when he noticed somebody duck back behind the curve in the road behind him. When he reached the spot there was only an elderly man with a stick some distance away.

Hood left the car. He walked along the quiet road, took the steps down to the beach and sat on the shingle with his back to the sea-wall waiting for dark.

It was a warm night with a moon. Hood stood in the shadow on the quay looking round. Everything was quiet. The clock of the church opposite struck one – then, in the odd Midi fashion, one again.

The fisherman's boat was still at the same mooring, about fifty yards away. Hood prayed the owner hadn't taken away the oars; but it wasn't likely. He went quietly along, keeping close to the wall, to the next wedge of shadow. There was no sign of Lobar's men. Stepping over to the mooring, he pulled the boat in and quietly got down into it.

The oars were in the bottom. He fitted them and paddled the boat gently out past the breakwater. He continued rowing until he was well offshore. Then he shipped the oars and started the motor. It made a loud chugging. He throttled down, trying to reduce the noise. It didn't make much difference. He swung the boat towards the *Triton.*

It was windless and the sea was dead calm. At some distance from the *Triton,* he stopped the motor, took out the oars again and began rowing. The *Triton* was not showing many lights. Hood steered for a point astern of her. An approach from the stern would reduce the chance of being seen. Slowly he drew level. She looked very big from the small boat.

When he was full astern, he turned in towards her. Standing, he faced round and pushed the oars, keeping his eyes on the *Triton.* He could not see a look-out. The motor-launch was not at the boom, which probably meant that Lobar was not on board. He paddled quietly. The set of the current was inclined to take him beyond the yacht and he had to bear on the starboard oar.

He pushed up right under the *Triton*'s stern, grabbed the rope ladder and made the boat fast. He shipped the oars, laid them in the bottom, got the ladder between his legs and cautiously climbed up. As his eyes came level with the deck he paused.

There was nobody in sight, though he could not see round the stern deckhouse. He grabbed the rail and pulled himself up. The ship was quiet. Next moment he was on deck. Flattening against the bulkhead, he edged round the starboard side of the deckhouse. No sign of movement. He tiptoed forward to the gate in the wire cage. It was open.

Hood went through and stood in the shadow. Somebody crossed the deck and went towards the fo'c'slc. Presently a match flared and a moment afterwards he made out the glow of two cigarettes. They were two of the crew.

Lobar's cabin, just forward, was in darkness. Hood edged towards it. He was about to reach for the door when he saw someone approaching along the deck. He drew back into a wedge of shadow. It was too late to move for better cover. He took out the Webley.

The man was coming straight for him. It was Perrin, in soft-soled shoes. Stock-still, Hood held his breath. Perrin went to the door of Lobar's cabin and stopped. He was four feet away, rattling a bunch of keys. Shining a torch, he picked out a key and unlocked the door. He went in, leaving it open a crack.

Was Sue Trenton in there?

Perrin switched on a light. It shone through the jalousie slats. Hood crept to the door and looked in. Perrin was bent doing something in the butler's pantry on the far side, his back turned. He had switched on the light in the pantry, leaving the cabin in semi-darkness; Hood could see there was nobody else there.

Hood eased open the door. His eyes on Perrin's back, the Webley covering him, he stepped silently into the cabin and slipped behind the drape of curtain. He stood waiting. Perrin seemed to be an age. At last he switched off the light in the pantry and came back into the cabin using his torch. He went out and locked the door behind him. Faintly Hood heard the rattle of keys as he retreated.

Hood stepped out, waited a moment, then struck a match, shielding it with his hand. It seemed the supreme opportunity to find out what went on below before he sought Sue Trenton. The match went out. He lit another, then using Lobar's desk lighter, he found a torch and slid back the frame and the Van Dyck portrait.

He tried the key Purdy had had made for the door below. It almost turned the lock. But it was only after a lot of manipulation that Hood managed to get the door open. Covering the torch with his hand so that it showed only a glimmer, he went down the ladder.

Everything was in darkness. At the bottom he moved cautiously along the alleyway, feeling for the door. He seemed to go on interminably and had an uncomfortable feeling that he was lost. He crept back and found the door. He was sweating. The key fitted. Hood opened the door. He winced at the loud creak it made.

There was complete darkness beyond. He had an impression of space. There was the smell of diesel oil and engine-room grease and something else, familiar but elusive. The torch showed another metal ladder going down. Hood drew the steel door to behind him and locked it. The sound made a reverberation – again the impression of space. He went down six steps, stopped and took his hand off the torch.

He was on a steel gallery, looking down at a long empty space shaped, as far as he could make out, like a rounded ship's keel. It might have been a cigar-shaped hold at the very bottom of the ship. All along it, like a spine, were curved chocks. They looked as if they were meant to receive the hull of some subsidiary vessel.

Slowly, Hood moved the torch round. Above the chocks were steel rings and chains attached to the *Triton*'s sides with gear for making the chains taut, once fixed to whatever they were to hold. At one end was an open watertight door. Beyond it, Hood saw a slightly smaller cigar-shaped chamber ending with another watertight door, shut.

He walked along the gallery, shining the torch. There was oil on the chocks and on the supplementary wood blocks lying about and a few inches of water at the bottom. Gauges and dials connected with piping. A lot of other mechanical gear was in racks, including tools and many large batteries. He counted six sizeable closed tanks disposed at intervals with flexible feed tubing attached to two of them.

Hood kept sniffing, trying to identify the familiar smell in the air. Suddenly the smell connected with words spoken in Conder's office that day when the two commanders from Naval Intelligence had told him about the *Triton* – hydrogen peroxide. He was smelling hydrogen peroxide. During the war, the Navy people had said, the Germans had used the heat energy given out when very concentrated hydrogen peroxide was mixed with water, to drive high-speed turbines, like the Walther turbine. The cost was staggering – a thousand times more than diesel oil, but undoubtedly worth it for special purposes. Then that was the secret of the *Triton*'s speed!

Yet Hood stood staring at the space below him, the watertight doors, the batteries, the tanks. *This* looked as if the *Triton* was a mother-ship to some other craft. Was that possible? He cursed at not having a camera, though it would be extremely difficult here to get any result.

He went to the end of the gallery. There was a cabin-like structure entirely closed in with a locked door. Tubes and insulated cables led into it. This, he thought, must be the navigation device.

Hood began to work on it. He tried everything he had been taught on the locks. He was unsuccessful. He could see no way of breaking into the thing. But he felt he could not give it up. He heard a small noise above and snapped the torch out.

There was silence. He waited but heard nothing more. He put the torch on again. With an iron bar, he might be able to force the door. He walked back along the gallery and leant over the hand-rail, shining the torch down into the darkness, looking for the tool-racks he had seen.

Something came round his throat and pulled him backwards. He went for his gun. But he was being pulled over backwards. He staggered, trying to loosen the grip. He felt the flesh of a huge hand. He fought for breath as the hand inexorably tightened. His lungs felt as if they were going to burst. Then he blacked out.

The throbbing in his throat was the first thing Hood felt as he opened his eyes. He was trussed to a heavy plank that extended beyond his feet and was propped up at an angle. It was some dimly-lit place, a room or cabin – if they were still on board the *Triton*. A feeble light came in through a grille somewhere above. His jaw was sore and he felt very stiff as if he had been beaten up while unconscious and kept bound for hours.

Then about twenty feet away he made out somebody tied hand and foot on a bed. It was Sue. Her head was turned away from him. She was quite still. Hood thought suddenly that she was dead and a sickened fury came over him. He tried to speak. His throat felt as if it had been rasped raw. He produced a croak. She stirred, then turned her head and looked at him mutely.

'Sue.' He had to make two shots at the phrase. 'You all right?'

'Ssh. Don't speak,' she said in a whisper.

'Where are they?'

She signalled with her eyes to the dark at the far end of the place.

'Hurt you?'

She was biting her lip. A bright light came on, making them both blink. Hood saw they were in a biggish oblong cabin with white tiled floor and shiny white clinical paint everywhere. There were a couple of ugly steel chairs, the bed, various hospital-like cabinets in white enamel and glass. It looked like a sick-bay. At one side was a dentist's chair and attendant bowl, drilling apparatus and so forth.

A sliding door opened, allowing a glimpse of another hospital-like area beyond, and Golos came in. He wore a singlet and blue dungarees. His monstrous hands hung at his sides. He stood in the centre of the cabin looking at Sue Trenton. She seemed to shrink in terror, shutting her eyes. The trace of a smile flickered on Golos's face. Then he stepped over to Hood and kicked away the bottom of the plank. Hood crashed painfully with it to the floor. His fingers were jammed underneath; the sharp edge had cut into his head.

He lay there looking up at Golos. Golos bent down and effortlessly lifted the plank into its former sloping position, but this time with Hood downward. Then he kicked the bottom away again.

Hood's forehead and nose hit the tiles full force. His head felt as if it were broken open. He managed to stay conscious. Golos lifted him again and propped him up. Hood blinked, trying to see. He felt the blood running from his nose. Sue was making a small frightened sound. Golos's hooded eyes went from one to the other of them.

In a moment, the door slid open again and Lobar came in. He was fastidiously dressed. He might have been entering some woman's boudoir. His dark suit was superbly cut; his linen gleamed, his shoes twinkled like mirrors; he was sobriety itself – no rings, no visible watch – but there was a glint of gold tooth in his smile as he contemplated Hood. His massive head shone. His lidless eye seemed extraordinarily large and glassy. He was smoking a big cigar.

With him entered an Oriental in a white surgical blouse. He stood in the rear.

'Good morning, Mr Hood,' Lobar said. 'I see Golos has been making you comfortable. He has a knack for these things. At one point, like the rest of us, he thought you had left us abruptly without bidding us farewell.' He turned to

Sue Trenton and gave an ironical little bow. 'Good morning to *you,* Miss Trenton. If you have lacked anything, I trust you will allow us to remedy that now?'

He drew luxuriously on his cigar, looking from one to the other. 'You make a charming pair, may I say. Who could not find pleasure in Miss Trenton's youth and naturalness? Or observe without approval the resource of Mr Hood? On the other hand, Mr Hood, you are inquisitive, which the old Chinese could never call a virtue. The superior man, they enjoined, should eradicate inquisitiveness at all costs, a precept I feel bound to follow. Don't you agree, Mr Hood?'

Hood looked at him. This belonged to the same order of ideas as being beheaded by a man in white tie and tails – the ceremonial accompaniment to cruelty. He had no illusion about what was coming. Lobar was going to have them both killed, probably after torture. Hood was very thirsty. He licked the blood from his lips.

'I believe in eliminating evil, Lobar,' he said. Behind the plank he was testing the rope binding him; it was an expert tie and offered little hope of loosening.

'Oh, evil! That would take us too far afield, Mr Hood.' Lobar chuckled. 'The old Chinese – you will forgive my reverting to them – the old Chinese had an admirable method with delinquent couples. They united them, bodily, grafted them one to the other and allowed them to grow together.'

An exclamation escaped Sue Trenton. Hood's glance went to the Oriental in the surgical blouse.

'But of course they had more time,' Lobar said. 'Now Mr Hood, you have first call on our treatment. Would you prefer to begin with, say, the dentist's drill? The Chinese pirates used to stick a carpenter's file a foot long between a man's teeth and work it with two hands. Here, we have the most up-to-date equipment for the convenience of our guests. Ching here is adept. He will drill your teeth beautifully, Mr Hood. He has his own method. He prefers to work from the outside, through the cheek.'

Ching evidently understood. He smiled, gave a bow and stepped to the dentist's chair. He touched a switch, reached for the apparatus and there was the whistle of a high-speed modern drill. Golos took the plank and dragged Hood across the floor. He lay one end of the plank on the arm of the chair and withdrew. Ching poised the needle-like drill. He held it delicately like a pen, as if he were about to add a touch to a drawing or begin a fine piece of calligraphy.

'Which eye would you like to have drilled first, Mr Hood?' Lobar said.

Sue Trenton screamed. Hood didn't know how much he could stand. He thought of the surgery men had borne before the advent of anaesthetics, removal of eyes, amputations and so on. He would go as far as he could, but the drill on his eye would surely break his control very rapidly. He said: 'Is there any object in this, Lobar, apart from your sadistic pleasure?'

Lobar rolled the cigar voluptuously between his lips. 'You are wrong, my friend. I do not get any pleasure from this sort of thing. It is necessary to kill you. You have killed men of mine. I will pay you the compliment of admitting that you are dangerous. You have given me much trouble and annoyance and I promise in consequence that you shall die in the most painful way possible. It is a principle much older than I am, of course, Mr Hood.'

'Old Chinese?'

Lobar smiled. 'Your accusation of me as a sort of inquisitor is entirely unfounded. Have I asked you for any information, Mr Hood? I have not. Do I propose to spare your life for some material consideration? I do not. Do I invite your spiritual reform? Neither that. I shall not even be here to witness your sufferings (which, I may say, will be as prolonged as the ingenuity of my people can make them). It happens that I must absent myself on urgent business. But that is not a thing I regret.'

'You will regret plenty, Lobar. We know about your business with Zarubino, the mimic.'

The faintest flicker of surprise showed on Lobar's face. He smiled. 'You must be gratified.'

'You won't get away with it,' Hood said.

'You are absurd, Mr Hood. You cannot prevent it. What's more, you make it sound like an improvisation. Everything, on the contrary, is arranged with great precision. All will go smoothly.'

'Zarubino, or Andreas as you call him, won't get within a mile of the place.' Hood wished he believed it.

Lobar made a gesture of impatience. 'He is on the spot already. You should wear ear-rings and tell fortunes, Mr Hood. Ching, give Mr Hood a hole for an ear-ring.'

'Yes, all 'ight.'

Hood felt the burning pain in his ear. Blood flowed. He gritted his teeth, tightening his muscles so as not to make a sound. If it hurt as much as this in his ear, it was going to be excruciating elsewhere.

The drill was through the flesh. 'Bigger,' Lobar said.

Ching worked it backwards and forwards in the hole. The whistle was frightful. Ching removed the drill. He stood looking at Lobar expectantly. Hood's ear felt on fire. He could just see Sue Trenton out of the corner of his eye. Her head was turned away.

'Would you like to tackle a molar, Ching?' Lobar said.

Ching nodded and bowed. He applied the drill to the skin of Hood's jaw about level with the back teeth. Hood felt the searing pain as the needle-point bit into his flesh. He forced his head back against the plank. He knew he was going to yell; he could help it.

'One minute,' Lobar gestured. Ching took the drill away. 'Ching, as you know, Mr Hood, is our acupuncture specialist. He is very skilful. A nerve is as fine as a hair, is it not? Ching can find it without error. Shall he demonstrate a jab in the sciatic nerve, Mr Hood? Or the trigeminal, the one in the face? It is extremely painful when irritated, the trigeminal. Drives people mad, they say.'

Ching nodded, grinning. He touched Hood's face with his

finger, outlining a branch of the nerve. Violently Hood jerked his head away. The movement made the plank slip from the chair and fall. Golos lifted it up. Lobar was looking at his watch.

'I fear I must go. I must ask you to excuse me, Mr Hood. As I was saying, indeed as you know, I have important affairs to attend to. They will not wait – and, after all, Golos here will take care of you. I leave everything confidently in Golos's hands.' His lip lifted in a smile. He spoke a few words to Golos, then said to Hood: 'I have recommended him to let you sample the pirates' method of hanging at some point – with a fishing-line. Miss Trenton will be cared for. It is unlikely that we will meet again. You have lost, Mr Hood. It is as simple as that. Goodbye.' He turned and went out.

Golos propped Hood in a corner, lit a cigarette and crossed to where Ching was wiping the drill. The two stood talking in low voices with their backs turned. Once Golos went to a bag in a corner, took out something and rejoined Ching. He kept looking over his shoulder at Sue Trenton.

Hood strained with all his strength at the rope binding his wrists; it was useless. The wound in his jaw hurt like hell. He wondered if, in the course of whatever they were going to do to him, he could find some way of hastening the end.

Golos turned and came towards him. Hood saw he held a reel of nylon fishing-line. Were they going to hang him at once, so as to have the girl alone? Rage filled him. He shouted at them. He could not control himself.

A huge palm rose, smothering his words, blacking out his view. The great fingers pressed unbearably on his temples. Hood gasped for breath. The cracks of light he could see dimmed. He lost consciousness.

He came to with excruciating pain cutting into his ankle. Detached from the plank but still bound, he was being hoisted by one leg to a hook in an overhead girder. They had pushed up his trouser leg and tied the fishing-line on the bare skin. It had already stripped the flesh. Golos held the reel. Only Hood's shoulders were resting on the floor.

Ching was looking on impassively. Hood could not see Sue. He tried to swing to see if they had taken her out, but Golos hauled. Pain shot up Hood's leg. He thought he was going to pass out again. He forced his shoulders back, taking all the weight he could. The blood was running down his leg.

All at once a buzzer sounded and a red light appeared above the door. Golos and Ching looked up at it; then exchanged glances. Golos hesitated, then quickly passed the reel end of the line under the arm of the dentist's chair and made it fast. He said something to Ching and went out.

Confusedly, Hood thought it must be some signal from another part of the ship, even from Lobar, who was ashore by now. He tried to get his free foot round the line to ease the strain. But this only made him raise his shoulders and bear more heavily on the line. Then great stabs of pain began shooting up his leg into the groin, as if some main branch of nerves was damaged. He screamed.

There was a movement at the edge of his field of vision – Sue.

'Oh, Charles. It's awful. They're devils.' She was sobbing.

The door opened. Hood saw two feet enter. His eyes followed the legs upwards; a dress, a hand holding his Webley. It was Ivory.

Her hair was disordered. There was a big bruise under one eye and some blood at the corner of her mouth. She was covering Ching with the gun.

'Ivory, for God's sake —'

'Keep quiet!' she said. She made Ching turn and face the bulkhead with raised arms. Quickly she glanced round, pulled open one of the cabinets and snatched a knife. In a stroke she had cut the fishing-line. Hood plumped, taking the fall on his free foot.

'Wrists – quick!' he said to her. She was kneeling by him. The gun was still aimed at Ching's back. Ching half looked over his shoulder.

'Get round!' she said, and he snapped back.

Hood's wrists came free. He rid himself of the remnants of rope, whispering urgently to her. 'Ivory, my girl, you're tremendous. You'll never know. What's happened? Give me the gun and get Sue free. What did they do to you?'

She passed him the Webley. He saw she had a tooth missing. With a gesture she pulled the dress off her shoulder, baring one breast.

'Christ,' said Hood. It was a mass of cigarette burns.

'Who – Lobar?' She nodded.

Now for the first time, Hood saw that she was breathing distressfully. She looked done in. Pulling the dress back, she stood up and went over to the bed. As she cut Sue free, Hood said: 'Golos is coming back in a minute. If you get out of here, jump over the side with Sue. There's a boat at the stern, tied up to the ladder. Keep that knife with you.'

'Can't make it.' She sat exhausted on the bed. Sue Trenton was on her feet.

'Yes, you can, with Sue. Listen, Ivory – Andreas has gone, has he?'

'Yes.'

'What did they have down below there, in the space at the bottom of the ship? Where the hydrogen tanks are. Do you know what I'm talking about?'

'Submarine.'

'A submarine!' Of course. Now he saw it. The *Triton* had been a mother-ship all right. The submarine had been housed in the space below, probably a small one, a four- or five-man vessel. The system of watertight doors allowed it to go out and return. With hydrogen turbines it would have high underwater speed and probably a good autonomous range.

'What were they doing, Ivory? Talk fast.'

'They been working on things underwater. Allied defences. All over the Mediterranean, laying apparatus which nullifies the defences without showing. Sent sub out all the time.'

'Whew!' From the secret papers he had seen and what Naval Intelligence had said in Conder's office, Hood knew that these underwater defences were among the most hush-hush devices in the west. As Conder had explained, it had been part of Lionel Crabb's assignment to find out if the *Sverdlov* or *Ordzhonikidze* had any equipment to counter them. 'Where is the sub now?'

'Left before we came here. I think to Dardanelles.'

'But why?' Ching moved. 'Hold it, Ching!' Hood said. The man froze. Hood snatched a hand-towel and held it to his cheek. 'Go on, Ivory.'

'They were using the sub, working with it; then Lobar had this mission with Andreas put to him. It meant interrupting work with the sub. Lobar was very angry. He didn't want to do it. He had to. So they evacuated the sub, near Turkey. First they tried to kill you. (Hood recalled the 'accident' with the van in Paris.) Then the idea was to keep you on board here while Andreas went on the mission to Paris. They said you wouldn't learn much, anyway.'

Ivory drooped. She looked as if she were going to faint. Hood shot out his arm to support her. In a flash, Ching had turned and jumped at him. Hood saw the glint of a knife. He had time to swing the revolver back on Ching. The hammer of the gun clicked on an empty chamber. He flung himself backwards on the bed, pulling trigger and hammer again for rapid fire. The gun went off. Ching had not had time to strike; he was about a foot away. Hood saw the bullet-hole appear in the corner of one eye.

As Ching fell on him, the door slid wide and Golos came in.

Hood thrust Ching's body aside. But before he could bring the gun up, Golos snatched a steel chair and threw it. The chair knocked the gun out of his grasp, but he managed to jump to his feet. Golos crouched and advanced on him. He held his hands before him, thumbs spread, like the great pincers of a crab. The mask of his face was sinister.

Sue Trenton screamed and recoiled. With a quick movement, Ivory bent and reached for the revolver. Her arm was extended, her head down as Golos sidestepped to her and grasped the back of her skull. His hand closed round it. His hooded eyes were not on the girl but on Hood.

With horror, Hood saw the hand tighten its grip. Ivory, bent double, could not move. She tried to say something. Then there was an appalling splintering sound, blood spurted out of Ivory's ear, and her body went limp.

Sue Trenton was screaming continuously.

'My God! You bastard!' Hood was white. He wanted to throw himself on Golos; but to get within range of those hands was suicide.

The plank was by the wall. He picked it up, smashed it at Golos. Golos dropped Ivory's head. His hand, smeared with blood, caught the end of the plank as it came round, wrenched it from Hood's grip as if it had been weightless and flung it aside. Ivory had slumped to the floor.

Golos crouched again, extending his hands, and moved on Hood. Hood knew that he had to keep clear. Once in Golos's grip it was all over.

Out of the corner of his eye he saw Sue Trenton edging towards the bed where the knife lay.

'Leave it alone! He'll kill you.'

Golos momentarily flicked a glance at Sue. Hood danced to one side, grabbed the fallen chair and jabbed it at Golos with all his force. Golos staggered. One leg hit him in the chest. He caught the chair. His lips curled back as he twisted the steel leg into a corkscrew. Hood was forced to drop it. Golos threw the chair across the room with a crash.

Sue flinched back with a scream. Golos was again momentarily distracted by her. It was obvious that he was anticipating dealing with her in his own way.

Hood had only a limited space in which to move beyond Golos's reach. Desperately his eyes searched for a weapon. On the floor was the hand-towel he had dropped. In a flash he stooped, snatched it up and flung it open in Golos's face. It gave him two seconds – the space it blocked Golos's vision. In the same movement, Hood sprang reaching for a glass jar on the shelf beside Golos. His hands clasped the jar.

As Golos brushed away the towel and swung for him, Hood smashed the big jar against the bulkhead.

The liquid contents spilled on the floor. Golos's heel slipped, his murderous hands momentarily flung up, and before he could catch his balance, Hood rammed the jagged glass edge into his face. He ground it into the flesh, gripping with both hands. The lower broken rim sliced a gash in Golos's throat. The upper rim hit his eyes.

Golos let out an animal howl of agony. One of his gripping hands touched Hood. Instantly, Hood let go of the remnant of the jar and sprang back. Golos dropped to his knees, still making wide gropings with his hands. One knee hit a fragment of jar. Blood kept squirting from his neck with the pumping of his heart. He fell forward. Hood raised the steel chair and smashed it with all his might on his skull.

Quickly he picked up the revolver. There were four rounds in it. 'Sue – come on!' She was standing in a corner, her hands to her mouth, petrified with horror. He put his arm round her. 'We have to break for it. Take that knife and stick by me.'

Hood bent over Ivory. She was dead. He signalled to Sue to follow. The adjoining sick-bay was empty. It gave on to a short alleyway at the top of which they could see daylight.

'Keep close,' Hood said. He went up the companion with the revolver ready and looked out. The exit faced aft. The sun shone brightly. Three of the coloured seamen were standing together on deck. They pretended to take no notice of him. They were big powerful men.

'Come on, Sue.' He stepped out on deck, waited for her, took her arm. He looked over his shoulder. Three more men astern. Hood crouched and held the revolver close to his chest, concealed under his left elbow. He whispered to the girl: 'We are going to have trouble. Hold that knife with the point straight out, not down, and if you have to use it, just stick it forward, straight in the belly of the man who is tackling you. I can look after myself. Keep your nerve. There's a boat astern if you have to jump for it. Now walk forward close to me.'

They walked along the deck. The seamen had shifted and were standing across their path. 'What are they doing behind?' Hood said.

'Moving up with us.' Her voice trembled.

When they were three paces from the men, Hood said: 'Wait here. Watch them behind. When I say "run", run like mad for the stern.' He stepped forward, suddenly brought out the revolver and waved the men aside. The three seemed surprised at the sight of the gun. But the one in the middle shook his head. Hood waved them away again; they glowered. Their shoulders came down. Hood shot the left-hand man in the belly, quickly covered the man next to him. There was a moment of confusion. The shot man fell, making a noise.

'Run!'

She darted past them. The centre man struck with a knife. Hood side-stepped and tripped him. But the third man was on him, with the other group running up. Hood shot the third man in the face, turned and sprinted for the stern. With a shout of joy, he saw that Sue was through the wire caging. They had left it unlocked. They *had* to make it!

He swung round, covering the rest of the seamen. They were hanging back. Then just as he stepped through the gate, a man sprang from nowhere and slammed the gate on his hand. The Webley flew out of Hood's grip across the deck. Hood turned and ran, shouting: 'Get down. Quick!' She was aft, above the ladder and saw at once he had lost the gun.

'Down that ladder!' Two of his fingers had been painfully crushed by the slamming gate.

They were in the worst possible position on the ship. The seamen could approach on both sides to within a few feet behind the cover of the deckhouse. One concerted rush and it would be finished. He climbed over.

'Faster!' The wire gate had been flung open. He was a rung above her, telling her to haul the boat up with her foot.

They jumped in. Yelling 'Cast off!' Hood flung past her and sprang to the motor. He choked it and cranked. No result. Hardly pausing, he cranked again. He got no pressure. The motor didn't feel as if it were near starting. Furiously he wound the handle. Nothing doing. He flung up the cover, reaching for the fuel pump.

Sue gave a little sob. He looked up. She was still struggling to unloose the painter. At the same moment, Hood saw a row of brown heads over the ship's rail, looking down. Then just behind them, Perrin's head appeared. He pushed to the rail. He held an automatic.

'Sue – look out – duck!' Hood jumped forward, wrenched her back and down by the shoulder. He worked at the tie of rope and freed it. There was a shot. The bullet hit the gunwale.

'Run aft – and for God's sake, keep down!' he shouted to the girl. He hauled hard on the rope ladder and let go. But it gave the boat hardly any way. As he leapt back to the motor, Perrin fired again. It snicked the woodwork just ahead of him. Almost immediately there was another shot; one of the crew was shooting with the Webley. He cranked desperately. The motor gave a cough. He glanced up. What current there was, was slack and the boat was scarcely drifting. The motor would *not* respond.

The oars! They would give a chance. He made a dive for them in the bottom of the boat, hauled them out – and saw that a shot had snapped one of the cast-iron rowlocks.

Two shots. Behind him, Sue made an exclamation of pain. 'Hurt?' he called out.

'It's snicked my leg – nothing.'

They were offering themselves as targets! He dropped the oars, flung back to the motor. It produced another cough. He could feel some pressure.

'Oh, Charles – look! They've got —'

A man in engineer's overalls had appeared at the *Triton*'s rail. He had a sub-machine-gun. He handled it as if he were practised. He steadied it against a stanchion and took aim.

'Over the side! Get under the stern,' Hood yelled.

But Sue said again: 'Oh, Charles, look! *Look!*' – and looming round the headland of Cap Ferrat, moving majestically on to the scene, was the great buff hull of a liner. A thirty-thousand tonner! Hood could hardly believe it. She was close in, moving slowly. The rails were lined with passengers – decks of them – hundreds of them. *Orcades*. He could read the name on her bow. She must have just pulled out of Villefranche, on one of her cruise calls. They were suddenly the focus for a shipload of spectators!

Hood let out an insane cheer and waved. She was such a glorious return to sanity. 'Wave, Sue! For God's sake, wave! Keep on waving. Keep their eyes on us. Yell!'

As she stood up waving both arms, Hood bent to the motor again.

'Yoo-hoo! Coo-eee!' Sue was yelling at the top of her voice. People were waving back from the packed decks. Scarves zigzagged in salutation. Suddenly the *Triton*'s crew were gone. Perrin and the engineer with their guns had vanished with the rest. The great liner was full in view now. Answering calls to Sue's floated across the water. One of the watch on the bridge had a glass on them and several passengers were watching with binoculars.

Hood redoubled efforts with the motor. Suddenly it coughed, snuffled – and chugged into life. Carefully, Hood nursed it, strengthened it and slowly turned it up into a roar.

'Here we go, gal!' he yelled. 'Hold on.' He slipped in the clutch, veered and off they went for the shore. Hood opened her up.

'Give her a yell. She saved us.' They both yelled and waved at the liner and knew they were yelling out of sheer shattering nervous relief.

23

THE TRAFFIC at the Porte d'Italie was a tangled mass. There was a Metro and bus strike. Hood groaned. The driver had already done marvels in getting this far from the airfield in half an hour. Alongside, the driver of a Dauphine was leaning on his horn.

In the race to reach Paris in time, Hood had only been able to confide a brief message to Sue Trenton. Once ashore, they had phoned Purdy; the Consul was out. Hood had scribbled the message and told Sue to take it to Purdy for 'the same address as before' – the SIS office. Fortunately the snick in her leg was superficial. At Nice, Hood had used a Circle name to get a priority seat on a plane for Paris.

Purdy had evidently not even questioned the genuineness of the message. There were advantages in eager beavers! Hood had found a car waiting for him at Orly with Chuck Whitney, his assistant, and Henry Price, an SIS man whom Conder had flown in on emergency routine from Brussels. They told him it had been decided not to bring in the French Secret Service. The SDECE was a splendid organization. But apart from anything else, Conder had said, there was no point in giving it information about Hood's activities. This made things decidedly tricky. But Hood could see Conder's point. It was probably the Head Man's personal ruling.

Whitney had a slim athletic look with dark hair and blue eyes. Price was smaller but very tough. Hood had quickly filled them in. It looked as if they weren't going to reach the NATO building at the Porte Dauphine, on the other side of Paris, before the Council session began.

The jam as they tried to descend towards the Seine became monstrous. To improve things, the road was up. Cars were mounting the pavement, trying to get through.

'What happens when the rush hour starts?' Price said.

'They don't notice the difference.'

Forty minutes later they were at the Trocadero. Hood's jaw and ankle were giving him hell. The drill had started a toothache. He had only pieces of sticking-plaster over both wounds. Two fingernails had blackened on his right hand where the gate had slammed.

It took them ten minutes to circle the Place du Trocadero. The rain and heavy cloud were darkening the sky. Hood was tense with impatience.

'Drive between the trees, man, for God's sake!' Price called to the driver. The driver swung up on the central dirt alley running down the broad avenue and accelerated. Twenty other cars behind imitated them.

They reached a solid block at the Boulevard Lannes on the edge of the Bois de Boulogne. 'Come on,' said Hood, jumping out. They ran the quarter mile to the NATO building. Panting they went up the steps into the wide marble hall and made for a lift.

Two men in blue suits barred their way. 'Security desk first, please.'

The French clerk at the central security desk blinked at them. His eyes were small and set close together.

'We want to see Mr George Wetherby. It's urgent.' They had decided to put the whole thing to Wetherby who was Number 2 on the British delegation. Hood had once met him. To go to the security people would entail nameless complications, explanations and delay.

The man began thumbing awkwardly through an alphabetical list.

'British delegation,' Hood said impatiently.

'Oui, Monsieur,' the man said, continuing to thumb. He was about fifty and looked like a van-driver out of his element. He licked his thumb, turned another page, stared at it intently, turned another.

Hood looked round the hall. There were three entrances. The one they had used gave on to a tree-lined square of the Bois de Boulogne where children played in fine weather.

Another gave on to the Boulevard Lannes running alongside the building, and the third, on the opposite side, led out to one of the roads through the Bois. A good number of people were moving about the hall – newspapermen, men and women of the permanent staff, some arriving delegates. Groups were going in and out of the lifts. Now and then big black limousines drew up outside and solemn-looking men got out. There were security men by the lifts and the inner doors of the building.

'Hurry up, man,' Price said. The man at the desk was muttering silently, still gazing at his list.

'What's the matter?' Hood said. 'Christ, this is urgent. *Wetherby*. Do you understand?' He wondered if he could break for it. Wait till a lift was about to go, then force his way on at the last minute. But it would probably start some awful entanglement – and where would he look in the immense building?

At last the man picked up a phone, dialled and waited. Nothing happened. He hung on, looking dumber than ever. He blinked straight at them. Hood groaned with impatience. The man rang off and dialled again.

'Ullo? Dis. Ullo. Pouillard ici. Vezz-air ... Comment? Non, pas vu. J' suis seul ici. T'as pas mangé? Ben, non. Ecoute ... Vezz-air – ullo? Ullo-ullo ...? Couillon, il a raccroché.'

He redialled.

'Can't you *hurry*?'

'Ullo ... ullo-ullo? ... Dis ... Hein? ... Il t' la dit? Bon, c'est comme tu veux, hein? ... Dis ...'

'VEZZ-AIR-BEE!' bawled Hood.

'... Dis, Vezz-air-bee, c'est le six cent douze? ... Non, double-v. Bon. Merci ... T'a l'heure.'

'Six-twelve, let's go.' Hood was turning to go.

'Minute, Messieurs!' the man called out. 'Identity cards?'

Gritting his teeth, Hood handed over his passport; the others did likewise. The man began laboriously to copy out the details on a form. 'What's this for?'

'Laissez passer. Pas la peine de se facher, Monsieur.'

'Please forget it,' Hood said grimly, 'and *get on.*'

The man bent, concentrating heavily on the task. All at once, on the far side of the hall, Hood saw Andreas come in.

'There he is!'

Whitney and Price followed his look. Andreas had got out of a Rolls at the entrance on the Bois side where the permanent delegation offices were and was crossing to the nearby lift. He had on Richard Calvert's coat and hat and carried his briefcase. In every movement, every expression, he was Richard Calvert's double.

Spellbound, Hood watched him smile and raise his hand in salute to the doorman and the security man. It was uncanny. For a moment, Hood had the strange feeling that it really was Richard Calvert. Andreas put his hand in his pocket and showed something, presumably a pass. The security man glanced at it and saluted. The doorman had already rung for the lift.

Suddenly Hood was running across the intervening space of the hall with the other two behind him. They dodged staring officials, broke through groups of typists and were pushing their way among ranks of newspapermen. Ahead of them the lift door opened and Andreas stepped in. There was a fractional pause.

Struggling, Hood shouted: 'Andreas! Zarubino!'

Andreas's face did not change a fraction. The next instant, the liftman had shut the door and they were gone. As Hood and the other two broke through, they were grabbed from behind.

'What's all this?' They were security men from thc centre of the hall.

'That man who has just gone up is an imposter. He must be caught.'

'Who are you?'

'I'm here to see Mr George Wetherby, of the British delegation. It is urgent.'

'That was the British Ambassador who has just gone up.' There was a chorus from the doorman and others who had been standing by.

'It's Sir Richard Calvert. There's his car.'

'Comes in every day.'

'We been seeing him for two years.'

'Now what's all this about?'

Hood exploded. It was a chaotic moment. Andreas was up there in the British Ambassador's office, at his papers. In a few minutes he would be going into the Council meeting and the task of persuading anybody that he was not the real Richard Calvert would be increased a thousandfold, let alone getting them to bring him out. He had surely got Richard Calvert's keys to the safe. Hood imagined him ringing for Calvert's secretary. 'Oh, Alison, bring me the top-secret airfield file, will you?'

All at once, the man from the central security desk put his head into the group, blinking. 'Laissez passer.' He held out three passes.

Whitney grabbed them. 'Now for God's sake, let's get up there,' Hood said. The senior security man seemed to be impressed. 'All right.'

They crowded into the lift. There were Hood, Whitney and Price, three of the hall security men and the lift man. At the sixth floor, Hood said: 'Room 612,' and they ran down the corridor. Suddenly Hood called out: 'Wetherby!' George Wetherby's long elegant form was just coming out of a room ahead of them. He had a red dispatch case in his hand. They pulled up.

'Wait a minute – Charles Hood, isn't it?' Wetherby said.

'Yes. Listen. Can't explain. Have you seen Richard Calvert?'

'Yes. He's just come in. He's in his office.'

'Where is it?'

Wetherby pointed to a door farther down. 'He's pretty busy. Can't see anybody. Unless it's — '

Hood said: 'We have extra-territorial rights over these offices, haven't we?'

'Damned if I know. Probably have.'

Hood looked at Whitney and Price, then at the security men. 'Don't try to stop us.' He pulled out his gun, jerked his head to the other two. They went to the door. Softly, Hood turned the handle. The door was locked. With a gesture he posted Whitney outside and turned to Wetherby.

'Secretary?'

'This way.'

They ran to a door beyond and burst in. The two girl secretaries looked up startled. One held a tray with cups of tea. The other, at a filing cabinet, stared at Hood's revolver. The door to the Ambassador's room was shut.

Wetherby said: 'Alison, is the Ambassador — ?'

The door of the room opened and a uniformed messenger came briskly out. Hood had a glimpse of Andreas, standing just inside the room, with a sheaf of documents in his hand. Andreas glanced up as the door was about to shut. Hood jumped forward. There was a confused bustle. The messenger and the girl with the tea blocked the way. The girl dodged maddeningly back and forth with the cups, dropped them, screamed. Hood flung himself at the door. It was locked. Andreas had seen him!

He turned to Wetherby: 'Quick! Any other exits?'

Wetherby hesitated. 'I don't think – wait a minute, there's the conference-room on the other side. I must say, I don't follow what you're after.'

'For God's sake where's the conference-room?'

Wetherby headed out into the corridor again, they ran back past Whitney and turned at the far end into a cross-corridor. There were rows of identical office doors. Wetherby threw open the second. They paused staring at the long empty baize-covered table, the door of the Ambassador's office ajar at the far end. Price ran forward, scanned the inner office. 'Gone,' he called.

Hood swore.

'Can I ask what this is about?' Wetherby said.

'That was an enemy agent, not Richard Calvert. He has all Dick's papers.'

'Good God!'

'In a matter of minutes he can be out of here. Is there an emergency alarm system?'

'I suppose so. If there is, we've never used it. Difficult now anyway: the Council meeting is going to begin any minute. He can't get far if we —'

'The man can change his appearance twice a minute.'

'What!'

Hood thought fast. A lift appeared at the end of the corridor. 'Hold it!' Hood called out and gesticulated. Price ran to hold the lift. 'Listen, Wetherby,' Hood said. 'As soon as we're below, get security to send out a general alarm. Stop everybody leaving the building. We'll be outside. If you get him, hold him and it doesn't matter what anybody says, it doesn't matter what you think yourself, *he is not Richard Calvert*. Come on, Chuck,' he called out to Whitney. They ran for the lift.

Outside, on the Boulevard Lannes, the traffic jam had miraculously dissolved. A stream of other cars was flowing through the Bois de Boulogne.

'By God, he's got away with it.'

They looked at each other. Hood knew it was so. Lobar had been ready for an emergency. 'Come on.' They ran to the taxi rank in the Avenue Bugeaud.

'Fourteen rue Dubosc.'

'Near the Opera?' the taxi man said.

'Right,' Hood said. 'Fast as you can.'

The traffic was still entangled in the centre of the city. At the Boulevard des Italiens they left the taxi and hurried through the evening crowds. Fourteen rue Dubosc was a tall narrow-fronted block of what had once been flats but were now mostly offices, with an insurance firm on the ground floor.

They left Price at the street door and went in. The place

was dingy. It looked as if it had remained untouched since Louis Napoleon's day. An ancient hydraulic lift was stopped at the first floor. It was, as Tookey Tate had said, pushed up by a sort of greasy steel stalk which rose out of the ground.

'This is the place,' Hood said.

They summoned the lift and got in. Hood pressed the button for the top floor; the lift gave a hiss and a sigh, as if it were lamenting the effort, and slowly rose. The building was quiet. They passed the second floor and the third. There was the sound of a door slamming above. Their eyes met.

The lift was just coming level with the fourth floor landing. Hood opened the doors. The lift quivered to a stop with another hiss. They stepped out. Hood peered upward. For a moment, after the door had slammed, they had heard steps coming down. Now they had ceased. There was silence. Whoever it was had halted on the stairs above.

Hood stepped back. Chuck Whitney took out his gun. They stood close to the wall of the staircase, waiting. In a moment, a shadow moved somewhere above. There was no sound. Whoever it was paused again, evidently suspicious. Then they saw the shadow again, lower down. Something creaked faintly.

All at once, a head appeared over the banisters. It was Lobar. He saw them. His head vanished at once.

With a shout, Hood sprang forward up the stairs. They could hear Lobar running up ahead of them. As Hood reached the fifth floor landing, Lobar was a flight above, turning towards the sixth. It was the top floor. They could hear him grunting; but he was extraordinarily agile. Hood strained to catch him.

There was a flash and a loud bang. Hood was on his face. The shot ricocheted off the wall. They heard Lobar running on – and were up after him. Lobar evidently saw that he had no time to get into the top floor flat. As he reached the landing, Hood fired. But Lobar was through a dark opening on the far side.

Hood shouldered the flat door. It was locked. He jerked

his head to Whitney to get in. 'Watch the service stairs!' He went towards the dark corner.

'Look out for that gun!' Whitney yelled.

Hood felt a draught of night air on his face. There was a short corridor and a flight of stairs. At the top he saw the night sky. It was the roof. He cocked the gun, thumb holding the hammer, and pulled the trigger. Only the pressure of his thumb kept the gun from going off – the instantaneous firing method. He went up slowly. He crouched, stepped out on to the roof. There was another flash as Lobar shot again. Hood was behind the dark mass of a chimney. He had a bare glimpse of Lobar moving quickly away – and fired. He couldn't tell whether he had hit him. Lobar had vanished.

As Hood sprang after him, some obstacle at ankle-height tripped him. He fell, the revolver was knocked from his grip and he heard it slither, then clatter somewhere far below.

He bent down, feeling round for the obstacle. It was a radio aerial lead. Two feet to his right, the roof sloped. He backed away. On the left, the roof extended flat, interspersed with chimneys, over the adjoining block. There was a blaze of light from the batteries of arc lamps on the far edge. It was the Place de l'Opera with the flood lights on the Opera façade.

Hood moved across the roof towards the big lights. Lobar stepped out in front of him.

Hood knocked his arm up and gave a right jab to the face. The shot went wide. Lobar smashed the gun down with all his weight. Hood barely had time to avoid it, but stuck a foot out and as Lobar crashed, he kicked the gun out of his grasp.

Lobar's free hand gripped his ankle and wrenched it from under him. Hood went over. At once, Lobar was up, aiming a kick at his head. The toe-cap caught Hood viciously above the ear. The dark swam. Hood managed to roll away. Then Lobar was running along the edge of the roof among the arcs and a mass of cables. It must be a way of escape! He was lifting an arm to shield his eyes from the glare.

Hood got up and raced after him. As Lobar turned, Hood

caught him under the chin with the heel of his hand. Lobar staggered. Hood wrenched off a half-eaten iron cap from the chimney-pot alongside and smashed it in Lobar's face. Lobar rocked back and crashed into one of the lights. There was a shattering of glass, an electric flash and a sudden patch of darkness. Lobar screamed. Hood smelt burning. His foot slipped on the edge of the roof. He groped wildly, caught a cable and crawled back.

He could hear Lobar breathing harshly near by but couldn't see. The fierce glare blinded him. Something hit him hard in the chest and flattened him. He shook his head. Against the sky, he saw Lobar above him, raising a heavy tripod with both hands above his head. He tried to scramble away. The tripod caught his shoulder and knocked him over again. He thought he was going to pass out. A tiny voice shouted at him: 'Keep moving, or he'll get you. Keep moving!' Mechanically, like a punch-drunk boxer, he moved leg and arms. He was vaguely aware that he might be crawling towards the edge of the roof. Darkness and the blazing light swirled together. He gasped for breath. His vision managed to focus.

Lobar was coming at him again. Hood gathered all his strength. He got to his feet. As Lobar came in, he hit him with everything he had in the solar plexus. Lobar's head came forward. Swiftly grabbing the back of Lobar's head with both hands, he rammed it down harder, at the same time driving his right knee up to meet the descending face. His knee met Lobar's face with a terrific crunch. Lobar tottered back. Hood sprang in and got a choke hold round the great throat. Groggily, Lobar tried to shove him away. Hood hung on.

A big floodlight was smoking behind them. Lobar faltered. His heel caught a cable. He tripped backwards against the floodlight. He let out a strangled roar as the heat bit into him. Violently he heaved, straining to keep his neck and head from the searing metal. Hood gritted his teeth and held him arched back over it.

Lobar's clothes began to burn. Then his flesh sizzled. Hood was choking and coughing with the fumes. Lobar groped in the air. There was a sickening smell. Hood forced him backwards. Lobar was going limp. Loops of cable hung by the arc. Hood let go with one hand and grabbed them and lashed them round Lobar, binding him over the drum of the light. Lobar twitched. There was a louder sizzle. Lobar's mouth opened in a hideous grimace. The lidless eye bulged. He made inarticulate sounds. Hood pulled the cable taut round a bar of the metal frame.

'That's for Ivory,' he gasped.

He turned away and picked his way across the roof. He was swaying. He stopped for a moment to recover; then as he reached the landing, Whitney came out of the open door of the flat. 'Hell,' he said, seeing Hood's cut face and rumpled suit. 'What happened?'

'Finished him.' Hood was still winded. 'It was the head villain. Where's the other one?'

'Nobody else in the place. I checked the service door but it was locked on the inside. The key's still there.'

'You mean he hasn't come back here?'

'Looks like it. You all right, Charles?'

Hood nodded. But he waved aside the cigarette Whitney held out. The wound in his jaw and his tooth were hurting badly. He brushed a hand perfunctorily over his suit. 'Nothing from Price below?'

'Not a thing.'

They went into the flat and rang Wetherby's office. Andreas had not been found. Hood rang off.

'Better have this.' Whitney had found a bottle of whisky and poured a shot. Hood gulped it. They went downstairs. Price hadn't spotted anybody. With caution, they questioned the *concierge*. No, she said, only Monsieur Roland, thc stout Monsieur of the sixth floor, had come in this afternoon. (This was obviously Lobar.) They moved discreetly away along the pavement.

Hood cursed with frustration. 'They're probably micro-copying those papers right now. *We've got to find him.*'

Then a sign opposite caught his eye. *La gaine Naughty.* Corsets! He grabbed Whitney's arm. 'What's the date?'

'Date? Twenty-first of April.'

'The twenty-first of April.' He had abruptly remembered the invitation card he had seen in Andreas's cabin. 'By the eleven thousand virgins of Cologne, that's it! Come on. A taxi. Hey, taxi! Taxi!'

'Where are we going?'

They bundled into the taxi. 'Hotel Albert VI. And make it fast. I don't care what traffic rules you break, if there are any rules. Fast!'

'What's the idea, Charles?'

Hood said: 'You two had better get ready to look like corset buyers.'

The traffic, if anything, was worse. But the driver, a young man with a pale knobby face, was full of poetic zest. Clipping corners and swerving round islands on the wrong side, he told them that taxi-driving in ordinary times lacked adventure. These were the moments when a taxi-driver really lived! The entire city was a challenge. The basis of his technique was to scare other drivers out of the way by recklessness. He ignored No Turn signs, took short cuts up one-way streets. Police stared, then shrugged. The driver waved to them. 'They're not stopping anybody to give out tickets tonight,' he laughed. He swerved between a converging Peugeot and a Renault van, blaring his horn. At last he pulled up outside the Albert VI.

'That was Napoleonic,' Hood said, giving him a note.

They hurried across the pavement. The hotel lobby was animated. They looked round. Hood glimpsed a horse-hair plume and a splash of scarlet. 'This way,' he said.

They crossed to the staircase leading down. It was lined with Republican Guards – gilt helmets with plumes, blue coats with scarlet facings, white trousers, shiny boots. The guards held their drawn sabres, at the salute, in front of their noses. At the top was a discreet notice: *Chambre Syndicale de la Gaine*.

The other two looked dubiously at Hood. 'You sure this is right?'

'Where's the royalty?'

'Our man's here; it's a professional corset show.'

Price jerked his head towards the resplendent guards. 'All this for corsets?'

'They're all wearing them.' As they went down, Hood said: 'Listen, you two, for God's sake, don't start looking shocked. This is strictly professional, see? You're blasé. You've seen it all for years. You design the damn things. Keep your eyes out for Andreas.'

At the bottom of the stairs, an ambassadorial-looking group in tails and dinner-jackets was bowing to them and smiling. Hood produced his Competitions Licence with the ape photograph. He bowed to the sleekest-looking of the ambassadors. He felt all in, but drove himself on.

'Hood and Partners, Corsetry Limited.'

'*Comment?*'

'You know, the Tuck Me Belt and Teazem Bra.'

'*La carte d'invitation, Monsieur?*' smiled the ambassador, playing a small invisible concertina. 'Zee invitation carte, you 'ave?'

Hood looked astonished. He stuck to English. 'But we gave it up when we came in. We've just been called out to the telephone by the Minister of Trade.'

The ambassador smiled. His hands squeezed the concertina. He plainly only half understood. He looked round at the other senior diplomatists.

'It was your colleague who let us out – where is he?' Hood said.

Puzzled looks. Hood pretended to see somebody over their shoulders in the room beyond and made vigorous signs. 'Coming, old boy,' he called. He waved the Competitions Licence at the ambassador again. 'We're doing a special Teazem job for the Debutantes' Ball at the Chateau de

Versailles.' He cupped palms under imaginary breasts. 'N'est-ce pas?'

The ambassador's eyebrows went up. He bowed deeply. The others parted ranks and bowed them through.

The vast room was crowded. Rows of men and women sat round a narrow raised gangway curving round the room in the shape of a horseshoe. There were billows of cigarette smoke. The lights in the body of the room were dimmed but a series of spots brilliantly picked out the gangway.

'Spread a bit,' Hood whispered. 'Keep watching me.'

At that moment, a girl came through the curtains at the far side. She was a very pretty blonde with dimples. As she reached the gangway she shrugged the wrapper from her shoulders and discarded it.

Hood heard Price's gasp as he moved away. The girl was modelling a belt somewhat smaller than a bikini and a narrow strip bra. The black stockings, suspenders and high heels added to her sexiness.

'Voici *Abandon*,' murmured a voice over a loudspeaker.

The girl paraded saucily along the gangway, pausing now and then, turning, striking poses. Even a corset, Hood thought with amusement, was ultimately meant for display, an adjunct of female vanity. There could hardly be a more enviable profession in the world for a woman than that of a model – displaying herself before other women.

The girl passed in front of him. She had a beauty spot high up on the inside of her thigh. As she reached the end of the gangway, there was applause from the crowd.

Hood scanned the faces. The corset trade was taking notes, turning round talking to each other, lighting cigarettes. There were plenty of men. He couldn't see Andreas.

A sophisticated brunette came out. She turned her back to drop her wrapper, turned round again on her high heels. Her hands were revealingly over her nude breasts. She stepped forward. Her skin showed under the openwork of the black corsets. She paused provokingly, straddled her legs and twisted slowly at the hips.

'Voici *Révélation*,' cooed the loudspeaker.

Murmurs of approval from the crowd. The girl turned. The open meshes disclosed invitingly her *derrière*. She bent over. There was a brief, too, too brief glimpse of the promised land – then she was striding on, smiling, one arm waving free.

To the left, Hood saw Price red-faced, trying to look the bored professional buyer, scribbling in a notebook. On the other side, Whitney twiggled his eyebrows and signalled Whew!

Hood threaded his way among the standing onlookers. He wondered how long the display had been in progress. It was highly unlikely that Andreas had already come and gone. Yet he could easily be missed in this crush. The dimness of the room didn't help. Some of the spectators were no more than silhouettes.

Another model was out. Between the intervening heads and shoulders, Hood saw a nude back, a long leg. Just below, in the front row, was a free chair. He caught Whitney's eye, then shouldered through.

'Excuse me.' Reluctantly the onlookers made way. Hood crouched as he went down the gangway and reached the chair. A massive woman in the next seat thrust her arm out. 'C'est pris, c'est pris!'

Hood nodded and sat down. The woman continued to argue and expostulate. Hood took no notice. The position gave him a better view of the room. The model was on the farther side. He searched the rows of faces. No Andreas.

There was a certain amount of movement at the rear. Craning, he saw one or two people leaving. It occurred to him that if Andreas had come here, he was disguised. There was an area to his right masked by a column. He leant forward to get a view of it. The woman next to him was fidgeting and muttering.

'Voici *Coucou*.'

The new model came sauntering forward and stopped just above Hood. Hood looked up. The target area, so shadowy in the corset advertisements, loomed there. The mystery was dissipated. She wore nothing underneath – no doubt the quintessence of professionalism. The bra was all support with two little round holes at the centre of each cup. Cuckoo! the girl's two pink tips seemed to be greeting the audience. She was very close. Hood could see the texture of her skin. She unhooked a suspender, took the corset's lower edge and rolled up a flap, demonstrating the thing's flexibility. There was a murmur of appreciation.

Somebody tapped Hood's shoulder. 'My place!' It was a masculine-looking woman with a tie.

'Excuse me.' Hood got up. A suspender belt wouldn't do anything for *her*, at any rate.

Then, going back along the passage between the chairs, he saw Andreas. Andreas was squeezing past knees in the middle of a row on the far side. He was in a hurry and kept glancing up at the model. Hood thought fantastically for a moment that he might know her and be going to meet her. Then he realized that Andreas had seen him. He had shown himself in the seat.

He thrust his way among the onlookers at the back, ran towards the far side. He had lost Whitney and Price. Painfully he collided with a man, knocking his hurt ankle. It was some official who wanted to be argumentative. Hood thrust him off. He broke through a group applauding the model who had just appeared, pushed a way, among protests, to the back row of chairs.

The next passage between the chairs was yards farther round. Andreas had reached it but saw him again and doubled back, running. Hood trod on feet, forcing his way along. There were indignant and angry cries. He could hear a stir behind him. Whitney and Price were evidently trying to join him and having trouble.

As he reached the passage between the chairs, Andreas was standing transfixed and hesitant at the foot of the model on the gangway. She had just struck the favourite 'shy' pose of the corset ads – face averted, bosom up, one long leg back and belly and generating zone thrust forward.

'Voici *Take Me*' huskily breathed the microphone voice.

A photographer was taking her; he had his camera almost touching her thighs and was working away.

Andreas jumped up beside her. One hand was gripping a fat briefcase. His face gleamed with a terrible joy mingled with fear. He looked odd and a little absurd in his formal clothes. In the first sudden hush of surprise as everybody watched, he extended a hand towards the girl. He seemed almost overcome with temptation to caress her. There was an enthralled silence. The extended hand touched the offering. The audience roared. The girl looked round startled, stepped back.

Andreas came to himself. He sprang past her, ran along the gangway. In a moment he had disappeared behind the curtain. Hood reached the gangway, jumped up and raced after him. The audience was on its feet. Flinging the curtain aside, Hood ran into a big vestibule full of models and dressers. It was a tableau. They were all poised, startled at Andreas's sudden appearance among them and the noise from the audience. Some of the girls were standing in corsets waiting to go on, others in wrappers. A few were nude. Several screamed. Some of the nude ones just looked coolly and didn't try to cover up. Hood saw there was only one door, on the far side.

He bounded for it. Outside was a corridor and stone stairs up. He took the stairs three at a time, hearing a door slam above. He paused on the first landing. No, not here.

He leapt up the next flight to the floor above. Suddenly the sound of shattering glass came from beyond the door. He wrenched it open. It was a dead end. He ran back past the landing to the turn of the passage on the opposite side.

Halfway down was a waist-high window, the pane smashed. As he reached it, Whitney came round the turn behind him. Then, out of the window, Hood saw Andreas.

He was clinging with his fingertips and the toes of his

shoes to two tiny ledges, trying to work his way along. He had the briefcase in his teeth. He was only about six feet beyond the window.

'Oh, my God,' Hood said quietly. Whitney came up. Hood put a hand on his arm, motioning him to silence. Chest heaving, Whitney looked out. He gritted his teeth in a grimace, glanced back at Hood. They did not speak.

Andreas worked his way a few inches farther along the ledge. His neck was quivering with the effort to hold the briefcase. Appalled, they saw his fingers beginning to slip. He had cut them on the glass. The blood made them slippery. Slowly, the fingers slipped until only the very tips were clinging to the stone. They shook with the force of the grip. Andreas was staring bolt-eyed at the stone in front of him. All at once, his hands slid away, he shouted, tipped back and fell.

Hood looked away. He made an effort. 'Chuck, go down and get that briefcase. Be quick. Better not go back that way. Meet me on the corner of the Champs-Elysées.'

The Head Man picked up a signal from his desk. 'The *Triton* limped into the Black Sea at seven o'clock last night, in spite of an extensively damaged port side after collision with the British steamer *Stanford*. Too bad.'

'We did our best, sir,' Conder said.

The Head Man nodded. There was the ghost of a smile on his enigmatic face. 'By the way Hood, Richard Calvert wants to know when he's going to see you again. Some picture hc wants your advice on.'

'Is he all right?'

'Absolutely. He was bored being locked up, that's all. They knocked him about a bit, but wouldn't do anything more without orders from Lobar.'

Conder said: 'The SDECE are pretty angry. They realize a good deal has been going on but don't know what.'

'Very well, if that's all.' The Head Man stood up. 'Thank you, Charles.' They shook hands.

Back in Conder's office, Hood said to Miss Markham, Conder's secretary: 'Put a call in to Nice for me, will you, Sophie?'

'Who do you want, the Consul again?'

'No. This time it's a night club; it's called Le Nichon.

'What does that mean?'

'Well, roughly, a charming bulge.'

She eyed him obliquely. When the call came it was Kit on the line. 'Good God, it's Pinkerton.'

'How's your appetite, my girl?'

'Um.'

'Listen, Kit, there are reasons why I can't return to your haven of peace and rest straight away. Which means you must come to London. Tell Jojo you want some leave. There's a ticket waiting for you at the British Consul's in Nice. He will wire me when you're arriving and I'll meet you at the airport. All right?'

'I'll be there tomorrow night.'

'Kit, how about flying down to Malaga or somewhere?'

'Yes, yes – but the night *after*.'

THE END